JDkkins.
JD

CO 2 55 123

C000263288

The Cry of the Children

The Cry
of the Children

DC 12.2.01

EMMA DALLY

LITTLE, BROWN AND COMPANY

A *Little, Brown* Book

First published in Great Britain in 1997
by Little, Brown and Company

Copyright © 1997 Emma Dally

The moral right of the author has been asserted.

A CIP catalogue record for this book
is available from the British Library.

ISBN 0 316 88291 7

Typeset in Times by
Palimpsest Book Production Limited,
Polmont, Stirlingshire
Printed and bound in Great Britain by
Creative Print & Design (Wales), Ebbw Vale, Gwent

Little, Brown and Company (UK)
Brettenham House
Lancaster Place
London WC2E 7EN

For my siblings,
Simon, Mark, Jane, John and Adam

Do ye hear the children weeping, O my brothers,
  Ere the sorrow comes with years?
They are leaning their young heads against their mothers,
  And *that* cannot stop their tears.

from 'The Cry of the Children' by Elizabeth Barrett Browning

PROLOGUE

London's Kentish Town in the late 1960s. A place of change and social upheaval. One hundred years before, the Midland Railway cut a heartless gash through the area, across the playground of St Luke's School in Islip Street, dividing one part of Kentish Town from another and cutting off the whole of Kentish Town from the green, open spaces of Parliament Hill and Hampstead Heath.

For one hundred years, the railway industry smothered the streets with filthy sooty air, mucky debris from the steam trains and shunters' yards in Kentish Town and in Camden Town, just down the road. Large, drifting particles of soot blackened the bricks and windows of the Victorian terraced houses of this north London village which, before the trains, had been regarded as a healthy country retreat for city dwellers. The railway made the winter air a thick yellow, the summer air a choking grey.

During this period, people who could choose generally shunned Kentish Town, preferring instead the leafy suburbs or the fresher villages of Hampstead and Highgate further north.

Now it was changing. In the 1960s, a decade after the steam engines had been replaced by electric trains, and the clean air legislation prohibited the burning of coal fires in domestic grates, the air was clearer and cleaner. Young professionals who could not afford the areas their parents moved to in the Forties and Fifties, were turning their attention to Kentish Town, attracted by its Victorian family houses with decent-sized gardens, and by its proximity to the city centre.

The other new immigrants of the Sixties were also arriving from abroad – Cyprus, India and Pakistan – adding to the social mix and, with their corner shops, were offering exotic, unfamiliar foods and smells, and slowly changing the landscape and character of the smaller streets off Kentish Town Road.

In 1968, Kentish Town Road itself remained much the same as it had for years, with its Boots the Chemist, Sketchleys, West the butcher, Woolworths and the Post Office. Although the trams no longer trundled up the hill, the road was as congested as ever by traffic, the cars, taxis and red double-decker buses jostling for space on the main artery to the north.

A pedestrian walking up from the Northwestern Polytechnic at the junction of Prince of Wales Road would pass the Saxone Footwear shop and Jennings, the solicitor. The Scotch Wool Shop stood next to Broadmead Radio and TV, which rented out most of the televisions in the council flats on the Torriano or Peckwater Estates. Walking on up the road, the pedestrian passed the Wimpy Bar and the Council for Unmarried Mothers, the Nina Hunt School of Dancing and Dawson & Briant, the jewellers.

As this story begins, Sainsbury's is advertising in the local papers for staff to work in its new self-service store, which will compete with the Tesco at the top of Fortess Road. Tesco now has late-night shopping on Fridays and has just started to give away Green Shield Stamps. In

Highgate Road, the ABC cinema – once called the Forum – is showing a new film, *Camelot*, starring Richard Burton and Vanessa Redgrave.

Over the last few years, Camden Council has bought up at least half of the properties in the area and is currently locked in battles with numerous Residents' Groups and Housing Associations about whether the mid-Victorian terraces should be renovated or flattened to make way for vast housing estates of high-rise blocks. As the new house-owners do up their homes (gentrification is beginning), squatters are moving into and occupying the council's many empty properties, to be sharp, nagging thorns in the councillors' sides.

There is squalor but there is also care. In the summer of 1968, as America fights a war in Vietnam and the whole world seems to seethe with rebellion and revolt, many back gardens in Kentish Town are quiet, well tended and verdant. Flowers bloom, trees grow. Blackbirds sing loudly and pull worms from the surprisingly fertile soil.

That pedestrian walking up Kentish Town Road might buy some milk and cheese at the Express Dairy, order some fresh cod fillets at W. Starling, the fishmonger, and purchase a couple of punnets of strawberries and a pound of ripe plums from Lipman's, before popping into the new premises of the public library to borrow the latest new novels.

Concentrating on the errands of the day, and shutting out the sounds of the busy street, that person, like everyone else walking outside at that moment, will not hear another sound in Kentish Town.

It is the sound of a child crying, sobbing quietly. A little girl locked in a small room in a big house. No one hears her. They never do.

When she is finally released from her prison, her eyes will be dry. Her eyelids will flicker. She is just a child and quite powerless. But she is clever, and ambitious. And she knows that she will not be powerless for ever.

CHAPTER 1

May, 1997

Distant Voices

Lunchtime in Shepherd's Bush, London. It is a sunny May day. A tall, lean-limbed woman walks down the street. Her flat leather sandals slap on the hot pavement. On her slender body she wears a simple white sleeveless blouse, and a dusty pink denim skirt swings around her long legs.

Two bare-chested builders sit on a flight of steps eating thick fried egg sandwiches. They simultaneously eye up the woman as she goes past. One of them, a chunky young man with curly blond hair, wipes the egg yolk off his rough chin and is tempted to whistle. He particularly fancies older women.

But something holds him back. Perhaps the look on this woman's face prevents him from doing what usually comes so spontaneously to him. Today, however, even he is sensitive enough to guess that perhaps a cocky message from him is not appropriate.

The woman has a pleasant face – still pretty, even though she must be in her late thirties, the young builder reckons. She has large chocolate-brown eyes, wide cheekbones, small chin – framed by a well-cut bob of brown hair.

As she walks by, the woman's dark brown eyes do not notice the presence of the admiring builders. Nor do they take in the smile from Mehmet, the gentle Asian grocer who is stacking his fruit and vegetables in artistically shaped piles on the wooden shelving outside his small, crowded corner shop. Mehmet is used to exchanging greetings with the woman, but he, too, knows that she is troubled today. He thinks she looks a little less worried than she did when she walked past an hour earlier but he can tell that all is not well with her.

In fact, Mehmet has been thinking for some time now that something was up with her. The sparkle in her eyes is less bright, her smile less ready than when she and her handsome husband first moved to the neighbourhood three years ago.

A devoted family man with four healthy children (three sturdy sons and a daughter), Mehmet is fairly sure of the reason for the woman's troubled expression, and when he discusses his theory with his placid fecund wife, she agrees with him.

The woman turns into Melrose Gardens. If she could read Mehmet's thoughts, she would tell him his theory is right. She is a woman in crisis. Until recently, she has always regarded herself as a perfectly normal person. Now she feels herself turning into a very abnormal person. At the moment she does not think that life can get much worse.

Unfortunately (or perhaps fortunately), she does not realise that it can indeed get worse, and that it will. She also does not know that the telephone she can hear ringing as she turns the key in the lock marks the beginning of the next stage of her life. And that this stage is going to be far harder than anything she has ever encountered before.

*   *   *

The telephone was ringing as Lucy came in through the door of her flat. By the time she reached it, the ringing had stopped. Never mind. If it was important the person would ring again. She retrieved the bag she had flung down in the hall and began to unpack her shopping in the small fitted kitchen.

She made herself a tomato sandwich and settled down at the kitchen table to read the newspaper with conscious satisfaction. Lunchtime was her favourite time of day. Her husband, Simon, who had worked in a newspaper office for over ten years, laughed at her for it. For in spite of being freelance and able to organise her days as she liked, Lucy liked to stick to office hours, starting work promptly at nine am and working through until twelve forty-five pm. She would look forward to catching up with the news during her lunch hour.

Simon thought she was absurd. 'The whole point of being your own boss is that you can work when you like,' he laughed. 'You can work at night and go to the cinema in the afternoon and avoid the crowds.'

Lucy disagreed. 'It still makes me feel as if I'm bunking off school,' she replied.

'You're just not a natural freelance. Perhaps you should work in an office again,' Simon said.

'I didn't become a freelance by choice,' she reminded him sharply.

This morning, of course, had been disrupted by the visit to the doctor, so she had not got much work done. She was copy-editing a dreary consumer guide to family law and had promised the publisher that she would finish it by the end of the week. She would probably have to work late into the night.

The telephone rang again just as she bit into her sandwich.

Damn! She hated to be disturbed while eating, and she had forgotten to put on the answering machine. She could not just let it ring, she was incapable of ignoring it.

To her relief, it was Rosie.

'Lucy Montague! I've been trying to get hold of you all morning.'

'I've been out. I had to see the doctor.'

'Everything okay?' Rosie was briefly, but genuinely, concerned. 'At least, nothing serious?'

'No, nothing serious. I just felt I had to do something about the fact that I can't get pregnant. I can't go on like this for much longer and I've asked to be referred to a specialist.'

'Ah. Oddly enough, that's what I was ringing about,' said Rosie.

Lucy sensed a suspicious cheerfulness in her voice. She waited.

'I wondered if you would mind doing a small interview on just that subject for me. Please say if you really don't want to, but we're desperate to get hold of someone. The person we lined up let us down at the last minute and it occurred to me that you might just agree to do it . . . Of course, I'll understand entirely if you don't want to do it,' she added disingenuously.

Lucy smiled. She was used to helping Rosie out at the last minute. Rosie was Associate Editor on a woman's magazine, in charge of features, and she shamelessly used her friends as interviewees whenever necessary. Over the past two years, Lucy had been interviewed about six or seven aspects of her deeply interesting life experience. How the children of doctors view their own health; being made redundant; freelancing; one was about having a homosexual brother (that was strictly anonymous, as was the one about oral sex). In fact, Lucy's life could be mapped out through the pages of *High Spirits*. As could the lives of most of Rosie's friends.

At least Rosie did talk to real people nowadays. She had found herself in big trouble with her editor last year when it was discovered that she had written a series of articles without interviewing a single real person. She had simply made them all up.

'Real people never say the right things,' Rosie defended herself. 'I can think up much more interesting and apt quotes than your average person. Sometimes you find people who've done something interesting but when it comes to talking about it, they might as well be pond life.'

'That's not the point,' snapped her editor. 'Do that again and you're out.'

Of course, the editor knew and Rosie knew that this was not true. Rosie was far too valuable to the magazine. She was full of ideas for every section, from features to fashion, she wrote like an angel about any subject, and she worked all hours. Rosie was headed for stardom, and everyone knew it. She was frequently approached by rival magazines and she was clearly just waiting for the right offer to come along. Indeed, when Rosie won a major media award for that same series of articles (submitted before the misdemeanour had been discovered), nothing was said about it. Proud to have an award-winning journalist on her team, the editor put up Rosie's salary, gave her a generous clothes allowance, and prayed that *Private Eye* never found out the truth.

'You can be interviewed anonymously, Lucy,' Rosie continued. 'I wouldn't expect you to put your name to it . . . we'll just describe you as Milly, a thirty-five-year-old lawyer.'

'That's what you called me in that article on blow jobs,' laughed Lucy.

'No, I've never used the name Milly before.'

'I mean the thirty-five-year-old lawyer.'

'No, you were thirty-four last time.'

Lucy sighed wearily. 'Yeah, from blow jobs at thirty-four to IVF at thirty-five. Except that I'm thirty-seven.'

'That's a small detail,' replied Rosie. 'Oh, go on, sweetheart, say you'll do it, please. I'm really desperate. This last woman got cold feet at the last minute. I told her she'd be anonymous but she's terrified her mother-in-law will recognise her and make trouble for her and her husband. Ridiculous! But you can't make someone talk if they don't want to.'

'No, indeed.' Lucy did not feel sure about what she was agreeing to.

It had been hard enough talking to her GP that morning about what was going on. Her doctor had quite shaken her up, talking about unconscious reasons for infertility, and she had not yet had a chance to think about it properly.

But the visit to the doctor had shaken her up in some way that made her feel slightly different about it, too. She was surprised to hear herself agreeing to Rosie's request. 'All right,' she said. 'I'll do it, as a favour to you, Rosie, but you owe me one . . . Tell the journalist to ring me this evening at about six thirty, before Simon gets home.'

'You're a true doll.' She could hear Rosie blow a kiss down the phone. 'Thanks.'

Lucy went back to her sandwich and newspaper, trying to concentrate on the daily news again. Instead, she found herself replaying her visit to the doctor that morning.

Lucy had always liked Dr Kenny, who was not much older than Lucy herself and had an endearingly friendly, no-nonsense manner. She even liked her enough to forgive her for having young children. She had once seen the doctor shopping in Marks & Spencer with a toddler and an infant in a buggy; the toddler, she had noted with satisfaction, was howling its head off.

But here Dr Kenny was in a professional role. When Lucy sat down in the chair next to the doctor's desk and burst into tears, Dr Kenny had handed her a box of tissues and waited in silence for her to stop. When Lucy managed to blurt out that she had decided that perhaps it was time to be referred to the fertility clinic – or was it the infertility clinic? – Dr Kenny had nodded and smiled, and said, 'Of course.'

If Lucy had a complaint about Dr Kenny it was that she was sometimes just too correct in her behaviour. The health centre was very geared up for counselling and therapies of various kinds, so it was no surprise when her doctor stared at her and said, 'Perhaps you should think about talking to someone about what you're going through.'

Lucy sniffed through her tears and frowned. 'What do you mean?'

The doctor shuffled her papers. She was clearly treading carefully. 'I am going to refer you to the clinic at the hospital but it may take a while to get an appointment. It seems to me that you are possibly more upset about your difficulties in starting a family than you think.'

Lucy rolled her wet eyes.

'It sometimes helps to talk about your feelings,' Dr Kenny continued, 'get them out and not keep them bottled up.'

Lucy felt herself cringing. This intelligent woman was sounding like something out of Rosie's magazine. 'I don't need to talk to anyone I don't know,' she said. 'I talk to my friends.'

The doctor smiled. 'Fair enough. Sometimes friends are

all you need. But sometimes they're not. Just remember that if you do feel the need to see someone, we can arrange it. Just let me know.'

Biting the inside of her lip, Lucy smiled. She was grateful for the concern, if nothing else. She did not feel she got much real support from anyone around her but that was mainly her own fault; she did not like to talk to anyone about her problem.

The doctor continued. 'You know, there's been quite a bit of research done on why people don't conceive. Psychological factors can play a large part.'

'So what?' Lucy snapped, taken aback by her own rudeness.

Dr Kenny paused and smiled again. 'I'm just saying that sometimes there can be a psychological component.'

'You mean that I unconsciously don't want to be a mother? Unable? Unready? Unwilling? That sort of thing?' Lucy scratched her forehead and looked defiantly at her.

Dr Kenny shrugged. 'I don't mean anything specific. It's just that a lot of women can go for years with unexplained infertility – when there's no obvious reason – and suddenly find themselves pregnant. As far as I'm concerned, yours is unexplained. All the preliminary tests have shown that you're ovulating. You've never had a pelvic infection, so far as you know, Simon is producing perfectly good sperm, and plenty of them. Yet you're not getting pregnant. It can often be like this. There is no obvious reason and then suddenly it happens. We all know about couples who have been trying for years to adopt a baby and then suddenly the woman finds herself pregnant with no help at all.'

'Of course I've heard of that,' Lucy said impatiently. 'But I don't see what it's got to do with me. I'm sure there's something physically wrong and since those first investigations I've had over the last three years have not thrown anything up, I feel time is running out. I want to get to a clinic and be investigated properly. A year ago I still thought it was just a matter of time. Now I have less time to play with. I'm thirty-seven. I can't afford to wait much longer.'

Dr Kenny nodded. 'Fine. I'll write to the consultant today. They're very good at the Hammersmith.' She scribbled in her notes, looked up and smiled. Lucy's time was over.

Lucy picked up her bag and rose from the chair. 'Thank you for all your help. I'll let you know how I get on.'

The doctor nodded gently. She did not seem to have taken offence at Lucy's rejection of psychological help. 'Let me know if you haven't heard from the hospital within three weeks.' She caught Lucy's eye. 'And you may be right. Perhaps they'll pinpoint the problem at the clinic and fix it. Physiological problems are usually the easiest to fix . . . But I think you'll be all right. Most couples end up with the baby they want nowadays, whatever the original problem is.'

Biting into her tomato sandwich, Lucy thought that she was not about to tell anyone that her doctor thought it was all in the mind, but she was aware that something inside her had eased. As she ran water into the kettle for coffee, she realised that she could manage to talk about it to a stranger. Perhaps it was good to talk, just to articulate and clarify her thoughts about the whole business. And it might also help someone else in the same situation to learn that she's not alone, that she's not the only one.

The kettle boiled. As Lucy poured the water on to the instant coffee, she chuckled at how Rosie had persuaded her to be interviewed. Rosie was so clever, and so incorrigible! And she had always been like this. She had an inborn talent for getting her own way in the most charming manner imaginable.

At university, where they had first met and become friends, Rosie edited the student newspaper, took the leading roles in the productions of the drama club, and made all her own clothes from designs she had pinched from the swanky boutique in the high street. In her second year, she had been banned from several clothes shops in the town after being regularly spotted measuring up the seams of dresses and writing down the details in a red notebook. The shops naturally thought she was a spy for a rival in the garment industry but in fact she simply went back to her lodgings and cut out her own paper patterns to recreate the dresses on her old Singer sewing machine.

On top of all this activity, Rosie always had a string of boyfriends waiting for her favours. She treated all of them quite badly and Lucy was forever handing out comforting cups of tea to the latest reject. They trooped round regularly to their shared flat in the hope of a reconciliation, only to find that Rosie was out with somebody else.

The only time Lucy ever showed any disapproval was when Rosie slept with three men in one day, dashing from one set of digs to another across town and back, until she returned home, alone and exhausted.

But even then Rosie was immune to criticism. 'The trouble is,' she said artlessly, as she collapsed on the sofa, 'I like all these boys in their way, and I don't like to hurt anyone's feelings. I can't bear to reject any of them. You know, Tom's much better in bed than Bill but Bill always makes me laugh. And Martin's so spiritual – he's teaching me Tantric sex, though I don't think it's really for me. It probably suits B-type personalities more. And then James, well, poor old James. I haven't got the heart to disentangle myself, he's insecure enough as it is . . .'

Rosie's looks always attracted attention. She had thick glossy brown hair and the most unusual mouth with naturally dark-red lips which turned up at the corners to give her a permanently content and bemused expression. Ripe and buxom, with a small waist, she had always dressed well, from her home-made dresses at university to the Nicole Farhi suits she could afford now that her magazine salary was topped up with a dress allowance – all part of her 'package' from the magazine.

Lucy always loved Rosie's company. Rosie's mind was as vivacious and lively as her body, and made Lucy feel more alive in her presence. She was full of ideas and laughter, and she could rarely sit still for a moment. It was no wonder that men were always attracted to her. But Rosie always manipulated them as she wanted. Unlike most people, she did not seem to be longing to find a partner with whom she could settle down and reproduce. 'If I have a biological clock at all, it must be electronic – because I can't hear it ticking,' she would say with a laugh.

For Rosie, work took precedence over the boyfriends. She just wanted to do interesting and stimulating work and have a good time. And the fact that Rosie was not longing to settle down and have babies made her a safe friend for Lucy. Unlike many of Lucy's old friends, Rosie was not going to go off and betray her by getting pregnant!

Of course, all that running around at university had been in the late Seventies, before anyone had ever heard of AIDS. Fired up by the women's liberation movement and easy access to contraception, women were encouraged to flex their sexual muscles and enjoy them without the risk of disapproval or fatal disease. In those days, all you had to fear was pregnancy.

Lucy often reflected on the irony of that. All those years spent trying not to get pregnant. All those days following a rather too carefree night anxiously waiting for the stomach cramps and dark menstrual blood. How welcome they had been then! Now the telltale twinge in her belly and the blood flowing through her cervix each month sent her plunging into gloom.

With her thoughts back on her infertility, she wondered if she was really ready to be interviewed by a complete stranger about something so personal.

The journalist telephoned at exactly six thirty, by which time Lucy had begun to feel agitated. She did not know whether her nerve would abandon her and leave her to sob pathetically into the receiver and blurt out her misery. Talking to her doctor that morning had brought on tears; she had no idea whether this favour to Rosie was going to be better or worse. Was she going to find herself blubbing uncontrollably? Pushing back the nervousness, she reminded herself sharply that she had agreed to do this interview, so there was no going back now . . .

Lucy did not catch the woman's first name and she had forgotten to ask Rosie what she was called. It hardly mattered. In fact, the more anonymity on all sides, the better, especially if she was going to cry.

The woman was a sympathetic and sensitive interviewer with an attractive husky voice. At one point Lucy thought it sounded a little familiar. But Lucy was surprised to find how easy it was to talk like this over the telephone, to recount her experiences over the past four years. She told her the whole story, about how she used to be a book editor in a publishing company, how she got married to Simon, a journalist and the Deputy Editor of a local newspaper in south London. She used to have a wonderful job, she told her, but then everything changed. There were cutbacks and 'downsizing' and she found herself being laid off with a bit of redundancy money and a lot of rejections from other publishing houses that were also shedding staff.

It was at this point, she explained, that she had decided to look on the bright side, and to regard this event as no bad thing. She and Simon decided that now was probably the time to start a family, as they had always planned to do. If Lucy could build up enough contacts doing freelance editing, she would be able to work from home and be available for the children.

Such hopes! Lucy felt such sadness as she described the excitement of having her coil removed by the GP, and being tested for rubella in preparation for conception. Then there was the joy of having sex without contraception. In those early days, the knowledge that it might result in a baby added a thrilling edge to sex. Their sex life during those early months seemed electrified by the possibility of creating a new life, by their sense of omnipotence. 'We had sex at every opportunity,' Lucy laughed, 'in bed, on the kitchen floor, across Simon's desk, against the washing machine . . .'

She had not expected to get pregnant straight away (though she had secretly hoped to). For the first three months, when her periods came on the dot, on the twenty-seventh day of every cycle, she tried not to be disheartened. She knew it could take time. But gradually her feelings changed. The onset of each monthly period was marked in her diary with a large, disappointed 'P'. Friends who had started trying to get pregnant around the same time would suddenly announce their success, and then fall quiet. Most disappeared; Lucy could not bear to see them in their fecund happiness.

Month after month went by. Sex became a chore. The four days of the month during which she was supposed to be fertile became crucial, marked out in red in the calendar in her head. One night Simon had flu and simply did not have the energy to arouse himself in any way – he could barely lift his head off the pillow.

Lucy sat downstairs and wept into glasses of neat whisky, bitterly disappointed that that month's chance was lost.

Into the mouthpiece of the telephone, she described the isolation and anger of being infertile, of how she felt excluded from ordinary life. Although she deliberately avoided her friends as they settled into domestic family living, she still could not avoid the rest of the world. Everywhere she looked, there were pregnant women, and the streets were crowded with women holding toddlers and pushing buggies. Nappy advertisements filled the television screens night after night. Novels were full of descriptions of childbirth and mother love. Even the children's section in the local library seemed to accentuate her misery as she walked past the door.

Her despair was a repeating pattern, following her menstrual cycle relentlessly, month after month. It disappeared for the four days after ovulation, allowing Lucy's spirits to rise each month as the twenty-seventh day approached. Then they would crash at the first twinge of cramp in her belly, and the painful lumpiness in her breasts followed by the unkind presence of blood cleansing her womb, washing away that month's ovum and all chances of its fusion, implantation and survival.

Then there was the pressure she felt from her mother

to produce a grandchild. She did not describe in full her mother's tactlessness or insensitivity, but she did describe the sense she often felt of her parents' disappointment when she was with them now. Omitting the fact that her brother Andrew was unlikely to produce grandchildren, ever, Lucy did hint that if her parents were ever to have grandchildren, they would only be from her.

Lucy also realised, but did not say it, that there was a hope deep inside her that if she could produce a grandchild, then her parents might become a bit happier, that her mother would stop henpecking and her father would stop retreating from the world. A child might give them a new interest and bring them alive again.

Perhaps it was talking to a faceless stranger on the telephone but Lucy found it surprisingly easy to articulate thoughts and feelings she had never expressed before. She talked about the loneliness of infertility, how it set her apart from the rest of the world. 'I have become painfully sensitive,' she explained, 'to the most innocent enquiry from anyone who asks if I have children or am planning to have them. I blush bright pink and feel almost attacked and exposed. The worst of it,' she continued, 'is that I have actually become quite phobic about children. I avoid them if I can. I no longer see old friends who have children and I tend only to mix with couples without children. It's pathetic, isn't it?' Saying all this made her feel like a sad person.

But there were some things she did not divulge to this journalist, and never would divulge to anyone, such as the time the telephone had rung at six o'clock one morning when she and Simon were fast asleep. Simon answered the phone. The exclamations and joy in his voice said it all. His sister's firstborn was a boy. A twelve-hour labour. Mother and baby were doing well. As Simon went into the kitchen to put on the kettle, too excited to go back to sleep, Lucy turned her face to the wall and wept.

Nor did she mention how the romantic weekend in Rome (carefully scheduled to tie in with her fertile days of the month) was ruined for her by the presence of a bawling baby in the row behind them on the flight home.

For years Lucy could hardly bear to admit to anyone that there was something wrong. Seeking medical help would be an admission of need. Simon had persuaded her that they should at least do the basic tests to check that all was well, so she had gone along with that. Anything that did not mean going to hospital. As the daughter of a doctor, she had mixed feelings about hospitals and clinics. The thought of invasive medical tests made her panic. She could not bear the idea of having metal instruments inside her, fiddling with her reproductive organs. She even thought that if she ended up with a baby at the end of that, it might be a metal robot.

'But now the time has come for me to brave the next step,' she said, 'since just letting Nature run its course has not worked. That's a change in my thinking. I'm not sure what I'm going to do if they start talking about laparoscopies or hysterosalpingography, or other ways of fiddling around with your insides. But,' she said with a light laugh, 'I'll have to deal with that when it comes to it.'

She told the journalist how it had affected her relationship with Simon and how it had put pressure on him to have sex on certain days of the month and be kind and supportive when her period started. 'But Simon has always been wonderful,' she said. 'And continues to be so. Luckily he has never had a burning desire to reproduce himself, so he never makes me feel I'm letting him down as well as myself. He's a brick,' she added, 'and always has been.'

She had said far too much, she knew. All this woman had

wanted from her was a few quotes. 'I'm sorry to rabbit on,' she said. 'I don't know what came over me.'

'That's all right,' replied the woman on the other end of the phone, 'you've said some very interesting things and given me some strong lines.' She paused and said, 'Thank you so much, Lucy. I do wish you luck. I hope you get the children you want.'

Lucy's throat contracted at the genuine warmth of the remark. 'Thank you.' Her voice cracked. 'By the way,' she said, collecting herself, 'I didn't catch your name.' She had a sudden urge to connect with this woman.

'Vita. My name is Vita Cumming.'

'Vita.' Lucy repeated it. 'It's an unusual name. I knew a Vita once, a long time ago. There was a girl up the road from us called Vita.'

'What's your name? Is Montague your married name?'

'My maiden name is Butler.'

As she said it, a sharp shiver of excitement ran through her. She knew what the voice down the phone was going to say next.

'My maiden name is Valentine. I'm Vita Valentine. And you're Lucy Butler who used to live down the road. You're Dr Butler's daughter!'

'Yes,' Lucy whispered. An image appeared in her head, an image of a large rambling house with a vast garden in Kentish Town. There was shouting and laughter, and a crowd of chattering children jostling and playing together. There was a beautiful dark woman in a long exotically coloured kaftan, leaning on the arm of a tall, handsome blond man in the background. The adults were smiling, looking on, detached but proud.

Now she knew why the husky voice was familiar. She recognised it as the voice of her friend Vita, the friend she had during that long hot summer before her parents moved away to south London. She remembered her now, a pretty, vital girl whom she admired with a passion. A wonderful friend and, in some ways, it felt now as if she had been the most important friend she had ever had.

'What about you?' Lucy's voice was almost a whisper. 'Do you have children?' She dreaded the answer.

'Yes.' The reply sounded almost apologetic. 'I have two girls, eight and six.'

'And your husband, or partner? What does he do?' It was always a risky question but Lucy wanted to know.

The pause was followed by an unexpected answer. 'He's dead. He died three years ago. I'm a single mother.'

'I'm sorry,' said Lucy. 'How sad to be widowed so young.'

'Yes,' replied Vita, but she did not sound sad. 'Life goes on,' she said, 'especially when you have children. Oh shit, I'm sorry. Just what you don't need to hear again.'

'That's all right,' murmured Lucy.

Vita sounded excited. 'Now, do you think we should meet up? See what we both look like after all these years?'

'But, of course!' exclaimed Lucy, her heart pounding in her throat. 'We have to. God, how amazing! I'd love to see you again. Let's meet for a drink.' She was astonished by her excitement; it was almost uncontrollable. 'It will be wonderful to see you again after all this time.'

'Let's meet at the Groucho Club in town – do you go there? We'll meet up without my children – it sounds as if you've had enough torment over the past few years.'

That night at supper Lucy tried to tell Simon about the extraordinary coincidence of being interviewed by Vita Valentine. She tried hard to explain about the Valentine family and why she was so excited about making contact with Vita again. But Simon was keen to eat his pasta quickly and watch the highlights of the cricket on television. He did not express much interest in Lucy's news. Perhaps the Valentines did not sound interesting to him, or perhaps he felt uncomfortable because Lucy had gone public about their fertility problems. Simon was a taciturn man at the best of times, and he was also tired after a difficult day's work on the paper.

That night Lucy woke in the early hours thinking about Vita Valentine and her extraordinary family. She had thought about Vita frequently all her life, ever since her family had moved away from Kentish Town to Dulwich, in south London.

Simon's long, solid shape lay beside her. The night was quiet, apart from the occasional cat calling in the garden and the roar of cars speeding down Shepherd's Bush Road four hundred yards away.

Lucy moved over to cuddle up against Simon's back, fitting her body around his. She rubbed her nose against his skin and took in his heavy male smell. Her thoughts spun in her head.

Thinking it over in the warm bed, Lucy thought how odd it was that she and Vita had lost touch with each other so completely. Yet Lucy had thought about Vita and her family many times over the years, wondering what they were all up to. Certainly whenever she drove through Kentish Town, she thought about her friends from the past and all those things she used to do with them.

Once she had even plucked up the courage to ring them unexpectedly and see if she could pick up the threads of their friendship again, but when she looked them up in the telephone book there was no Valentine listed in Lady Margaret Road, NW5. They had moved away. The contact had gone.

Then the older she became, although the yearning to see them remained, Lucy also grew more fearful about actually meeting again. After all, Vita had never bothered to get in touch with her, either. Until today. And even that had been a surprise for both of them.

Lucy was nervous about it, there was no escaping that. What would Vita be like? What would she look like? What would she make of Lucy now? Would they have anything in common now that they were adults with lives of their own? Vita was a widow. She had married someone who had died. And she had children.

Lucy felt so inexperienced and childlike by comparison. Nothing had happened to her in her adult life to make her feel properly adult. She had hardly grown up and she felt that she would never grow up properly until she had produced a child, until she had become someone's mother.

'Life goes on,' Vita had said, 'especially if you have children.'

Vita had apologised for her tactless remark but it did raise an important question. But what if you do not have children? What if you want them and never get them? Does life still go on then?

Lucy scratched her leg and shifted position in the bed. She pushed the pillow under her neck and sighed deeply. As she lay there, her breathing gradually evened out and she slowly slipped back into sleep. Dreams filled her head. First she dreamed that she was surrounded by young children. They were all shouting at her and pulling her by the arms and clothes in different directions. Then she dreamed that she was in hospital where she had given birth to a baby with no backbone. She was crying but no one came to help her.

When the alarm clock went off at seven o'clock the next morning, Lucy was shaken awake by the bell, relieved that the start of the day had released her from the night terrors.

CHAPTER 2

July, 1968

The Family Up the Road

Lucy Butler was the nine-year-old daughter of a family doctor in Kentish Town. Her father, Gordon Butler, ran a small practice in Falkland Road. He was on his own but ran the practice with the help of his wife, Hilda, a former nurse. A quiet man, totally dedicated to his work and patients, he left the practical side of running the surgery, from the two ground-floor rooms of their three-storey terraced house, to Hilda and a part-time secretary.

Hilda Butler was a conscientious woman who enjoyed some pride in her own virtue. Thin and wiry, she was a woman in constant motion, tidying the sofa cushions, straightening the rugs, wiping the kitchen surfaces or patting her hair to check the state of its perm. Although she was no fool, she was prey to foolishness, of prejudice and irrational thought. In spite of her nursing training and marriage to a doctor, if pushed, she would opine that virtue could keep someone in the state of good health. And she was proud that she had not spent a day in bed for twenty years.

Hilda was well known in the neighbourhood for her

competence and efficiency. Her husband's patients tolerated her fussiness, which they put down to 'nerves' for they knew that Hilda was essentially kind at heart, and, when need be, got things done. And she was also always fair. If someone needed to see the doctor urgently, it was Hilda who decided who got through the door, and when. She never made mistakes and she made a conscious effort to be fair and decent to everyone, while remaining consistently firm with those who needed staunch handling.

Hilda's reward for such fairness was a high social standing. This meant a lot to her. As wife of the local family doctor, she was on a par with the vicar's wife – people came to her for advice and support – and she took her role and responsibilities seriously.

On Saturday afternoons, after the morning surgery and family lunch of roast chicken, peas and baked potatoes in their kitchen on the first floor, Lucy Butler loved to sit on the worn carpet that covered the floor of her father's surgery while he went through his notes and dictated letters for his secretary to type up on Monday morning.

The waiting room was on the ground floor in the front of the house, with the surgery at the back. The surgery was a comfortable, comforting room. On one side, against the wall, stood a high examining couch and a screen behind which patients could undress with some modesty. On the other side was a wall covered with bookshelves that were bowed from the weight of the medical textbooks and neat piles of issues of *The Lancet* and the *British Medical Journal* going back many years.

The third wall sported large photographs of her grandfather and great-grandfather, both doctors.

Against the fourth wall was a large wooden cabinet which was always kept locked. This was full of boxes of pills, powders, linctuses and capsules of all different shapes, sizes and colours.

Lucy always thought it odd that this cupboard was locked when her father was so careless about all the other drugs that came in, sent as samples by the drugs companies or handed in by patients who had given up on their treatment halfway through the course. She often watched him throw these samples carelessly into the bottom drawer of his desk, and wondered why he never bothered to lock them up with the rest of the medicines in the cabinet. When she asked him he would laugh and nod in agreement. 'You're right, I ought to lock them up or do something with them. I shouldn't leave them lying around. I'll get round to putting them away or throwing them away one day.'

But he never did.

During these quiet Saturday afternoons, Lucy liked to sit on the floor and leaf through the medical textbooks which revealed the shocking population of medical curiosities, the people doctors were really interested in. She was particularly fascinated by the grainy black-and-white photographs of Siamese twins, babies born physically joined. One of the pictures was of two live babies who were simply connected by skin. But the pictures that excited her most were of the ones that had two heads and bodies joined at the waist, with two arms each but only two legs between them. Those ones were dead. There was another picture she liked to pore over. This was of a living baby which looked normal in every way, except that it had one complete extra leg growing from its groin – the evidence of the second twin, the caption simply informed her.

She also liked to look at the children with Down's syndrome. She knew by heart the typical features of a Down's child – the eyes sloping upwards at the outer corners, the folds of skin covering the inner covers of the eye, the small facial features, the large protruding tongue, the short, broad hands with the inward curving little finger and the single transverse crease. Several people who looked like that – children and adults – came to her father's surgery once in a while. Her father explained to her that they had been born like that and they tended to be born to women who had babies late in life.

When Gordon Butler was in a light-hearted mood and not too busy, he would tell her what some of his patients had been up to the previous week, like the woman (he never revealed their names) who ate her prescription because she thought it was the treatment, and the man who was worried because every time he blew his nose his hair stood on end. (This was, in fact, true, Dr Butler recounted with a laugh. The fellow had an unusual sinus that ran up his forehead and under his scalp, causing the skin on his head to blow like a balloon when he blew his nose.) Dr Butler would chuckle in a gentle way about the patient he was particularly fond of – Henrietta, who was clearly a spastic, suffering from cerebral palsy. She could only have been born with it, he told Lucy, but he was too kind to contradict Henrietta's own version of her medical history – told to her by her mother – that she had been born perfect but then swallowed a nappy pin as a baby and this had worked its way through her body to ruin her backbone for ever.

Lucy knew many of the patients herself. She would see them coming into the house to sit patiently in the waiting room at the front of the house, and then she might see them another time in Kentish Town Road, at the fishmonger's or butcher, or browsing around the shelves in the library.

There was Elsie, the woman with popping eyes and hair falling out, who lived in a council flat in Bartholomew Road.

She would come with her ten-year-old son who had thick dark hair all over his face like a young werewolf. Then there was old Mr Potter, who lived in Ascham Street and suffered from patches of horrible red scaly skin all over his unhappy face. Lucy always felt sorry for him. Another regular visitor to the surgery was Miss Norris, a very thin lady whose enormous ankles swelled over the tops of her shoes as though someone had pumped water down inside the skin of her legs.

Otherwise Dr Butler attracted a lot of ordinary patients, with ordinary minor ailments and aches and pains. There were the young mothers with their chubby babies, the bent old ladies hobbling in with their corns and bunions, the elderly men with their rasping coughs and troublesome old war wounds. And some of them came to confirm that they were close to death.

It always saddened Lucy to hear that her father had just certified the death of someone she knew. Only last year old Mr Turner died, and she could hardly believe it. Frank Turner had lived in Falkland Road, just two doors down. He had always been so friendly towards her. He used to invite her in for tea and biscuits and tell her about his grandchildren, who lived in America and Australia. Then suddenly he was dead, a heart attack in his sleep. One day he was there, the next he was gone.

She had cried hard at that news. Her father had comforted her. 'Everyone has to die at some time,' he said. 'We're all mortal, even the Queen. And let me tell you that dying in your sleep isn't a bad way to go. That's the way I'd like to go myself.'

Lucy scowled. 'Oh, don't talk about you dying, Daddy,' she protested. 'I can't bear the thought.'

*   *   *

Dr Butler sat at his dark mahogany desk with his back to the cabinet. At thirty-five, he was a good-looking man with black hair showing streaks of grey. His gentle brown eyes and a quiet manner helped make him a popular doctor. He enjoyed his work and was a conscientious physician who had lived in Kentish Town for nearly ten years, since just before Lucy was born. With the help of his wife, he had built up a moderate-sized practice. Hilda had proved to be a great asset; she ran the practice as efficiently as she kept the home.

On the desk, below the photographs of his father and grandfather, was a large colour photograph of his children – nine-year-old Lucy, beaming at the camera, and seven-year-old Andrew, glancing shyly sideways, a smile perhaps about to appear on his lips.

There was another photograph of his wife in a tan leather frame. It was his favourite photograph of Hilda, taken soon after he had met her at University College Hospital, where he had trained as a doctor. She was a newly qualified nurse. In the photograph she was laughing, her curly brown hair thrown back off her face. She was looking so young and carefree then, long before their marriage and the arrival of the children. Well, they had indeed been more carefree then, in their early twenties, with their whole lives stretching out before them, before they had lived long enough to have experienced too many tragedies or dark moments. As a doctor, he saw such tragedies and dark moments all the time, but they were in other people's lives. The Butlers had, of course, had a few moments of sadness, but no more than the average.

It was quiet in the room. The clock ticked softly on the mantelpiece. Lucy felt peaceful and happy. The house was always blissfully quiet and still when her mother was out. She took the busy atmosphere away with her. That afternoon, Hilda Butler had taken Andrew over to Jones Brothers in the Holloway Road to get him fitted for new shoes.

The telephone rang at about three o'clock. Dr Butler answered it and listened before asking a few questions. 'I'll be along within fifteen minutes,' he said, and put down the phone.

'I have to make a home visit,' he told his daughter. 'It's just up the road. Do you want to come or stay here?'

'Can I stay here by myself?' Lucy was delighted that her father considered her old enough to stay.

As she said the words, she could see her father's face change, the expression suddenly uncertain. 'On second thoughts, I think you'd better come with me. Your mother might not be so pleased if she knew I'd left you on your own. You can come and wait for me while I see this young child. It's just up the hill. It won't take long . . .'

Lucy did not try to hide her disappointment. 'Oh, Daddy, I'm nine years old, and I'm perfectly old enough to be left alone. Please.'

Her father shook his head. 'I'm sorry, Lucy. You know if it were up to me, I'd let you stay. But your mother worries a lot and I think it would be better to ask her first rather than making a unilateral decision.'

Lucy did not know what unilateral meant. Normally she would have asked but she fell back into a sulky silence. She was tired of being treated like a baby. Her parents never let her do anything on her own or trusted her to be sensible.

Dr Butler picked up his heavy black leather bag. 'Come on, slowcoach, we'd better go and see this young patient. It's one of the Valentines, that family in the big house at the top of Lady Margaret Road. They've only recently registered with me, and I've hardly seen any of them. They seem like a healthy lot. There are a lot of children, about six or seven, I think, or maybe more.'

As father and daughter walked up the hill, Dr Butler thought how he was glad to have this opportunity to make contact with the family. His wife had told him they had registered, after their old family doctor in Tufnell Park had died and they did not like the new one who took over. Dr Butler remembered precisely when that was – in May. He remembered because it was around the time of the student riots in Paris. There was a lot of debate on the television and radio about students and student issues, and Anthony Valentine was often on as a guest, always very outspoken on behalf of the student cause. He was an academic of some sort.

Dr Butler noticed Anthony Valentine's name again in June when Danny the Red, one of the most famous students in Paris, came to Britain after a row about his visa. (Hilda had thought it wrong that he was granted a visa at all.) He came to take part in a BBC debate with students from other parts of the world. Anthony Valentine had taken part in that, too, totally on the side of the students, their sit-ins and complaints.

The Butlers learned from that debate that Anthony Valentine was a lecturer at the London School of Economics, where Danny the Red gave a talk to the students the day after.

Since then, the Butlers had occasionally seen Anthony on television discussing his views about the Student Question, or being quoted in the *Hampstead and Highgate Express* criticising Camden Council and the town planners for pulling down perfectly good houses and building characterless housing estates, all in the name of slum clearance and progress. He was very active in local politics and even seemed to support the squatters who had taken over many of the empty council houses scattered around the borough. Hilda did not approve of such things, but Dr Butler was undecided. As a doctor he had visited some pretty squalid homes and was aware of the disgusting conditions that many poor families were forced to live in. The council had a duty to build better homes for people to live in but Camden had been particularly bad about clearing houses and then doing nothing with them, allowing the empty houses to fall into even worse states of repair. If squatters moved in and did them up and looked after them, surely it was better than leaving them empty.

They had had squatters living two doors down from them for the past six months. Hilda had been most upset when they first pushed their way in and settled down there. The house had been lived in by an old patient of Dr Butler's, Frank Turner, a widower, who died in his sleep only last year. The house was already run down but it had fallen into an even worse state of repair very rapidly until it looked as if it was about to fall down brick by brick. Even Hilda had to admit that the young squatters – gentle people who wore flowing clothes and long hair – had improved the house no end. They removed the buddleia bushes from the crumbling mortar, replaced the rotting woodwork, patched up the masonry, painted the windows and door, and even planted brightly coloured flowers in the front and back gardens. The house had not looked so good in years.

No, thought Dr Butler, the squatting issue was not a simple one at all.

The Valentines' residence was a rambling double-fronted Victorian house at the top of the hill, just before Brecknock

Road, where Lady Margaret Road ran down towards Tufnell Park. Lucy had noticed this house before because its unusually massive size made it stand out from the others around it. Built in 1860 by a prosperous Victorian merchant who had made his fortune in railways, it was surrounded by a large walled garden shaded by tall poplar trees. From the top-floor windows there were sweeping views of London in every direction, to the Kent hills in the south, Hampstead Heath to the west, and the hills of Crouch End and Muswell Hill, and Alexandra Palace to the north. It was really a vast suburban villa amongst city terraces.

Lucy had often heard children's voices drifting over the garden wall. There were always lots of them, which had led her to believe that there were often parties going on from which she felt excluded. It had never occurred to her that they might just be the voices of the children who lived there.

It was about 3.15 when Dr Butler and his daughter stood on the blue-and-white ceramic tiles of the front doorstep and rang the bell.

The door was opened by a short woman with brown, shoulder-length hair. Lucy immediately noticed her straight sharp nose and thick, shapeless lips. Behind her, a small pretty child with long curly black hair and deep blue eyes clung to her skirt.

'Mrs Valentine?' Dr Butler was momentarily confused.

The woman stepped back, opening the door to let them step into the house. 'No, I'm the housekeeper,' she said. 'Mr and Mrs Valentine are out at a concert this afternoon. They left me instructions to call you if the child worsened. He's upstairs in bed. He was listless this morning and stayed in bed. But an hour or so ago he started vomiting. I called you after he was sick for the third time.'

She spoke softly but clearly with a distinct Welsh accent.

Her pale face showed little expression. She was not casual but she did not give the impression of being particularly worried, either.

Lucy smiled at the attractive little girl who was still holding on to the housekeeper's skirts. The child stuck out the pink tip of her tongue and curled it round the corner of her lips, in the manner of all the world's babies in moments of shyness, and looked away.

The housekeeper pushed the girl to the side with a firm gesture. 'Stand out of the way, Celestria,' she said. 'Let the doctor pass.' Then she started to lead Dr Butler towards the stairs.

Dr Butler hesitated. 'Is there somewhere my daughter can sit while I go upstairs? I apologise for having to bring her but my wife is out. I think she should stay downstairs while I see the patient.'

The housekeeper nodded. She opened a white door off the hall to the left of the stairs. 'You can wait for your father in here,' she said to Lucy.

Lucy wandered into the room. A dog, a brown cocker spaniel, was lying on a rug in front of the fireplace. It jumped to its feet when it heard her. For a second it eyed her nervously, but then relaxed and wagged its tail gently before settling down again, licking its chops.

Lucy sat down on a dark blue three-seater sofa, sinking into the comfortable soft cushions. Above the mantelpiece there were two life-size portrait paintings in ornate gilt frames. One was of a young woman of great loveliness, with huge dark eyes and long flowing black hair which fell in soft curls around her graceful neck and bare shoulders. Her face seemed perfectly proportioned and, draped in a diaphanous white shawl, she stared out at the world with a dreamy intelligence.

The other portrait was of a young blond man. Dressed in a crisp white shirt, open at the neck, he looked out boldly and confidently, his dark blue eyes proving the only colour against his pale skin and yellow-white hair.

Lucy was staring up at these portraits, and so engrossed that she did not hear the children come in.

She was startled by a voice behind her.

'Those are our parents.'

Lucy jumped and turned to see three girls standing in a row before the door. The dog jumped out of its basket and walked over to the girls, its claws clicking on the floorboards, its docked tail wagging in greeting.

The littlest girl bent down to pat the dog's head. 'Hello, Dido, lovely dog.' She kissed its ear and the dog licked the child's hand appreciatively.

'Hello, I'm Vita,' said the tallest of the three. She looked about the same age as Lucy, but she was tall and slender with thick black hair and dark eyes. She held out her hand. Lucy shook it shyly.

'Hello.'

'I'm nine,' said Vita. 'This is Perdita. She's eight, and this is Lorelei. She's five.'

Perdita and Lorelei stepped forward to shake Lucy's hand. These two did not smile but scrutinised her with their big calm eyes. Perdita's were as pale as Vita's were dark.

All three girls wore blue jeans and rather grubby white T-shirts.

Lucy realised then that these children were not unfamiliar to her. She had seen them many times in the street – either on bicycles or on roller skates, careering along the pavements as bold and carefree as any child she had ever seen. She had never seen them in the company of an adult, and Lucy had often been aware of her own envy of such freedom to roam at will.

Now that she could study them close up, Lucy was struck by how Vita and Perdita were beautiful, graceful and dark like their mother, though Vita had dark olive skin and Perdita had creamy white skin and a mole on her cheek. Lorelei, with her handsome wide cheekbones, white-blonde hair and deep blue eyes, evidently took after her father.

'The portraits were painted when our parents were students at Oxford,' continued Vita. 'They were very clever and the most handsome couple in their generation. These paintings were done by a friend of theirs who is now a very famous artist.

'They're older than that now, of course,' she added. 'The paintings were done fifteen years ago.'

Lucy nodded and smiled. Thinking of her own parents with their ordinary looks and features and their normal clothes, she found it impossible to imagine what it must be like to have parents who were so famously good-looking and handsome that they had to be painted. 'They're big pictures,' she murmured. 'It must have taken a long time to paint them,' she added.

The girls did not seem to notice the lameness of her comment. They now crowded round the sofa, quizzing Lucy relentlessly about herself. Where do you live? Where do you go to school? How old are you?

Glancing from one inquisitive face to another, Lucy told the girls what they wanted to know. She informed them that she lived in Falkland Road, just off Lady Margaret Road and opposite the Methodist church that was hardly ever used nowadays. She was nine years old, she told them. She attended St Luke's Church School in Islip Street, and when she was eleven she was going to go to Camden School for Girls.

As Lucy answered their questions, she found herself looking around the room. The large French doors were open on to the verdant back garden. The heavy maroon velvet curtains moved gently in the breeze which blew in from the outside. Three walls were crowded with pictures – oil paintings, watercolours, prints of all sizes. The fourth wall was lined with bookshelves, from floor to ceiling, all of them jammed tight with books. The small tables against the wall had colourful Tiffany glass lamps and simple Chinese vases of subtle delicate colours. The floor, dark polished boards with red and blue Persian carpets, bore piles of newspapers, magazines and reviews. Everywhere she looked there was something to read – books, newspapers, magazines and journals – *New Statesman*, *The Spectator*, *The Economist*, *New Scientist*, *The Times Literary Supplement*, *Vogue* and *Queen*.

A few minutes later the door opened again. The children stopped their chattering and fell silent as Olwyn the housekeeper came in carrying a round wooden tray with a glass of milk and a small plate of home-made butter biscuits. 'Here are some refreshments for you,' she said, without looking at Lucy. She was a short, stolid woman wearing a short skirt which stopped two inches above her fleshy knees.

Lorelei was stroking Dido, the dog, which backed away quietly and slunk off to its basket.

'Thank you,' replied Lucy. She watched in puzzlement as Dido nervously eyed the housekeeper.

Olwyn placed the tray quietly on the side table next to Lucy and left the room. None of the other girls said a word. It was an odd silence that had descended upon the room. But the moment the door clicked quietly behind the housekeeper, the children became animated again, and Dido's ears pricked up cheerfully.

'Are those just for me?' Lucy asked, greedily eyeing the pile of biscuits.

'Drink your milk and you can come and see my room, if you want.' Vita smiled at her with friendly openness.

'Don't you want a biscuit?' Lucy was puzzled that there was no milk and biscuits for the others.

Vita shook her head quickly. 'We're not supposed to eat between meals,' she said, 'and tea's in an hour.'

'Oh, that's what Olwyn says, anyway,' said Perdita with a quick laugh. 'But she's not here. I'll certainly have half a biscuit if there's one going.' She took Lucy's offering and ate it swiftly, wiping away any telltale crumbs off her red lips.

After Lucy had finished her snack, Vita took her on a tour of the house upstairs, all the while talking rapidly about her family.

'There are eight of us children. Our parents aren't even Catholics, they just like having children. Our mother was a twin and she has had two sets of twins herself – you know it runs in families. I might easily have twins myself when I have children. There's Constantine and Achilles, they're identical twins and they're fourteen. Then there's Byron, who's twelve. They all go to boarding school, where they have lots of fun. They're all out playing tennis on Parliament Hill this afternoon. They're very good at it. Then there's me, then Perdita, then there are the other twins, Lorelei and Florian. Last is Celestria, who's three.'

'What unusual names you all have,' remarked Lucy.

Vita nodded. 'Mmm. Our mother likes names,' she said. 'She says that sometimes a person's name is more interesting than its owner.'

Everywhere they walked in the house – up the stairs, along the corridors, into rooms – the walls were covered with bookshelves crammed with books, and any gaps between shelves were filled with pictures and ceramic pots.

Finally, Vita led Lucy into a bedroom and said, 'This is my room.' The walls were painted a sky blue. Bunk beds had been pushed against the wall, and on the walls were posters of the Beatles and the Rolling Stones. There was a record player in one corner and a box full of LPs. One poster of Paul McCartney was inscribed: 'To Vita, with all my loving, from Paul'.

Lucy looked at it with surprise. 'Is that really Paul McCartney's signature?'

Vita nodded casually. 'Yup. We've met the Beatles. They're friends of our parents. They've even been here to supper.'

Lucy was impressed. She had never heard the Beatles singing but she knew from her friends at school who were allowed to watch *Top of the Pops* that they were the coolest thing. It seemed astonishing that the Beatles had actually been to Kentish Town and eaten supper just a few hundred yards from her own house. Why, no one would believe her if she told them! She scrutinised the books stacked on the shelves running across the whole of one wall. 'You've got some great books here,' she told Vita. Lucy loved reading and always had at least three books out from Kentish Town Library at any one time.

'You can borrow them whenever you like,' said Vita. 'So long as you return them.'

Lucy smiled gratefully at these words, for they suggested that she was going to see this interesting family again – and that Vita, at least, was happy to see more of her.

'Thank you,' she said.

Vita smiled back. 'Take one now, if you like, and bring it back when you've finished.'

Lucy knew exactly what she wanted. It was a beautiful old edition of *A Little Princess*. She had spotted it the moment she walked into the room. She had been planning to get it out of the library next time but this edition, with its gold lettering and old-fashioned pictures, was so interesting. And what a coincidence! She reached out and gently slid the book out of the shelf.

Vita nodded with approval. 'I love that book. It's one of my favourites. And that particular book used to belong to my grandmother. She gave it to me.'

Clutching *A Little Princess* under her arm, Lucy looked on with interest while Vita then showed off her collection of fossils.

'I found them in Sussex, near my grandmother's house,' she said. 'It's very chalky around there, and good for fossils.'

A voice was calling from downstairs: 'Vita! Come down now. Dr Butler is leaving.'

Vita pulled on Lucy's sleeve. 'You've got to go,' she told her. 'But you must come again soon.' Her smile was warm, her pink lips revealing small white teeth. She spoke with the confidence of an adult. 'Any time.'

'Thank you,' said Lucy. 'I'd like that.'

As they walked down the stairs Lucy could see her father by the front door, dressed in his brown corduroy trousers and green tweed jacket, giving instructions to the housekeeper.

A small, sturdy dark-haired boy of about eight suddenly appeared from a doorway, crept across the hall and disappeared down the basement steps.

'Is that one of your brothers?' asked Lucy.

Vita frowned. 'Who, him? No. That's just the Brat,' she said dismissively. She turned away and said no more.

There was no time to find out more. Lucy's father turned and reached out his arm for her. 'There you are, Lucy,' he said. 'Time to go home now. The patient is quite comfortable.'

Olwyn the housekeeper had opened the front door for them. As father and daughter walked out into the garden, and the heavy door was closing behind them, Lucy heard the sweetest words she could have hoped for.

'See you again soon,' Vita called. 'I hope you'll visit us again.'

At supper at the Butlers' house in Falkland Road that evening, Lucy listened as her parents discussed Dr Butler's visit to the Valentine family. Andrew, as always, was lost in his seven-year-old thoughts at the other end of the table. Hilda Butler was noticeably interested in the fact that her husband had been to their house that afternoon, and she quizzed him in detail about what it was like inside.

Dr Butler slit open his baked potato and spooned in a slab of yellow butter. He shook his head and frowned.

'I wasn't there to inspect the decor, Hilda. I had a sick child to attend to.'

'It is very big with lots of rooms,' Lucy offered. 'There are books everywhere you look – on the walls and the floors, too. It's crammed with things, beautiful things to look at.'

'Such as?' demanded her mother.

'Oh, beautiful bowls, rugs, vases and statues, and stained-glass table lamps, things like that.'

Hilda nodded in the ostentatiously knowing way she had. Lucy could guess that her mother was mentally tut-tutting at the amount of dusting such objects required. She did not give her the pleasure of knowing about the light film of London dust that lay on the bowls, vases and statues, or how untidy the place had been with piles of books stashed in corners on the floor and mountains of dirty clothes in the children's bedrooms.

'I met some of the children, too,' she went on. 'They were very friendly. One of them, Vita, said I should come again.'

'How many children are there?' asked her mother. 'I know there are a lot of them.'

'Eight.'

'Oh, they must be Catholics, having that many children.' Mrs Butler seemed pleased to have worked out something else. 'That explains why I never see them in church.'

'Perhaps they simply don't go to church,' said Dr Butler. 'That's possible.'

'No, they're not Catholics,' chimed in Lucy. 'Vita specifically told me they're not.'

Her mother did not seem to hear. 'They must be well off to be able to afford so many children.'

'I expect there's a bit of private money there,' replied Dr Butler. 'The house seems to be full of heirlooms.'

'What's an heirloom?' asked Andrew from the end of the table, where he had been struggling with his baked potato and listening quietly.

'Don't talk with your mouth full, Andrew,' his mother said tolerantly. 'Hold your knife and fork properly. And please, darling, sit up straight!'

Lucy caught Andrew's eye and smiled sympathetically as their parents continued to exchange what bits of information they had about the Valentine family. Lucy lapped it all up as she heard the snippets of information and gossip.

'He's very left-wing, the husband, isn't he?' Lucy could

tell from the sharpness in her mother's voice that this was not necessarily a good thing – whatever it meant to be 'left-wing'.

'He certainly doesn't seem to side with the Establishment, in anything he says or writes,' replied Dr Butler. His own political views were neutral except when it came to the National Health Service, which he loved dearly and defended passionately.

Mrs Butler's attention switched to Mrs Valentine. 'She is very good-looking, I have to say that. I see her sometimes in Kentish Town Road. She wafts about in long kaftans and the most unsuitable kinds of clothes. Her mind always strikes me as being somewhere else. I've stood behind her in the butcher's on more than one occasion when she's held up the queue while she scrabbles around for her shopping list, which she's usually lost somewhere among the folds of her garments.

'But I don't think she has much to do with the house, really. That housekeeper of hers is always doing the household shopping, as far as I can tell. I'm not sure how much she does with the children, either. Seraphina Valentine – isn't Seraphina her name? – extraordinary, isn't it . . . ?'

As her parents continued to discuss the Valentines, Lucy learned that Seraphina was a writer and artist who had had some success at both.

'She writes poetry, I think, and novels. I've seen her books in the bookshop,' said Hilda. 'Historical novels – not really my sort of thing.' Her own taste ran more to straightforward romantic fiction. 'And once when we went to the Camden Arts Centre there was an exhibition of her paintings. Not to my liking at all. Very modern.'

Now Lucy's mother struck her final blow.

'It makes you wonder, though, doesn't it? To go out to a

concert when one of your little ones is ill. Fancy leaving it
to the housekeeper to arrange for the doctor to come.'

'That's a bit harsh, Hilda,' said Dr Butler. 'People are
allowed to enjoy themselves, and the child was not that
ill.'

'But they didn't know that, did they? Besides, I don't trust
anyone who hands over her children to another woman to
look after. What's she doing having so many children if
she's not going to look after them herself?'

'Perhaps that's precisely why she does have so many
children . . .' muttered Dr Butler drily, impressed by his
own insight.

Ignoring him, Hilda went on cataloguing her disapproval. 'And I always see them running around the place,
unsupervised, in a way that *I* would never tolerate. Shaking
her head, she declared that the Valentines were 'bohemians'.
The tone in her voice made it plain to Lucy that they were
not quite as wonderful as she, Lucy, thought, that there was
something other people did not like about them.

As a result, Lucy was fascinated by her mother's reaction
to the Valentines. They seemed to bring out all sorts of
opinions she probably knew her mother had, but she had
never heard them expressed before.

But in spite of this disapproval, Lucy could tell that the
Valentines fascinated her mother, just as they fascinated
her.

After supper, Lucy went to bed and settled down to her
evening reading of *The Lion, the Witch and the Wardrobe*.
She had started it the week before and was enjoying it a lot
but now she could not wait to finish it so that she could
begin reading Vita's copy of *A Little Princess*, which now
lay on her bedside table. Lucy had placed it there carefully
so that she could see it even when she was lying down with

her head on the pillow. Earlier, she had run her fingers over the soft brown binding and admired the delicate tissue paper covering the pretty coloured picture plates inside.

Immersed in the world of Narnia, Lucy did not hear Andrew come into her room.

'Hello,' he said.

Lucy turned to look at him. She smiled. He looked cute, dressed in his stripy blue pyjamas and sucking his thumb.

Climbing on to Lucy's bed, he snuggled down next to her, as he did every night.

Lucy smiled again and moved over to make room for him. She liked her little brother and was always pleased when he asked for things from her.

'Read a book to me, Lucy,' said Andrew. 'Read me some more of *The Lion, the Witch and the Wardrobe*. When you've finished, I'll read it myself but I like the way you say it out aloud.'

So Lucy read to Andrew for ten minutes until his eyelids closed and he fell into a deep sleep beside her.

Dr Butler came up to say goodnight and to move Andrew back to his own bed. 'Goodnight, Lucy,' he said, as he turned off the light, the sleeping boy in his arms. 'It sounds as if you've made some new friends today.'

Snuggling down in her warm bed, Lucy still felt exhilarated by the afternoon's visit. Her head was swimming with images from the Valentine house up the road. How happy she was that those girls had been friendly. It would be wonderful if her father were right – she would so much like to be friends with them!

Lucy turned over restlessly. The more she thought back on the day, the more she felt that she had been on some electrifying journey to a new and exotic land. She had not known that people could live like that, surrounded by hundreds of books and beautiful objects – the richness of the velvet curtains, the deep warm colours of the rugs on the floor, the bright modern prints and the thickly textured oil paintings in their gilt frames, even the freshness of the breeze from the garden – and have so little regard for untidiness or dust. These were the two things that her mother could not abide.

Her eyelids fluttered and she let out a drowsy sigh. Lucy fell asleep trying to imagine what she would have been like if chance had made her be born into the Valentine family instead of her own. She would have liked to be Vita's twin. How lucky she would have been then!

CHAPTER 3

May, 1997

Old Friends

The night before her planned meeting with the adult Vita Valentine, Lucy was tense and nervous. At home in bed, her jaw felt tight and rigid, her teeth clenched. Even a bit of warm bedtime sex did not help her relax much, but then sex rarely helped her relax nowadays, now that it had become associated with procreation and nothing more. Sleep finally came by midnight but Lucy was dismayed to find herself awake again three hours later after an unpleasant dream about blind babies encircling her and reaching out their chubby arms to her in despair. Why was she suddenly dreaming these awful baby dreams?

Simon lay in a deep sleep beside her, his curly hair just visible under the blue duvet. His breathing was deep and regular. Lucky sod, he never had trouble getting to sleep – or staying there, for that matter. Simon was such an uncomplicated man. Phlegmatic and calm at all times, nothing fazed him. Or at least it never appeared to.

Her thoughts spun around her head as she thought about the Valentines again. Vita she remembered as a striking beauty, with long black hair, white skin and flashing black eyes. Thinking about her, Lucy felt quite old and faded, particularly since she knew that Vita was also a mother, something Lucy herself had been unable to achieve at this great age of thirty-seven. Thirty-seven! With no children and no significant career to speak of! Here was Vita with two young children *and* a successful career as a journalist. Now she was aware of it, she had seen Vita's byline in numerous publications. Lucy felt as if she had done nothing by comparison.

But if thoughts of Vita made Lucy feel inadequate, then memories of the Valentine parents made her feel even worse. They couldn't have been much older than Lucy was now, yet at that time they were famous. And they had eight children! How could she fail to feel she had just wasted her life in the face of that?

The birds outside the window were starting up the first notes of the dawn chorus. Why could she not sleep? There was no hope; her thoughts churned on round and round her head.

Well, at least, she thought, she was still married and seemed to have been quite successful at that. Lucy consoled herself with the other fact that Vita had told her, that Vita was widowed. So not everything could be perfect for her. Terrible things had happened in her life. Lucy felt a pang of guilt about feeling glad that life was not perfect for Vita Valentine. She was not glad that Vita had been widowed but she was glad to know that she had not always had a charmed life.

Now she was more awake, Lucy realised how much she was clenching her jaw. Sleep had not entirely gone away, it hovered about her. Her thoughts were slipping in and out of consciousness as she recalled that first visit to the Valentine house with her father that Saturday afternoon. Was it a dream or memory when she saw in her head the group of

Valentine children crowding around her in a big room filled with beautiful objects? Were they dreams or flashes of broken memory, these feelings that she experienced now? There was the deep longing to be part of that household, her excitement at being in their presence, her great joy at being accepted as a friend of Vita and Perdita, her younger sister.

Dreaming and not dreaming, she visualised the wonderful paradise of the grandmother's house in the country, swimming in the river nearby, running through water meadows, the long grass tickling her bare legs as a crowd of children ran chasing each other and falling over in their excitement.

The dawn chorus grew louder. Lucy was awake but she realised that she had a smile on her lips. What great friends they had been that summer, those Valentine girls!

Lucy rolled over. Tucking the pillow under her neck, she tried to get more comfortable. So long ago. She had been nine. It was the year they went to Norfolk for their summer holiday for the third year running. It was the year *Yellow Submarine* came out, and when the Beatles opened their shop in Baker Street. The Valentines had known the Beatles, she remembered that, too.

She had a strange memory – or was it a dream? – of her father laughing and making jokes. Lucy could almost feel the happy atmosphere in the house. Was she imagining it or did she have a memory of her mother sitting at the table, smiling and relaxed? Hilda is looking across the table at her husband, the doctor, a proud look on her face as he talks and laughs in an animated way. Was there a time when her parents had enjoyed each other's company and relished family life?

Her thoughts were drifting out of control. Oh, it must be a dream. Lucy frowned in the grey dawn light as she worked through another strange thought. She had been nine when her parents moved away from Kentish Town. They moved soon after that amazing summer. What was so astonishing to her now was that Lucy had only known the Valentines for a very short time, for that one summer of 1968, yet it always felt as if it had been years. The Valentine family had impressed itself in her consciousness so deeply that she was always surprised to remind herself that their intense relationship had not lasted for years.

And yet, once her father got that other job in south London and they moved, it seemed that she had no more contact with the family. That was strange, but indeed, she had no recollection of seeing Vita – or any of them – after the move. She did not remember even keeping in touch by letter. How odd that so much of that summer had become a part of her and other bits were so dark. Memory was a strange thing. And the strangest thing was the feeling she had that life had somehow become completely different after her family moved away from Kentish Town. Maddeningly, she could not remember why. What was it that made one remember some things and not others?

Oh, she was tired. She lay awake for a while longer until finally sleep did overcome her. Her steady soft breathing began just as she had started to wonder again what Vita Valentine would look like.

They were to meet at the Groucho Club at seven. Vita lived in West Hampstead, Lucy in Shepherd's Bush, so it was easier for them both to travel into the centre of town and meet there. And Vita was a member.

Lucy had been to the Groucho Club a few times with Rosie, who had been a member from the early days, and she was not delighted by the choice. Those crowds of noisy, confident young people made her nervous, but she did not have an alternative venue to suggest.

Lucy arrived early and sat on the sofa in the foyer waiting for Vita to arrive. Sitting perched on the edge of the seat, she watched the cocky journalists and young advertising executives, dressed in their slick suits, walk in through the revolving doors, kissing each other on the cheeks, greeting each other with loud exclamations of joy and delight. The short skirts, well-toned bodies, high heels, and air of self-importance made Lucy want to shrink away and disappear into the upholstery, so unconfident and small she felt.

Vita was late and Lucy's discomfort grew, sitting there on the green sofa. She tried to look casual and offhand, and listened in to several banal conversations one advertising executive had on his mobile phone, talking loudly so that all could hear.

Just when Lucy was beginning to think she had got the date wrong, Vita walked in through the door. Lucy recognised her immediately, though it was twenty-eight years since their last meeting. Jumping to her feet, Lucy smiled with obvious relief.

'Hello, Vita.'

The thick hair was still black, pulled back off her face and tied in a loose plait down her back. Her skin still had that olive Mediterranean sheen inherited from her maternal grandmother, and her eyelids still looked heavy over her dark eyes. Her features were clean and strong. Lucy instantly recalled the portrait of Seraphina Valentine on the wall in the sitting room. Vita had grown up to look just like her mother. She held out her hand to Lucy and smiled, showing a flash of strong white teeth. As Lucy responded, she placed her other hand over Lucy's, pulling her to her, and kissed her on the cheek. 'Hello, there! You look just the same. And you look wonderful!'

Lucy blushed. She did not feel wonderful at all, and Vita's well-cut black suit made her feel even more dowdy in her neat little Marks & Spencer skirt and blouse, and her polished brown shoes from Next.

'What will you have to drink?' Vita asked, leading Lucy into the bar and waving casually to the waiter.

'What are you drinking?' Lucy asked.

'Large Scotch on the rocks.'

'I'll have a white wine spritzer,' replied Lucy.

They sat side by side on a lumpy blue sofa under the window, oblivious to the noisy crowd surrounding them in the bar. It was odd at first as they slowly filled each other in on their lives since the age of nine. In her husky voice, now made even huskier by the untipped Gauloises she consumed in great numbers, Vita told Lucy about her family's activities. The whole family moved, in 1969, to California, where Anthony Valentine was given a teaching post at Berkeley. The children all went to American schools but then came home to go to university at Oxford.

'We all went to Oxford. It was expected of us.' She said this breezily but without boasting. 'I read English and my sister Celestria read medicine. She's a consultant paediatrician in Yorkshire. Everyone else read law, including Perdita, whom I'm sure you remember. Perdita's a barrister here in London, but my older brothers – Achilles, Constantine and Byron – they're all lawyers in the States. They have a law firm together in Washington DC, and specialise in civil rights cases. And Florian and Lorelei, the other twins, are solicitors with their own firm down in Croydon. They concentrate mainly on legal aid and mental health cases.'

'So they're all left-wing, like your parents . . .'

Vita looked at her curiously for a moment. Then she laughed. 'I don't think any of them are particularly interested in politics, but I suppose there seems to be a family gene that wants to make things better in the world.' Pausing briefly, she added without looking directly at Lucy, 'Or perhaps there's a need to look after the underdog . . .'

'And are they all married?' Lucy wanted to know all the details. 'Do they have children?'

To her surprise, Vita shook her head. 'Some got married but they all seem to have split up. I'm the only one with children, and all the others seem a bit hopeless when it comes to relationships. I don't know if they're going to reproduce or not. I do know that Perdita certainly doesn't want children, and Celestria seems too busy looking after other people's children to have much time for a social life. The rest, I don't know . . .'

'That must be sad for your parents,' said Lucy, thinking of her own mother's longing for the next generation.

But Vita shrugged. 'Oh, I don't think they're bothered. They're not particularly interested in grandchildren. They hardly see my children. They still live in California and rarely come to Europe nowadays. We talk on the telephone.'

It was clear that she did not want to dwell on her parents, and she proceeded to tell Lucy more about her adult life. Soon after graduating, she married a fellow graduate from Oxford. He was a brilliant classicist, quite exceptional, who got a starred First and an academic post at Queen's College. But in his early thirties he became very peculiar, she said. He started to do odd things and was finally diagnosed as manic-depressive. By that time, they had two young children.

'Until I had children I was working as a journalist on the *Oxford Mail* but I stopped working the minute the children came along.' She paused. 'At the time it seemed very unfeminist to do such a thing, and I was criticised by several of my female colleagues on the paper. But I really wanted to look after them myself. It was important to me, for one reason or another,' she added softly.

'When the little one was just two,' she continued, 'Chris became out of control. He stopped taking his pills and ran up massive credit card bills, bought two new cars and a whole Smallbone kitchen one weekend. Then a week later he flew to Rio de Janeiro and back. He offered three people jobs on the plane.

'Immediately after that, the low started and he became more depressed than I'd ever seen him before. After a while he began to get better again and I thought he was all right. But then on Easter Sunday, he shot himself in the garden of a cottage we had rented for the holidays. I don't know where he got the gun from. It was a 12-bore shotgun. He put the muzzle in his mouth and lay on top of it so that the kickback wouldn't throw him off target. I found him when I came back from a walk with the children . . .' A deep line ran down her forehead as she toyed thoughtfully with her glass. 'I relive that scene every week of my life, and I still have a section of his skull, which I picked up afterwards.' Raising her head, she looked directly into Lucy's eyes. 'It's very smooth,' she said.

Lucy wanted to reach over and touch Vita, but she held back. 'I'm so sorry,' she said. 'It must have been terrible.'

Vita shrugged. 'Yes, it was. But the worst thing was that I was almost relieved when he killed himself. It was really the only way out of what had become a nightmare for him, for all of us.'

There was a brief, awkward silence as Lucy tried to imagine what Vita had gone through.

Then Vita sat up straighter and asked in a brighter voice, 'What about you, then?' It was clear that she was not hoping for pity.

'Well, there's not much more to tell you, really. I've had an unexciting sort of life,' apologised Lucy. 'I went to York University and then got a job in publishing. The worst thing that happened was that I got made redundant. I got married five years ago and I am still happily and boringly married. Simon is Deputy Editor of the *South London Examiner*, where he's been for years. He is not the ambitious type, he's happy on the paper, and I think just likes a relatively quiet life.'

It was Lucy's friend Rosie who had first introduced Lucy to Simon. She had met him at a dinner party and then invited him to a small drinks party of her own. Amazingly, Rosie had not slept with him. 'Grab him before I do,' Rosie had whispered soon after she had introduced him to Lucy on that occasion. Shoving the chilli dip under Lucy's nose, she hissed, 'Offer him some of this – it's nice and spicy.' Rosie placed her mouth against Lucy's ear. 'Go for it! You deserve him and I *think* he deserves you.'

The start of the relationship was simple and straight-forward. Simon and Lucy had taken to each other at that party. Simon invited Lucy out the next week and it grew from there. Simon was a great letter writer and proceeded to flood Lucy with long and passionate declarations of love.

Their relationship had grown slowly, thrived and flour-ished over the years. It had survived the few calamities, such as Lucy's redundancy, and they had weathered the unpredictable storms of infertility for a long time without breaking up, as many couples did.

Lucy looked sadly at Vita. 'The major event in my life is a non-event – I just haven't managed to conceive. And now I'm really beginning to feel that time is running out . . .'

'What about your parents?' asked Vita. 'Is your father still practising?'

'Yes. He's coming up to retirement soon but he's still working as a family doctor in Dulwich. He's been doing that since we moved away from Kentish Town.'

'And your mother,' asked Vita, 'she's still going?'

Yes, Lucy told her, her mother was still going. What she did not say was that her mother was more of the same – fussy and anxious, worrying about minor details and avoiding important issues. Lucy did not want to say too much about her mother's henpecking and constant nagging of her father. Age and experience had helped Lucy realise that her mother behaved in such a tight and rigid way because what was going on inside her head felt so messy and unbounded that she was terrified that it might become unleashed. Hilda needed to keep that internal chaos under control at all cost.

'My mother's not an easy woman to live with, but my father's worked out his own way of handling her. I suppose that's what couples do when they've been together a long time.'

Again, she did not describe in full her father opting out of conversation and family discussions in order to avoid arguments with his wife. It seemed that he always gave in to her. Lucy could tell that her father felt it was just not worth standing up to Hilda. It was just not worth getting into conflict with her, for whenever he did, Hilda would retreat to the bedroom in distress and tears, and Gordon would not have won any victory. As a result, Gordon Butler spent much of his spare time concentrating on his own interests

– listening to the opera on weekend afternoons, gardening, and reading detective novels.

'My parents have developed their own way of dealing with each other,' repeated Lucy sadly.

Vita raised her eyebrows and gave Lucy a cynical smile. 'My parents have never had that problem. They've always been more interested in each other and their work than in anyone else.'

There was another uncomfortable pause as Lucy could not think of how to respond. In the past, she had never once thought to criticise the Valentine parents in any way. They had seemed like dream parents to her at the time.

In her confusion, she found herself asking a question she would normally avoid. 'Tell me about your children . . .' But at the moment she had a singular feeling of closeness to Vita, as though they had been friends all their lives and had seen each other only last week rather than almost thirty years ago.

Vita looked pleased and opened her black leather handbag. Lifting out a photograph, she handed it to Lucy. Two black-haired girls with dark eyes and long eyelashes were standing with their arms around each other's shoulders and giggling into the camera.

'They're beautiful,' said Lucy. 'They look very lively.' A twinge of envy ran through her. 'They look just like you.'

Vita smiled. 'They're good girls. They've survived everything very well, so far.'

She went on to explain that she had a local woman – a mother herself – who looked after them after school and during the holidays, but as a freelance journalist she was working at home most of the day.

'I can keep a good eye on things,' she said, 'and make

sure everything's okay. She comes on a daily basis – I'd never have a live-in nanny.'

For a moment Lucy thought that a strange look came into Vita's face and, as she caught Vita's eye, a peculiar feeling spread over Lucy herself. She felt distinctly uneasy, but had no idea why.

'So, tell me about the rest of your family,' she said. The two women drank some more. The strange feelings receded and disappeared as the effects of the wine crept through her body. Lucy sank back on to the sofa. She was beginning to feel very relaxed and comfortable in Vita's company again. They drank some more and talked and laughed, still ignoring the crowds around them.

'Do you remember the time we ran that funny old go-cart down Lady Margaret Road at about five in the morning? And the time we left our footprints in the wet cement on the building site?'

Vita giggled and nodded. 'We had great fun,' she agreed. 'I remember a lot about that time, actually.'

Lucy felt a flicker of pleasure at the words.

'That holiday I had with you and your family up in Norfolk,' said Vita, 'that was lovely.'

'Did you enjoy that? I don't remember it being particularly memorable. I always worried that you were bored with my family. Yours always seemed so much more exciting.'

'Oh, I wasn't bored. I liked your parents a lot, especially your father. He was so great to talk to, and I learned a lot from him. He liked children, you could always tell that about him. He was interested in what children had to say. That's quite rare in an adult.'

Lucy looked thoughtful. 'It's interesting that you say that. Thinking about it, my father's been pretty good as a parent, to me. I've probably never properly appreciated how much he's supported me over the years. Mind you, I don't think he had particularly high expectations for me because I was a girl. It was different for my brother. When Andrew decided he didn't want to be a doctor, even after going through medical school and qualifying, my parents were disappointed. I think Dad's always felt that Andrew let him down because he did not become the fourth generation to go into medicine. He's still hoping, of course, but he won't get his wish. Andrew is far too happy not being a doctor – he runs his own computer graphics company, and loves it.'

As Lucy spoke she realised that Vita was looking distracted. Perhaps she was bored by Lucy's tale, or perhaps she was disappointed after meeting her old friend.

But Vita looked up at her again with an enigmatic smile on her red lips. 'It seemed to me that you were pretty lucky with your parents . . .' Her voice tailed off. Looking at her watch, she grimaced in dismay. 'Oh, I've got to get home, I'm afraid, before the children go to bed.'

She got to her feet. It was time to go.

As Lucy jumped to her feet also, she felt an impulsive rush of warmth towards Vita. 'You must come over for a drink and meet Simon,' Lucy said generously. 'Being journalists, you probably know all sorts of people in common.'

They parted on the mosaic ducks on the step of the Groucho Club, hugging each other tight. Vita smelled of expensive French scent.

'I'm glad we met up again,' Vita said in a forthright tone of voice as she stepped back. 'It's been great seeing you.'

'Oh yes,' said Lucy. 'Same here.' She felt quite dazed by the success of their meeting. It had been far better than anything she might have imagined.

Vita set off for Piccadilly and Lucy headed towards Tottenham Court Road tube. Lucy's spirits were soaring, and she suddenly recalled this same elation from the old days; Vita had always had this effect on her; it seemed as if nothing had changed.

Feeling quite high, Lucy sat on the edge of her seat in the tube train home. Her head buzzed with memories of that summer of 1968. Most of the memories came into her head vivid and unprompted, but there were others, too, vaguer ones. But whenever she tried to concentrate on these, they hovered in her mind and then veered off into the blackness beyond her mental reach. A peculiar sense of frustration came over her, as if some elusive thing were allowing her to go so far and no farther.

The excitement of meeting with Vita Valentine was forgotten two days later when she received the telephone call from Patrick Toller, her brother's live-in partner.

It was a call she had been awaiting for four years.

'Andrew's in the hospital,' Patrick said. His voice trembled. 'He's got PCP. They say they think he'll be all right, they've got it in time.

'He's at the Middlesex if you want to visit him. I'll be there this evening, too. Andrew wants you to call your parents and tell them.'

Lucy put down the phone. Her lips trembled like a child's as she fought back tears. It had started now. This was it. Patrick's news heralded what would be a quickening downward spiral of hospital admissions until death.

Until now, in spite of being HIV-positive, Andrew had been perfectly healthy. After an attack of shingles four years before, which was what prompted him to be tested for HIV, his health had been fine. He was a tall, strapping young man who played tennis and swam regularly. He always looked so well.

But Lucy knew that the virus would eventually win. She had read enough to know that the HIV-positive status eventually led to 'full-blown AIDS', that, in spite of the efforts of modern medicine to combat the disease, the virus gradually destroyed the body's immune system until the significant illnesses started, creeping up relentlessly, slowly destroying strong resilient human tissue and finally reducing it to a feeble mass of skin and bone. She did not know exactly what lay in store for her little brother, but she knew his future was going to be wretched.

PCP. This was a new term to her. She looked it up in her book on AIDS, which she had surreptitiously bought at Waterstones a year ago, and found that the initials stood for '*Pneumocystis carinii* pneumonia'. *Pneumocystis carinii*, the book explained, was a parasite that commonly caused lung infection and pneumonia in people with HIV infection. 'It is not known to cause illness in people with healthy immune systems. In many cases, PCP is an AIDS-defining illness. The immune deficiency syndrome makes its presence known as diseases appear that are caused by microbes ordinarily living in perfectly healthy human beings whose normal body defences prevent disease.'

Patrick had said that Andrew wanted her to tell their parents. This was the hardest bit. At some level Lucy felt angry with Andrew for dumping that task on her; he could have told them himself.

Yet Andrew had hardly seen his parents in five years. They could barely control their anger and annoyance over Andrew's rejection of a career as a doctor after all that time at medical school, when they'd been so proud of him. He had qualified, got his medical degree, but then announced that he did not want to practise as a doctor. His parents were disbelieving at the time, certain that he would change his mind.

But then Andrew packed up his backpack and set off for a trip around the world 'to find himself'. After spending two years in Australia, he returned to London a happier-looking man and now certain that he did not want to be a doctor.

In Australia he had discovered a talent for art and design which he had also combined with computer skills. He intended to set up a design company and have nothing to do with medicine at all.

He looked fit and well, slimmer and well-toned. When he introduced Lucy to his partner Patrick, Lucy was shocked at first, but then when she thought about it, she was not so surprised. The signals had all been there for many years – the absence of obvious girlfriends, the men's perfume, the fastidious dressing, the increasingly exaggerated gestures and mannerisms.

Andrew's parents concentrated their annoyance on his refusal to be a doctor. His sexuality was never discussed. Both the Butler parents had found Andrew's rejection of medicine difficult to accept, though it was Gordon who generally found it easier to accept what his children actually were, even if he had to struggle with himself a little. Hilda Butler, by contrast, had a tendency to expect things of people and then be disappointed and unforgiving when they didn't turn out that way.

Lucy always felt that by not becoming a nurse and marrying a successful doctor as Hilda had done, she herself had failed her mother. And by not producing grandchildren, she had failed her even more.

But at least she continued to have a relationship with her parents, while Andrew did not. Whenever his name came up in her parents' presence, her father would busy himself with the newspaper while Hilda pursed her lips, and allowed her eyes to take on a glassy stare.

*   *   *

Now Lucy had to tell her parents of Andrew's condition, when they had never even acknowledged that he was homosexual. Her hands shook as she tapped out the phone number and held the receiver against her head.

As always, her mother answered the telephone. Without any other warning, Lucy just blurted it out: 'Andrew's in the hospital. He was admitted today.'

She heard her mother let out a little gasp at the other end. The unguarded gasp of a mother.

Lucy had decided in advance not to let her mother do any of the talking. She had a message to convey, and convey it she would.

'He's in the Middlesex. I'm going to see him this evening but he'd like to see you, too. He specially asked me to call you.'

There was hesitation at the other end. Then a quiet voice. 'But what's wrong with him? Is it something serious?'

'He has pneumonia, Mother. But they say he's going to be all right.' She did not add, 'this time'; but that was what she was thinking. 'He'll be in for a few days,' she added.

There was a silence on the other end, then her father got on the line. Hilda had handed the receiver to him.

'What's all this then, Lucy?' Lucy repeated what she had told her mother, aware from the grunts on the other end that her father was taking it all in. He had worked out what was going on.

'He's in the Calder Ward,' she said. 'You can go and visit at any time . . .' She hesitated before saying more. But she decided to anyway. 'It's the AIDS ward, Daddy.' Her words spilled out as she broke down at the words.

Dr Butler's voice was calm and gentle. 'Yes,' he said, 'I thought it might be. Don't worry,' he added with an uncharacteristic firmness in his voice. 'We'll be there. Tell Andrew, when you see him, that we'll both be in to see him tomorrow.'

As she put down the phone, Lucy heard Simon, home from work, coming in through the front door. She stumbled across the room and threw herself into his arms.

That night she dreamed that she gave birth to a baby with two heads. One head was laughing and jeering at her; the other was crying pitifully. She woke up sweating, greatly relieved that she had been spared the task of killing the monster and both its heads.

CHAPTER 4

July, 1968

Paradise Found

Vita Valentine rang Lucy the next day, just as the Butlers were beginning to get ready for church.

'I wondered if you would like to come over to play this morning,' she said.

A thrill ran through Lucy as she heard these words. Vita wanted her company. She wanted to be her friend. Vita's voice was strong and confident. 'You can stay for lunch as well, if you like.'

To Lucy's surprise, her mother seemed pleased to hear about the invitation. In fact, for a momentary flash, she thought she looked excited.

'Tell Vita you can go up after church. I'll drop you round myself. They're only a minute away from St Benet's. I'd like to meet the mother,' she added softly, almost to herself.

A few minutes later, Mrs Butler's mouth twitched. She had been thinking. 'So it doesn't look as though they are churchgoers,' she said.

Dr Butler smoothed his hair against his scalp with the palm of his hand. 'Plenty of people are churchgoers without going to church every week, Hilda. We're in the minority nowadays.'

His wife ignored him. Humming softly, she straightened Andrew's collar and tie and checked her lipstick in the hall mirror. 'Ready everyone?'

Then, as she did every Sunday morning at ten minutes to eleven, she opened the front door, ushered her family out before her, and set off up the road to pray.

Seraphina Valentine, *née* Wilkinson, was an identical twin. She and her sister Araminta had been recognised as the most beautiful girls of their generation at Oxford where they graced the corridors of St Hilda's. From their Spanish mother they had inherited their thick black hair and lustrous brown-black eyes. Both were scholars, and they were identical in almost every way, though Seraphina was left-handed and Araminta right-handed. In temperament, too, they differed. Araminta enjoyed the privileges of their diplomatic upbringing and was attracted to conservative young men in striped shirts who shared her father's conventional beliefs. Seraphina, on the other hand, suffered frissons of guilt about her family's wealth, and invariably drifted towards clever young men whose political beliefs were at odds with those of her father. It was inevitable that she should end up with Anthony Valentine, who was recognised as not only the cleverest student in his year but also an intelligent left-wing thinker. He took a First with little effort and was immediately offered an academic post at the London School of Economics, hotbed of the student politics that he relished so much.

Nowadays, Anthony Valentine was renowned as the students' friend and eloquent expert on popular youth culture, with weekly columns in the *New Statesman* and the

Guardian and frequent invitations to speak at demonstrations and rallies and to appear as a pundit of television talk shows.

So Seraphina married Anthony and, with two lots of twins, bore him eight children. They were part of the trendy set of young London intellectuals, and they were invited to every important happening and party in the capital, whether it was literary, artistic, political or social. They campaigned for everything that was fair and just. But they also loved and appreciated beautiful works of art, supported the underdog and were always outspoken in their views. They were also both talented in their own right. To the outside world, the Valentines seemed to be touched with magic.

Seraphina's twin sister, Araminta, meanwhile, married a weak-chinned young man in the Foreign Office. In spite of his feebleness in bed, he managed to sire four children within five years, after which Araminta was happy and relieved to move into her own bedroom and enjoy the life of a successful diplomat's wife. She devoted herself to a life of pleasure, her hospitality as famous as her infidelities.

When Vita Valentine opened the door to welcome Lucy, the rich smell of roasting meat and steamed pudding wafted out into the front porch.

Vita stood in the doorway smiling broadly. She put out her arm. 'How do you do, Mrs Butler? I'm so pleased that Lucy could come.' She beamed at Lucy.

Lucy smiled back shyly as her mother, somewhat ruffled, shook the child's hand. 'How do you do?'

'My mother says we'll bring Lucy home this afternoon,' continued Vita with the same tone of confidence. 'There's no need to collect her.'

As she spoke, a tall dark figure glided across the hall

towards them. Lucy recognised her immediately as the woman in the portrait – Seraphina Valentine. Although fifteen years older than her portrait, she was even more beautiful than her image, as though the bearing and births of eight children had, in some way, enhanced her physically. She was willowy and straight-backed, with thick black hair cascading halfway down her back and shoulders. She wore a long blue-and-white paisley skirt which brushed her ankles, and a sleeveless white bodice which was nipped at the waist and revealed firmly shaped sunburned arms.

Lucy bit her lip and stared in admiration. Mrs Valentine was so young! By comparison, her own mother seemed embarrassingly old and frumpy, with her church frock and hat, beige stockings and sensible shoes, not to mention her carefully permed hair (done every week at Daphne's Parlour down the road).

Lucy then noticed that Mrs Valentine wore no shoes. Under the flowing blue paisley, her bare tanned feet peeped out prettily.

Mrs Valentine held out her hand in welcome. 'I'm Seraphina Valentine,' she said with a charming smile. 'How do you do, Mrs Butler?'

Hilda Butler stammered out a response and again pushed out a stiff hand. Her daughter could see, with surprise, that her mother was nervous.

'Please call me Hilda,' she replied. 'It's very good of you to invite Lucy to play. Are you sure about having her stay for lunch? It's not too much trouble?'

Seraphina smiled. Her red lips parted. Her white teeth flashed. She seemed to have been put together without a fault.

'She can stay all day, if she wants. One more child around the place makes no difference at all. And she must stay for lunch, or there won't be time to settle in. Someone will bring her back this afternoon. We'll ring you if it's later than five.'

Lucy stepped into the house. She was aware of turning her back on the woman hovering in the porch. Lucy could not bring herself to turn back and say goodbye to the mother she was ashamed of.

To her relief, Dido, the dog, came bounding across the hall to greet her. She knelt down to pet it and concentrated on the brown spaniel until she heard the welcome click of the door latch.

That first Sunday lunch at the Valentine house changed Lucy's view of the world. It was the first time she realised that not everyone lived in the same way as her family.

First there was the scene in the sitting room, with the Sunday newspapers strewn around the room being read by various members of the family, small children kneeling on the floor around a game of *Monopoly* and two boys playing duets at the grand piano in the corner. Anthony Valentine sat back in a large armchair, one long leg crossed over the other, holding the newspaper up in front of him and laughing and commenting on things he was reading to nobody in particular. Mrs Valentine drifted in and out of the room in her bare feet and long skirt, carrying glasses of wine for her husband and herself and orange squash for the children. The delicious rich smell of roasting meat and vegetables seemed to float into every corner of the house.

When Vita introduced Lucy to her father, Anthony Valentine leaped to his feet and shook Lucy's hand vigorously.

'I hope you'll enjoy yourself,' he said with a broad grin. He was immensely tall and almost stooped to reach her hand. He was less like his portrait than his wife. He was broader and less blond, but still had fierce blue eyes and was very handsome. Before Lucy could force out an awkward reply, he sat down and disappeared behind the newspaper again.

'Come and play a game of *What*,' said Vita, 'we've just got time before lunch.'

They all sat down for lunch at two o'clock. Vita informed her that the whole family was together because the older boys were home from their boarding schools for the weekend. 'Mother loves to have us all around her,' she confided. 'We're her chicks.'

Indeed, Seraphina Valentine seemed in her element surrounded by her children, who clamoured for her attention and laughed and teased each other with a charming playfulness. To Lucy, so used to her frowning mother who was always worrying about whether things were going right, this smiling relaxed woman seemed like an angel.

'Now I want Lucy to come and sit next to me,' said Mrs Valentine, patting the chair next to her. 'I want to find out all about you.'

As Lucy slipped in beside her, Seraphina tossed back her hair and sighed happily. 'It is wonderful to have all our children here. It's not often that we're all together like this.'

Lucy looked around the table at the crowd of people. It was incredible to think that they were all one family. The parents at each end, the younger twins (Florian now quite recovered), the girls and the older boys who had travelled home from school for the weekend. And then there was the other little boy sitting in the middle. The one Vita had called the Brat.

He had straight brown hair which flopped down over his forehead. His watchful, closely spaced eyes and thin lips gave him a mean, pinched expression. Lucy noticed that he rarely smiled. He sat there hardly saying a word, humming quietly to himself and swinging his legs under the table. No one spoke to him in return.

Lucy scrutinised the older boys with care. The twins, both fourteen, had croaky voices on the verge of breaking. They were tall and blond like their father, and teased each other relentlessly, goosing each other every now and then with a poke in the ribs.

Anthony Valentine stood at one end of the long table sharpening the long carving knife. 'Remember now, all joints on the table will be carved!' He laughed and cast his sparkling blue eyes around the room as the children giggled guiltily and slipped their elbows down by their sides.

Mrs Valentine sat at the other end of the table. She looked relaxed and happy, occasionally pushing long wisps of black hair behind her long dangling Indian earrings. The table was laid casually with mismatched knives and forks placed haphazardly around the edge. Large jugs of water had been placed at each end and paper napkins in most of the places. Lucy took it all in with interest. What would her mother think of this, she with her perfect table settings and silver cutlery service – a wedding present from her own mother – all beautifully kept and polished and always put away after use in the teak canteen on the sideboard? Not much, she thought.

There was an empty place next to the Brat in the middle. Lucy eyed him discreetly. Who was this child?

Even as she wondered, Mrs Valentine reached over and touched her hand with her fingertips. 'Now, have you been introduced to everyone?' she asked. 'I hope Vita was polite enough to make sure you were . . .'

Vita looked up, caught out, a flush on her cheeks. 'I did, a bit . . .' Her voice tailed off.

Seraphina raised her head and tossed back her hair. The

sweet smile remained on her face. 'Now there's Constantine and Achilles, the elder twins, and Byron, all back from Bedales for a couple of days. Then you know Vita, of course, and Perdita and Lorelei, and Florian, now recovered, thank goodness, and our little baby Celestria. And then there's David, too, making it nine in all. He's one of the family, too. David is Olwyn's son. He's been here since he was three weeks old, haven't you, David?'

David nodded and said nothing.

Lucy could feel Vita shift in her seat and stiffen beside her. 'Everyone has such interesting names,' she said.

'Except the Brat,' Vita murmured so that only Lucy could hear.

Seraphina smiled. 'I adore interesting names,' she said. 'Probably because my own name was so unusual. It's from the Hebrew word *saraf* which means to burn. In the plural, *seraphim*, it means celestial beings.'

She looked around the table. 'Achilles, of course, was a hero in Greek mythology, and Constantine, which derives from the Latin which means constant, or firm, was the name of the first Christian Emperor. Celestria comes from the Latin *caelum*, which means heaven, or the home of gods and angels. Vita comes from the Latin, too, meaning life.' She tailed off as Olwyn entered the room carrying a large battered silver platter with a hefty roast leg of lamb.

It was the first time Lucy had looked at the housekeeper properly. Olwyn was short and heavy-set, with wide shoulders and hips, and thick legs. She wore a green knitted pullover and tight skirt which was pulled taut over her belly. Her short fair hair was cut in old-fashioned schoolgirl bangs, and her pale blue eyes were expressionless.

Olwyn placed the steaming meat before Anthony Valentine, who stood poised and ready with the freshly sharpened carving knife and fork.

Mrs Valentine clapped her hands lightly. 'Now, come now, children,' she exclaimed. 'Everyone help. Olwyn's not our servant, you know. Lucy, of course, is a guest, so she may stay seated.'

The children jumped to their feet and began to run in and out of the kitchen, carrying the bowls of potatoes, carrots, beans and steaming jugs of brown gravy. David joined in, too, but with a markedly slow reluctance.

Anthony Valentine stood at the end of the table and carved. He talked in a loud and passionate voice all the time, encouraging the children to talk, to tell him exactly what they thought about the week's events, and the exact reasons for their opinions. Anything and everything was analysed and discussed. No one had to agree. In fact, it was a good sign to disagree. 'What matters is that you have an opinion; it shows that you have thought about it properly and not just adopted some stupid received wisdom,' their father announced.

Lucy watched the scene with growing amazement. She listened to the older twins arguing with their parents not only about the tactics of students in Paris during the riots last May, or the graceful beauty of the Henry Moore exhibits at the new Hayward Gallery built on the South Bank, but also the merits of the Beatles. It astonished her. Her parents did not approve of the Beatles in any form. Her mother thought they were dirty and subversive, and her father thought they made a dreadful racket. The Valentines talked about the Beatles, the Rolling Stones and Bob Dylan as if they were as important as the opera her father liked to listen to on Sunday evenings.

In their mid-thirties, the Valentines made a striking couple. Eighteen years before, at Oxford, they had been a presence then. The impact they had on those who knew them now was just as strong, and Lucy was impressed.

The Valentine family had all settled down to the meal. 'I do like names,' Seraphina continued. She had a gentle singsong voice. 'It's important to have an unusual name, a name that means something interesting.

'Now, your name, Lucy, is the feminine form of Lucius, which comes from the Latin *lux*, meaning light. And what's your middle name?'

The dark eyes looked at her with interest.

'My middle name is Lorna. I'm Lucy Lorna.'

Seraphina nodded. 'How interesting. No doubt your mother named you after Lorna Doone, that romantic heroine of the book.'

Lucy stared at her blankly.

'The book, *Lorna Doone*,' Mrs Valentine repeated. She stared at the girl. 'No?'

Lucy shook her head slowly. 'I don't think so,' she said. 'I was just named after my Auntie Lorna, I think.'

Seraphina Valentine smiled, and squeezed Lucy's hand. 'I expect your aunt was named after Lorna Doone, then. A most popular book, it was, published in 1870, I believe. *Lorna Doone* was a great success and the name Lorna was just invented by the author. Then it became all the rage. It's a bit like the name Wendy. Did you know that Wendy is a made-up name? It was invented by a friend of James Barrie, who then used it in *Peter Pan*. Did you know that? So clever to make up a name that lasts. And, of course, Shakespeare invented the name Perdita, for the heroine of *The Winter's Tale*. It's derived from the Latin *perditus*, meaning lost . . .'

She looked over fondly at her second daughter who was reaching across the table for the bread.

'Don't reach, Perdita,' she called. 'Ask someone to pass you the bread.' She turned back to Lucy with a smile. 'Nobody could ever describe Perdita as lost,' she laughed lightly.

She scarcely paused as she quizzed Lucy about herself. 'Now, tell me what books you like to read – who is your favourite author?'

The conversation around the table turned to books and language. Olwyn and the children brought the food to the table, cleared the plates and brought the next course. Lucy noticed that David occasionally got to his feet to help but not often and certainly less often than the other children.

While the parents directed the conversation, Olwyn sat in the middle of the table watching the Valentine children eat, ticking them off quietly but sternly every now and then for talking with their mouths full or reaching across the table instead of asking for a dish to be passed. Every now and then, Anthony Valentine made some teasing remark to Olwyn, causing the housekeeper to laugh and reply quickly.

They talked of books and films and music. They laughed and argued and thumped the table. Lucy sat beside Seraphina Valentine feeling quite intoxicated by the atmosphere. Never had she seen adults behaving with such abandon or talking to their children as though their opinions mattered. By the end of the meal, she felt she had fallen in love with the Valentine parents and longed to be included in their brood.

'Now where do you live, Lucy?' Anthony Valentine asked.

'Falkland Road,' she replied shyly, aware that everyone was looking at her.

Anthony nodded. 'Where in Falkland Road?'

'Opposite the Wesleyan Chapel.'

'Ah,' he replied, 'the poor ignored Wesleyan Chapel. Built in such Gothic splendour a century ago, and regarded for so long as the most important free church in the district. Now it's hardly used at all. There used to be so many Methodists in Kentish Town. That's why Gospel Oak is called that – it's where the early Methodists taught the gospel, out in the open air. And that's where the council is now pulling down perfectly good houses to build those ghastly housing estates.'

'There's talk of the Methodists doing a straight swap with the Roman Catholics,' said Olwyn. 'The Catholic church in Fortess Road is much too small for them all.'

'I haven't noticed you going to chapel very often, Olwyn,' teased Anthony, helping himself to some more red wine.

Olwyn smirked. 'No, I don't think chapel and I mix too well nowadays. I spent too much time going to chapel as a young girl, I did, back in Cardigan when I was a child. I had enough chapel then to last for the rest of my life.'

Seraphina turned to Lucy. 'Did you know that the Welsh have traditionally run the dairies in north London for years?'

Olwyn nodded. 'That they did. I grew up on a farm in the wilds of Wales and came to London to seek my fame and fortune. In the early days I stayed with some relatives who ran a dairy in Finsbury Park. The milk came from the farms in my area of Cardigan. All the Welsh milk went to London and came back to Wales as English butter! In London, we used to speak Welsh all the time to each other. Once someone on the bus going down Holloway Road heard me and my cousin talking in Welsh and asked if we were Italian.'

Vita chimed in. 'Talking about the Catholics, they spill out into the street all day on Sundays, sometimes even out into the road.'

'Methodism saved this country from a serious popular revolt on the scale of the French Revolution,' said Anthony, getting into his stride. 'It really did make religion the opiate of the working class. But their membership has been plummeting over the past fifty years.' He lifted his glass of wine to his lips. 'They are partly to blame for this themselves because they will insist on teetotalism. Not much fun for anyone . . .'

As the conversation moved about from adult to child and back again, Lucy listened in awe. This was so different from the weekly Sunday lunches at home, where her mother fussed about the table settings and nagged her and Andrew incessantly about their manners.

After lunch, Vita led Lucy out into the garden where they lay on their backs in the long grass, the hazy sun warming their bare arms and legs.

Lucy watched the swallows swooping above them in the blue sky.

'You're lucky to have so many brothers and sisters,' she said. But she was thinking: You're so lucky, full stop. You're so lucky to be in a family where everyone is interested in books and ideas and life in the outside world beyond work and the neighbours. She did not speak these last thoughts out aloud but they spun in her head as she stared up at the blue sky above.

Vita had found a ladybird on the leaf of a shrub and was trying to persuade it to walk on her arm. 'Mmm,' she replied.

'It must be wonderful to have such a big family . . .'

'It's okay,' said Vita without enthusiasm. She did not seem interested in talking about it.

The girls fell into silence again and then Lucy's curiosity

grew. She wanted to know everything about this family she wanted to be part of. Vita patiently answered her questions.

'The twins and Byron go to Bedales School, and the rest of us go to King Alfred's, another progressive school.'

'What's a progressive school?' Lucy had never heard of such a thing.

'It's not as strict as the normal type of school,' explained Vita. 'You don't wear uniform and the children are considered as important as the teachers. Even when we dance on the desks and do other naughty things, the teachers don't get really cross. It's great. And at Bedales the boys have midnight feasts and do all sorts of things they're not supposed to do. They're even allowed to smoke.' She paused and then added, 'I don't think they're allowed to smoke drugs, but I'm not sure.'

Lucy had never heard of people smoking drugs but her interest was elsewhere. 'And what about Olwyn? How long has Olwyn been your housekeeper?'

Vita rolled her eyes. 'She came when the Brat was three weeks old. She was training to be a social worker but she got pregnant. That meant that she had to give up her training and look for work. She's been here ever since.'

'So David's like another brother, in a way . . .'

Vita did not reply, and Lucy felt worried. She was desperate to keep the conversation going, to find out about all these people.

'Does David go to the same school as you or your brothers?'

Vita shook her head. 'The Brat? No, he goes to the school down the road. Olwyn couldn't afford to send him to our school.' She paused and added, 'Thank goodness.'

Lucy watched the ladybird clambering with some diffi-
culty on the fine hairs on Vita's arm. 'Why do you call
David the Brat all the time?'

Vita rolled over and suddenly scrambled to her feet. 'Oh,
I don't know,' she said casually. 'He just is one.' She did
not want to elaborate. She flicked the ladybird into the air
and jumped to her feet. 'Come on,' she said, 'let's find
Perdita.'

CHAPTER 5

May, 1997

Life and Death

Lucy received a letter from the fertility clinic surprisingly quickly. They had a last-minute cancellation and could fit her in. At least she was not going to have to wait for months, as she had expected, but she was suddenly anxious about being sucked into the hospital system. She had been feeling under the weather recently, which she put down to her sadness about the condition of her brother Andrew.

The clinic was busy. There were only two doctors on duty, the consultant – a tall, handsome man with thick grey hair and a pinstriped suit under his white coat – and his senior registrar.

Women sat in rows along the corridor, some flicking through the old magazines on offer, some just staring sadly into space. The pain of their failed attempts to procreate was clearly evident on their faces.

A few women were accompanied by their husbands. These too were also sad-looking people who sat slumped in chairs next to their wives, turning the pages of the women's magazines with a terrible listlessness.

The queue moved slowly. It was humid. Every ten minutes or so the nurse would call out someone's name. A woman would get to her feet, be weighed in full view of everyone and then taken off to a cubicle to undress and await the arrival of the man who may or may not provide them with the answer to their dreams.

Lucy tried to read her book and fight off her growing impatience with the delay. She had already been waiting forty minutes after her appointment time. When her annoyance had grown particularly strong, she reminded herself that she was lucky to have got an appointment so quickly. She should be grateful that she was there at all, she told herself.

As she sat there staring at the pistachio green walls and the health posters Blu-Tacked to them, she thought about the night before when Vita had come over for a drink. Lucy had wanted Simon to meet her important friend from the past. Simon was not a particularly sociable man and Lucy was surprised and pleased by how well he and Vita had got on. Being journalists, they had a lot of common ground and acquaintances they both knew. They shared their opinions of stroppy editors, lazy writers and people who ripped off other people's work. The evening had been a success on all sides. Vita told Lucy that her sister Perdita wanted to see her again, too, and Lucy agreed to a day when the three of them could meet up again.

Another patient had been called. Lucy thought of Andrew in a ward two floors below her now. She was planning to visit him afterwards if she had time.

Andrew was back in the hospital again and very low in spirits. After his first attack of PCP, he had been discharged from hospital within a week. For a while he had been feeling fine again, though rather nauseous from the Septrin he was taking for the pneumonia. Then just three days ago he had started getting attacks of diarrhoea which did not stop. He could not control it at home and had to go into the hospital. There they told him he now had *cryptosporidium*, a parasite that lives in the drinking water, which they could not eliminate from his system. They also thought he showed signs of pneumonia again. They admitted him to try to control his gut and check again on the state of his lungs.

'They all appear kind and well meaning,' Andrew had said during his first stay, 'but I know better than most people that to them I am basically only a case study. I'm a specimen who can help them learn more about HIV. I'd do the same in their position but I'm not. All I want is a bit of peace and quiet at home.'

Now he had been hauled in again so that the doctors could learn some more.

Upstairs at the infertility clinic, it was Lucy's turn at last. She had waited an hour. Four years and one hour. She was weighed and taken into a cubicle to get changed. Dressed in a starched blue hospital gown, she smiled at the tall handsome consultant as he came into the room.

'Good morning, Mrs Montague.' He had a friendly face and an avuncular manner. His smile seemed genuine.

He studied Dr Kenny's letter of referral and then turned to her. 'You've been trying to conceive for four years.'

'That's right.' Lucy tried to smile back and make her voice sound bright and cheerful. She could not bear to be identified with the sad team of women sitting outside in those chairs in the corridor.

'And you've never been pregnant before? No accidents? Abortions? Miscarriages?'

She knew he had to ask such a question. It was relevant for him to know if she had ever conceived in her life. It was not a nosey question about her sexual history.

She shook her head. 'No, nothing.'

'All right, pop yourself up on the bed and let's have a look at you.'

Lucy lay on her back with her legs bent while the doctor prodded and probed her body, gently, carefully. He felt her breasts and around under her arms. She was vaguely aware that her breasts felt heavy and tender to his touch.

The doctor's face was inscrutable but he seemed to be spending a long time feeling around her lower belly, gently and quietly.

'When did you say your last period was?'

She had to think for a moment. Normally she knew exactly when it was but since she had admitted that she needed help, she had stopped counting. 'About three weeks ago.'

'And it was a normal period.'

It came out as neither a statement nor a question. Lucy had no sense of what he meant.

'I think so.' Creeping up from deep inside her came a fear that something was wrong. Something very serious. She tried to remember. He had to know all the facts. 'But when I think about it, it was perhaps a little lighter than usual. It didn't last very long. But it was definitely a period. It came on the dot, on the twenty-seventh day of my cycle.'

She remembered her sorrow only too well. And she remembered thinking that perhaps her period was light because she was going into an early menopause, just to finish things off for her.

'Anyway, I think we missed the fertile days that month because my husband was away,' she added ruefully.

'And the period before that? That was normal?'

'As far as I remember, yes.'

All periods had become the same to Lucy, the bloody messenger of death. If not the death of a fertilised ovum, a death of another tiny part of her. Sometimes she felt as though there was not much left alive in her.

The consultant had finished. 'All right, sit up, Mrs Montague. I'm not going to do an internal examination today.'

Lucy stared at him. 'Why not?' Her throat tightened with fear. It was cancer. He was going to tell her that something was wrong, so dreadful that she should stop thinking about something as trivial as infertility. She clenched her fists over the edge of the bed.

The doctor turned to look at her. His eyes were kind and intelligent. 'I wouldn't say this if I weren't certain because I know how painful it is for you ladies when you cannot conceive.'

Lucy stared at him. This was not making sense. He did not look serious in a worried sort of way. But then doctors are used to conveying bad news.

'The fact is,' he continued, 'you appear to be pregnant. As soon as you can you should make an appointment on the other side of the building in the antenatal clinic.'

'Pregnant?' Lucy was dazed. She sat rigid in her position.

The doctor smiled at her and patted her hand. 'You have what we call a "waiting list" pregnancy. It's more common than you'd think. Sometimes just the very fact that you know your problem is going to be taken seriously at last can do something to the reproductive system. It's very mysterious. A little tender loving care can do all sorts of wonderful things.'

'But my periods . . . I've been having periods. How can I be pregnant? And how can I possibly be pregnant when we didn't even have sex at the right time last month?'

'My guess is that you conceived the month before, so you were already pregnant last month. Your last two periods have not been real periods, even though they seemed to be normal to you. As you said, the last one was a bit lighter. It's possible to have some breakthrough bleeding at the time when you would have had a period, which makes the woman think she's having periods. I've known of cases where the woman has had a monthly bleed throughout the nine months of her pregnancy.

'But by my examination I should think you are approximately ten weeks pregnant.'

Lucy began to laugh, suddenly and uncontrollably. Tears of joy filled her eyes. 'Thank you so much,' she said. She wanted to leap up and hug him. 'Thank you so much. I can't believe it. It's such a shock.'

She climbed down from the bed. Her legs were trembling. 'I can't thank you enough.'

The doctor smiled. 'You don't need to thank me, but I'll look forward to seeing you in the other clinic. You can get dressed now.' As he left the room, Lucy was too grateful to him for being the bearer of such good news to be annoyed by the patronising little pat he gave her on the knee.

Lucy dressed as quickly as her shaking hands would allow, fumbling with the buttons on her blouse and pulling her pants on backwards by mistake. She could not stop grinning and shaking her head in disbelief. Within a minute, she had gone from being miserable to a state of ecstasy. Everything about life had changed.

Not everything, of course. Lucy skipped out of the clinic, leaving all the sad women behind, joyful in her knowledge that she was no longer one of them. Avoiding the lift, she ran quickly down the stairs to visit Andrew.

The moment she stepped into the ward, she automatically

collected herself. Her ecstasy seemed inappropriate and insensitive in such a place.

Lucy was no longer bothered when she walked into AIDS wards at the hospital. Her first visit had been quite different. Before she went, just the thought of it had made her rigid with apprehension – afraid of what she might see but also even more afraid of how she might react, particularly at the sight of her brother.

It had indeed been a harrowing experience, seeing those rows of stricken young men, some blind, some constantly vomiting into buckets at their bedsides, wasted and anaemic, staring listlessly around them, all hope gone. But having visited him a few times at the hospital, Lucy had become used to it. It had become horribly unshocking.

Andrew was dozing when Lucy first arrived. She stood by his bed for a few minutes looking at him. As if he sensed her presence through his sleep, he stirred and opened his eyes. He smiled sleepily at her.

Lucy took his long bony fingers in her hand and leaned over to kiss him on the cheek. This was a gesture of greeting she had made herself do ostentatiously for four years, ever since Andrew had told her he was HIV-positive, but she was ashamed that even now, she avoided touching his lips. The AIDS virus cannot be passed on by social kissing – even deep French kissing, she knew that. HIV is a very fragile virus and it is difficult to become infected by it, she knew all that, too. She knew that it was impossible to get it from lavatory seats, sharing eating utensils, mosquitoes and, yes, kissing. But there was always that shameful little irrational uncertainty inside – and still she could not touch his lips. She did not want his saliva on hers.

Andrew had lost even more weight since her last visit. His six feet four inch frame had lost a lot of muscle and he was beginning to look like the skinny, stick-legged seven-year-old she knew as a child. As an adult, he had grown into a big strapping fellow, a brother a girl could be proud of.

But his skin was a good colour and, in fact, compared with some of the other patients in the ward, he looked quite robust. He was thin for him but not that thin.

While it was comforting to realise that, it was also worrying to think about how much further Andrew had to go before he looked like some of the other men in the ward, like his neighbour in the next bed, for instance. The poor man, who had a good job in a local authority, looked like somebody out of Belsen. His huge eyes had sunk into deep sockets and stared out at the world looking dazed and listless. His hair was dull and brittle, and the skin on his bony limbs was peeling.

He had been there when Andrew had first been admitted, three weeks before. Then he had had much more flesh on his bones and had been sitting up and chatting to a jolly group of friends who had come to visit him after work – clever, decent young people with good jobs and happy lives.

He had deteriorated a lot since Lucy had last seen him. There were many new faces in the ward, some looking remarkably healthy and normal, others evidently suffering from all sorts of opportunistic infections. One man opposite lay in bed, listless, his face covered with a mass of bluish red patches, the telltale signs of Kaposi's sarcoma, or KS, as those in the know called it.

Lucy had read up about KS, as she had about all sorts of AIDS illnesses. She knew that it was named after Moritz Kaposi, a professor of dermatology at the University of Vienna Medical School who in 1879 described an entity he called 'multiple pigment sarcoma', consisting of a group of reddish brown or bluish red nodules, usually a quarter of an inch in diameter, anywhere on the skin. In patients with HIV, KS is another AIDS-defining illness. Though not life-threatening in itself, it can be horribly disfiguring if it spreads across the face, and can cause serious problems if it spreads internally.

Lucy handed Andrew the giant Galaxy chocolate bar she had bought in the kiosk in the hospital lobby. He had always adored chocolate; she brought him some on every visit. 'This should keep you going.'

'The parents came to see me again,' Andrew said, tearing the paper off the chocolate and nibbling at a corner.

Lucy waited for more.

'Dad's fine but I think Mum finds it unbearable. She sits by my bed looking for an excuse to scarper.'

'At least she's visiting you,' said Lucy. 'I was afraid she might be too frightened to come into an AIDS ward.'

Andrew smiled ruefully. 'I think Dad managed to assert himself for the first time ever and gave her a talking to.' He sighed again. 'Still, we have nothing to say to each other, the parents and I. They sit here more or less in silence until it seems an acceptable time to leave.'

Remembering her dream-memory, Lucy asked, 'Do you recall a time when the parents were happy together?'

Andrew looked thoughtful. 'I think there was, a long long time ago, and so long ago that it doesn't matter. And I don't care, not after the way they've behaved towards me.

'I'm just a big disappointment to them, I suppose,' he continued. 'Not only did I not become a doctor, like a dutiful son, but I also turned out to be a faggot. Now I'm dying in such a way that all their friends will know that I am a faggot, that I have sex with men, when Mum's probably managed to keep it all a big secret up to now.'

It was not the first time that Andrew had talked like this. Over the past few weeks he had become somewhat obsessed with his parents' behaviour towards him. Lucy did not contradict him because much of what he said was true but she did wish that Andrew would stop tormenting himself about it. He had to let it go.

'Well, at least they came to see you,' she said. 'You know lots of people are rejected by their parents when they tell them they're HIV.'

'Yes, yes. I hardly need to be told that.'

'I do think Mother loves you, Andrew, she's just incapable of showing it.'

'If she can't show it, then she might as well not feel it.'

Andrew's voice was bitter. He turned away but at the angle, Lucy could see his eyes glistening. 'She doesn't kiss me when she comes,' he said softly. 'But then, what do I care?'

Lucy was silent for a moment, then she said, 'I think you do care, Andrew. I think you care quite a lot.'

Andrew turned back his head quickly as if to argue, but then he said softly, 'What day is it today? I lose track so quickly in here. What's the date?'

'It's May the thirtieth.'

Andrew looked up at the ceiling and sighed. 'It's odd to think I'm going to die. I know we all die at some point but it's a weird feeling knowing that it's imminent. It's weird to know that this time next year I'm probably not going to be here. It's odd to look at a calendar, and look at the days between now and Christmas and think that on one of those days, I shall probably die. One of those days will be my deathday. You will know that, and Patrick and Mum and Dad will know that date and you'll all remember it every year. It's a peculiar feeling to know that I'm definitely going to die young, that I shall never grow old. You will only remember me at this age or younger.'

Lucy grabbed his hand. 'That's not true, Andrew, you know that that's not true. Many people live for ten, fifteen years with HIV. There's no reason to suppose you'll die so soon. The advances they've made with drugs to treat all these things that go wrong mean that you can be treated.'

'Only until the next thing goes wrong.' Andrew's eyes were filling with tears as he fixed them on his sister.

'I've been thinking about this a lot, Lucy,' he said. 'I'm not interested in struggling on until the bitter end. I don't want to have my body giving up on me bit by bit. I'm very vain and I don't want to be covered with KS like that bloke over there. I'm terrified of going blind, and lots of people get this horrible virus in the eyes. Then lots of people get dementia. That would be even worse. But I couldn't bear any of these things happening. They're just not worth it.'

'What's not worth it?'

Andrew drew a quick breath. 'I'll kill myself before I get to that stage.' He spoke in a fierce hiss and stared at her defiantly.

Lucy stared back and nodded gently. 'I understand,' she said finally.

Andrew pushed himself up on his elbow. 'The problem with all this is knowing when to do it. It's a question of balance, of getting the timing right.' He was suddenly animated. 'I want to go on for as long as I can enjoy myself but if I leave it too late I may suddenly find myself trapped in hospital where I won't get the opportunity, or be too incapacitated to carry it out. That's my fear.'

He had obviously been thinking all this out for a long time. 'You will help me, won't you, Lucy? When the time comes, you'll be there for me?'

Lucy did not know exactly what her brother was saying. She assumed that through the gay network Andrew had the means to do away with himself. Surely he had been given specific instructions – like swallowing a handful of tranquillisers, drinking several large whiskies and placing a plastic bag over your head. If you breathe gently, you just gradually go to sleep. That was the way she remembered Bruno Bettelheim, the child psychiatrist, did himself in when he had had enough of life. Surely Andrew had done his homework. The thought of the act itself was too painful to think about in much detail and probably the less she knew, the better. He was right. She could not argue against him.

'You know I'll always be here for you,' she whispered. 'I've always supported whatever you've wanted to do.'

She swallowed hard. 'But, Andrew, you will tell me, won't you? You will tell me if you're going to do it, so I can say goodbye.'

He turned away and loosened his hold on her hand. 'I don't know if I can promise that,' he said flatly. 'In some ways I think it's better just to do it without a fuss, without telling anyone. Probably Patrick will be the only one to know. And perhaps I won't even tell him when the time comes . . .'

They sat in silence for a few minutes. Then Andrew spoke again. 'I've been doing a lot of reading about death lately. We know so little about it. Why should it be worse than sleep? Socrates said that, just before he died after taking poison. He said, "If it was an annihilation of our being, it is still an improvement to enter a long and peaceful night. We feel nothing sweeter in life than a deep and tranquil rest and sleep, without dreams."'

Lucy smiled. 'Good for Socrates,' she murmured.

There was no more to say about this. Then Lucy remembered her own good news. She smiled. 'By the way,' she said quietly, 'you're going to be an uncle. Believe it or not, I've just been told that I'm two and a half months pregnant. You're the first to know. The baby's due in January, so you'll just have to stick around until then.'

Her brother smiled. 'Well done,' he said. 'I'm very pleased for you and Simon. I know how much that means to you. I'd love to have had children myself . . .' His voice tailed off and then he said, 'I would love to stick around to see my nephew or niece, but it would be foolish of me to make any promises now. Mind you, there is one promise I'll make, and that is that the minute I get out of here – with any luck by the weekend – I'll buy a bottle of champagne and we'll drink a toast to the future member of the family.'

Andrew collapsed into the pillow, his eyelids drooped. 'I'm tired,' he said. 'This bloody tiredness sweeps over me and I can't fight it.'

Lucy got to her feet. 'I'll leave you to rest,' she said. 'By the way, I've been meaning to ask you if you remember the Valentine family when we lived in Kentish Town. I don't expect you do because they were my friends rather than yours, and you were only seven. I recently met one of the girls again . . .'

Andrew was smiling sleepily. 'I do remember them,' he murmured. 'There were lots of children . . . the girls were very powerful . . . there was a nanny with mean eyes . . .' His voice faded and suddenly he was silent with sleep.

Lucy tiptoed away from the bed and out of the ward. She left the hospital feeling closer to Andrew than she had since she was a child. Somehow the teenage years and then adulthood had conspired to force the two of them apart. They remained close in spirit but work and their respective relationships meant that they never had time alone together and so never had the chance to talk about their parents in any detail.

How she longed for them all to be friends! Lucy had the strongest urge to get Andrew and her parents reconciled – she only hoped it would be possible before it was too late.

Lucy told Simon the good news when he came home from work. His joy showed her that he had been more worried about their fertility problems than he had previously let on. He kissed her and hugged her tight. 'I'm so happy for you,' he said. But the sentimental shimmer in his eyes told her that he was happy for himself too.

They drove down to Lucy's parents' house in Dulwich, south London. Lucy had decided to surprise them with her news in person. Simon drove rather recklessly as the truth about Lucy's condition gradually sank in. He talked and joked incessantly.

'The responsibility! Now we really are grown-up! No more lie-ins on Sunday mornings, that's what they all say. No more hangovers. And if it's a boy I'll have every excuse to spend my Saturday afternoons watching cricket matches . . .'

Lucy smirked. 'You might have a cricket-mad daughter, you know. And you're jumping the gun a bit. It hasn't been born yet. Let's get there first.' She felt supremely content and contained in a way that she had not for many years. 'Besides,' she added, 'remember what Vita said the other day: with children, it's the first few years that are really hard. When they're old enough, you can bribe them with TV or treats if you want to get the occasional lie-in.'

Simon laughed. 'I hope she's right, I hope our kids don't turn out to be incorruptible. Oh, the joys of daytime television! Our parents never had anything like that when we were growing up.'

He fell silent and looked thoughtful. As they stopped at some traffic lights, Simon peered at Lucy. 'Does this mean that I have to get a more ambitious job?'

'I won't make you do that,' laughed Lucy, 'but you may have to limit your book collecting for a few years, or decades.'

Simon had only a few hobbies. He liked watching but not playing cricket, and he liked reading. Recently he had begun to collect first editions of modern crime novels, rummaging through second-hand bookshops and car boot sales, and poring over the catalogues of second-hand book dealers. He already had an impressive collection of Ruth Rendells, Patricia Highsmiths, P.D. Jameses and Elmore Leonards. He liked to boast about how little he paid for the books but Lucy suspected that he did not always reveal the true sum that he spent each month on this habit. It had become a joke between them.

'At least I don't bet on the horses like some of the blokes on the paper. The Features Editor loses forty quid a week, and at least my books should grow in value!'

Lucy smiled at Simon and placed her hand on his leg. She could feel the muscle in his thigh tense up as he shifted gear. A warm tingle ran through her. It seemed as if all their difficulties were over. 'And I'm pleased you liked Vita so much the other day. I was afraid you wouldn't. I thought you might find her too assertive.'

Vita had taken up Lucy's invitation to have a drink and meet Simon one evening. Simon was not keen on particularly confident, 'aggressive' women. Although he tolerated Rosie, he often found her uncomfortably over-bearing. 'I think it's interesting that you are attracted to assertive women as friends, when you're not overtly like that yourself.'

It made Lucy chuckle. 'Perhaps I choose them because you're less likely to run off with them.'

Simon smiled wryly. 'Yes, but I did like Vita. I thought she was interesting. I've noticed her byline in the nationals for some time. She's done some good campaigning pieces on various social issues which I like. And it may be that she could do some pieces for us – she's got a good eye for a story. I was pleased that she didn't seem to think it beneath her to write for a local rag.'

For all his apparent lack of ambition, Simon loved working on a local paper because a good local paper – as his was – could truly affect ordinary people's lives in a way that a national newspaper could not. A newspaper campaigning, for instance, for traffic-calming humps in the road outside the primary school, or rooting out dishonest landlords, could do far more good than any of the high-minded broadsheets some of his more ambitious mates had moved on to.

Lucy respected Simon for that and she never put pressure on him to go for more glamorous jobs on the nationals, where he would certainly have less influence in the world than he did now.

'I did like Vita,' Simon was saying. 'She's good-looking, too,' he added with a lascivious grin.

Lucy sat back in her seat and allowed her head to roll gently on the head rest behind her. Suddenly life seemed simple and sweet. When their prospects had seemed so grim before, now they suddenly had a future – at least, seven months ahead and beyond, they did. From bumping along the bottom, she had now shot up to the heights of ecstasy. She was excited about telling her parents and looked forward to seeing the look on their faces at the news. That should cheer them up, she thought. Again she hoped that the baby would give her mother something new to think about, so she would stop fussing about the house and bullying Lucy's father. But then, she hoped that Andrew's condition would have done that, too.

As if Simon had been reading this last thought of hers, he said, 'Well, now your father will really have to believe that Andrew is never going to follow in his footsteps. I've always felt that deep down Gordon still thinks that Andrew is suddenly going to decide to practise as a doctor, after all.'

Lucy nodded. 'Daddy's so proud of the family tradition – his grandfather, his father and then himself – and it was always expected of the sons of the family. All my childhood, my parents talked about Andrew going to medical school. No other options were ever considered. And they certainly never thought I should go to medical school. A nursing training would have been acceptable – like my mother's – but not medical school.'

'So Andrew conformed until he actually qualified,' said Simon. 'Then he turned his back on it all. That must have hurt your parents.'

'Yes, he turned his back on them, too, really. They've never properly forgiven him.' Lucy paused. 'Still, I would hope that they are no longer fretting about whether Andrew is going to continue the family tradition when Daddy retires next year. All they need to worry about now is how many months, or years, Andrew's got left.'

They drove on over Battersea Bridge and down through Brixton and Herne Hill towards Dulwich, where Lucy's parents still lived in the house they had moved to from Kentish Town at the end of the 1960s.

*   *   *

Lucy's announcement of her good news caused great rejoicing at her parents' home during the early part of the evening. Hilda hugged and kissed both her daughter and son-in-law and Dr Butler pulled out a bottle of champagne, given to him last Christmas by a grateful patient. They sat in the sitting room with the French doors open sipping the fizzy wine and talking animatedly about the little object buried deep inside Lucy, a little object that was part of all of them. It was now all right to talk about it. But as the evening wore on, the earlier levity and feeling of hope gradually fell away bit by bit as people switched their thoughts from the future of the unborn to the remaining life of the about-to-die. It was mostly unspoken, however, Andrew's name was hardly mentioned, though his presence hovered over the dinner table like Banquo's ghost.

When Lucy tried to ask her mother about Andrew, their conversation became a tangled mess.

'You saw Andrew,' Lucy said quietly.

Hilda had picked up the bowl of French beans and offered them to Simon. 'That's right,' she said quickly. 'Would you like some beans, Simon? They're from the garden.'

Lucy was used to her mother's evasiveness and was not ready to give up easily. 'How did you find him?'

Her mother glanced up at her sharply. Her expression was pinched and taut. 'What do you mean?'

'Andrew,' continued Lucy. 'When you saw him, how did you find him?'

'We found him in the ward.' Her mother pursed her lips and helped herself to some beans.

Now Lucy retreated. What was the point?

Her father cleared his throat. 'We thought Andrew had lost a lot of weight,' he said. 'A considerable amount.'

After that, Hilda made it impossible to try again. She began to talk incessantly, jumping from one topic to another as though a silence in the conversation would allow something nasty to creep in. And news about the baby had given her a great opportunity for such chatter. It was as if she had shoved Andrew's ghostly presence out into the cold and slammed the door behind him. She launched into a monologue: 'I can't wait to let everyone know,' she said. 'At last I'm going to be a grandmother. I shall start knitting straight away. Now, where are you going to have the baby? I hope you're not thinking of having it at home, not at your age. I wonder what it'll be. I suppose you'll be able to find out, with all the tests they do nowadays, but I think it's fun not to know, it's far more exciting to find out at the birth.'

Lucy endured the rest of the meal in silence. Then she cleared the table and left her mother talking rapidly to a tolerant Simon in the sitting room while she and her father washed the dishes.

'Does Mother care about Andrew at all?' Lucy did not look at her father as she spoke. 'She's hardly mentioned him all evening. In fact, she's positively avoided talking about him.'

Dr Butler dried the glasses with the checked dishcloth and placed them carefully in the sideboard. 'Yes, she does, of course,' he said. 'But she's very excited by your news, as you can tell, and so am I.' He paused. 'But your mother has had a big shock, you know, and it will take a while for her to get over it.'

Lucy sniffed. 'Well, she'd better hurry up before it's too late.'

'You know it's difficult for a religious woman like your mother to get a grip on homosexuality.'

Lucy turned to look at her father. 'Why don't you tell her to stop being so ridiculous, then? Why can't you make her see sense?'

Her father looked away. 'I've done my best,' he said. 'I don't think I can do any more.'

Lucy sniffed again dismissively, causing her father to look up quickly.

'Don't judge her too harshly,' he said quietly. 'Your mother's not perfect, just as none of us is perfect. She's had a few blows in her life and it takes a while to recover each time.' He paused and then continued. 'Sometimes it's not possible to recover completely. But I do believe she'll come through this all right.'

Lucy looked up. 'What blows? What blows has she had?' Her mother had always seemed so simple, her life so straightforward, it seemed to her, a housewife and mother, the wife of a doctor. She looked straight at her father, challenging him to explain.

Dr Butler stared back, tempted to explain about the tragedies and disappointments that had become the barnacles of their married life. But now was not the time.

'One day I'll tell you about it,' he said. 'Not now. Pass me that pot. It needs a good rub.'

Lucy handed him the orange Le Creuset dish and turned to finish washing the plates in silence, making a conscious decision to think about something other than Andrew. She switched her thoughts to the drink she had arranged to have with the Valentine sisters later that week, and she realised that she felt oddly nervous about meeting up with Perdita again.

Lucy had arranged to meet the Valentine sisters in a bar in Covent Garden. Vita had been adamant about getting Lucy

and Perdita together when she had been for a drink to meet
Simon. 'Perdita wants to see you,' she said.

Lucy had been surprised. She did not remember having
a particularly strong attachment to Perdita. In fact, when
she thought about Perdita, or tried to remember what she
had been like, all she could recall was a strange feeling of
wariness, an odd feeling of unease.

Lucy strode across a busy Covent Garden and found the
two sisters were already at the bar. They were sitting at a
table, three glasses and a bottle of white wine on the table
between them.

Vita jumped to her feet when she saw Lucy and greeted
her with a broad smile. 'There you are! And this is Perdita.'

Perdita rose to her feet, too, and reached out to shake
hands. Lucy recognised her straight away, the same pretty,
round face, the pale blue eyes, the dark mole on her cheek
and the glossy black hair. Straight from a day in court, she
looked severely smart in the dark clothes of her trade.

Perdita was smiling, but Lucy felt the pale eyes lacked
sincerity. She did not feel at ease.

'Have a drink,' Perdita said, pouring some of the wine
into the empty glass on the table.

It was a curious meeting and afterwards Lucy was not at
all sure what its purpose was. If Perdita had been keen to
see her, she still did not know why. It was almost as though
Perdita – now a successful barrister specialising in family
law and child abuse cases – had wanted to check her out,
to have a look at her twenty-eight years later.

No real contact was made between them that evening.
While Vita was friendly and talkative, and kept the conversation going, Perdita was closed and unforthcoming. Lucy
felt she was being inspected.

There was just one moment when Perdita turned her

impenetrable pale eyes on to Lucy and said abruptly, 'I suppose we only actually knew you for a few weeks one summer, didn't we?'

Lucy was eager to talk about their shared experience. 'Yes, that's right, though to me it seems much longer than that. I came to your house almost every day, as I remember, and I came to stay with you all at your grandmother's house, too. I was so amazed by the size of your family. There were so many of you, and your parents seemed so lovely and easygoing.' She laughed. 'They were such a contrast to mine!'

The sisters smiled and said nothing. Lucy suddenly remembered something. 'Didn't you have a nanny or housekeeper?'

It suddenly came to her, a vivid image of the housekeeper. She had a picture in her head of a stocky woman with plump knees serving up sausages and mashed potatoes to a crowd of noisy Valentine children around the table. 'And didn't she have a child, too? A boy. What was he called?'

A silence hung suspended in the space between them. Perdita sipped from her glass. 'David,' she said quietly. 'He was called David.'

There was something else, nagging in Lucy's brain. She tried to tease it out, but it stayed there. 'Yes, David, that's right. I'd forgotten. I only vaguely remember how he looked . . .'

Vita reached over and poured more wine into her glass. 'I'll get some peanuts,' she said, waving her arm to catch the waiter's attention.

'David,' Lucy repeated the name, trying to force an image of the boy into her head. 'He was about our age, wasn't he? And he got very ill . . .' Now it was coming back. She was shocked as the recollection came back with a jolt. 'Why, he died, didn't he?'

The sisters glanced at each other in a way that sent Lucy flying back to that summer. She remembered how they used to glance at each other like that in front of her, often when she had asked them something. It was a disturbingly familiar gesture.

Then Perdita nodded. 'That's right. He did die. He got very ill and died.'

Lucy was frowning. 'Yes, I remember that now. But what happened then? What happened to his mother? It must have been awful for her.'

Perdita and Vita nodded slowly and thoughtfully, in unison.

'Olwyn left us soon after David died,' said Vita. 'We did not keep in touch. I think she went back to her family in Wales.'

'And my family moved away, too,' said Lucy. She twisted the stem of her glass.

'That's right, you did,' replied Perdita. She spoke quietly, her eyes fixed on Lucy all the time.

Suddenly she smiled, revealing beautiful, even white teeth. 'Now, I understand that you are going to have a baby. That's wonderful news.'

Lucy nodded and smiled coyly. 'Yes,' she said. 'I'd almost given up hope.'

The topic was changed and the rest of the short evening was an odd and unexpected hour of small talk. Lucy sensed that Perdita had almost lost interest in her. She was certainly distracted.

The wine was finished and it was time to go. Lucy went home feeling quite dejected. Vita had been effusively friendly still, but Lucy left puzzling about why Perdita had been keen to see her in the first place. Perhaps it was just to be polite, but why? Perdita was a busy woman and they had not had the same strong bond between them that existed between Lucy and Vita. So why should she bother to fix up such a meeting? Lucy knew that there had to be some reason for it.

Lucy sat on the bus home feeling most peculiar. It was silly but it was almost as if Perdita had been checking her out in some way. But why and for what reason, she had no idea.

She was also bothered by the exchange about the house-keeper's boy, David. It was amazing that she had completely forgotten that he had died, and the discussion about him had just fizzled out like a dying sparkler. But there was something more; her gut feeling told her that. As she struggled to recall that ninth summer of her life, she was aware of an unsettling feeling in the pit of her stomach. She had no idea why; however hard she tried to catch the uneasiness and lay it out to dissect it, it remained elusive inside her, taunting her from a distance like some cruel school bully long ago.

That night the childmares returned. She dreamed that she gave birth to a perfect baby. She was ecstatic, filled with intense pleasure. The baby lay in her arms but as she gazed down at it she noticed that it had stopped breathing. In fact, it had never been breathing. The baby had been born dead but no one had noticed.

Lucy woke up crying. Why was she still having these dreams? She was pregnant. She was going to have a baby. Why was she still having these horrible dreams when there was no reason?

CHAPTER 6

July, 1968

Freedom

As she absorbed the first impressions of the Valentine family, Lucy realised that her experience of the Sunday lunch was unusual because the family was very rarely gathered all together in that way. The normal state of affairs was for everyone to be dashing one way or another, pursuing their own interests.

The next thing that struck her was the loving way in which Mr and Mrs Valentine behaved towards each other. They were very absorbed with each other, and clearly loved one another. They did not converse in the way her own parents did, in tight, barking outbursts with undercurrents that flowed on through the days and months without ever coming to the surface.

No, Anthony and Seraphina seemed openly to like one another, always attentive, listening to what the other had to say, laughing at each other's little ironies and engaging in rigorous playful arguments. It was a form of communication she had never seen before and it made her feel safe. They never seemed to argue about their children or drag their children into battles of will between them. It was always just the two of them.

She was equally impressed (the first time she witnessed it) by the way they touched in front of others. Although Lucy, of course, knew the facts of life, she could not even think that her parents ever had sex, ever mated like the dogs in the street. Her own and Andrew's existence proved that they had done it, twice, at least. But since then, surely, they had never touched each other in that way.

The Valentines, on the other hand, were like the young hippy couples she sometimes saw on Hampstead Heath or in Regent's Park where she would walk with her parents and brother on Sunday afternoons. They touched each other playfully, to interrupt a remark or catch each other's attention. They complimented each other on their looks or ideas. Once, Lucy watched on with astonishment while Anthony Valentine ran his hand over Seraphina's hip and the round of her buttock under her skirt. She was confused by a strange *frisson* of excitement that tugged at her chest.

The Valentines were indeed as sexually attracted to each other as they had ever been. Fortunately, Anthony's feelings for his wife were if anything enhanced throughout her six pregnancies. Many men are frightened by the physical manifestation of feminine fecundity but Anthony was drawn to it every time.

The children often witnessed their parents' day-to-day affection for each other but they did not see their father run his hand up their mother's leg while she was reaching up for a reference book from a high bookshelf, or see her turn around and thrust her leg between his as she reached up her arms and pressed her tongue deep into his mouth. They did not see the tussling and rolling on the bed, the sucking and licking, the stroking and the squeezing, arms and legs entwined, groaning and clinging to each other in joyful nympholepsy.

Anthony and Seraphina knew that they were lucky. In each other they had found a mate for life, someone each had grown with at the same pace. Their sexual energy and enthusiasm simply reflected the other mental and physical energy they shared. They each saw parts of themselves in the other. They were two halves who together made the whole.

To outsiders they were the perfect couple. To their children, they were ideal. Everyone told the young Valentines how clever and handsome and attractive their parents were. They had kudos at school for having famous parents, parents who stood up for their beliefs and made speeches against the Vietnam War and defended the rights of young students to have a voice of their own. And parents they called by their first names, Anthony and Seraphina, rather than Mummy and Daddy, or Mum and Dad, like the rest of the world.

Anthony Valentine was frequently seen on television with well-known people in, say, a delegation which included the philosopher A.J. Ayer, going to the American Embassy to protest against the trial of the famous Dr Spock in America. And Anthony Valentine was often there on the news and talk shows, having visited Paris during the May riots and being on friendly terms with the big student leaders in France and America.

Young people often admired him for saying things they felt but had never articulated before, while older members of the Establishment thought he was clever but probably in the pay of the Russians. Ordinary people who did not have very strong political views, such as Dr and Mrs Butler, thought that the Valentines were very clever but probably a bit too idealistic with it.

At the Valentine home, the parents were often there in the background – Seraphina in her study, painting or writing, and Anthony, if he wasn't at the LSE, would be holed up in his study too. Then they were not to be disturbed at any time, and children were not allowed to make noise outside their doors. The only time Lucy ever heard either Seraphina or Anthony Valentine get angry with their children was when one of them made too much noise outside their studies when they were trying to work.

Apart from that, there appeared to be no rules in the house. So, free in the day, the Valentine children, it seemed to Lucy, had the greatest fun. They rode their bikes all over the neighbourhood, through the wide leafy streets of Tufnell Park and Holloway, and through the rough estates of Somers Town and Kentish Town. They did not have to tell anyone where they were going or what they were doing. They simply knew that if they wanted to eat lunch or tea they had to be at the dining room table at certain times of the day.

In fact, the Valentine children saw very little of their parents. Anthony and Seraphina would emerge at six every evening for drinks after the children had eaten their high tea in the dining room. Olwyn prepared this meal each day, serving up enormous steaming dishes of shepherd's pie or Irish stew with Brussels sprouts and boiled potatoes.

There was a work rota written up and pinned to the wall in the kitchen. The tasks were all written down one side – the setting of the table, the clearing up, washing and drying – and the children's names were carefully written beside them. Everyone knew what to do and Lucy was impressed to see that they all did it, too, without complaining. For they seemed to know that once they had carried out their tasks, they were free from adult control.

David's name was also on the rota, though Lucy rarely saw the boy doing his jobs with the same diligence shown by the Valentines.

After tea, while Anthony and Seraphina sipped their cocktails in the sitting room, the children milled around them, playing the piano, arguing or playing cards. Half an hour was all the children had. Then it was time for the parents to go out, or simply to retire to their studies again while the children were marched off for their baths.

Those summer weeks seemed to go on for ever. Lucy had an open invitation to play at the Valentines' house whenever she wished. At first Hilda Butler worried that it was an intrusion for Lucy to go every day but after Seraphina Valentine had assured her for the fourth time that Lucy was genuinely welcome, Hilda Butler allowed herself to believe it. She also allowed Lucy to walk up the road on her own, which had never happened before. Perhaps seeing the Valentine children dashing unchaperoned around the neighbourhood had made her think that really it was safe to let Lucy out on her own to walk five hundred yards up the road. Or perhaps she was simply unable to reveal that until now she had accompanied Lucy everywhere. The reason did not matter; Lucy was ecstatic at her newfound freedom.

Gradually Lucy saw how the Valentine house operated. Although Seraphina and Anthony were often around in the day, they were also frequently out, either at work or attending concerts, poetry readings, art previews, the theatre or literary parties.

The person who really ran the household was Olwyn. She was the centre of the entire operation, organising the food and meal times, and the children's work rota, managing the two cleaning ladies, buying clothes for the children, dressing, washing and feeding them.

When Olwyn was not washing or feeding them, the children were free to run wild. That first week of the holidays, the older boys initiated a project to build a tree house in the garden. It was a tremendous effort and all the children became involved. They drew up the plans, carried the planks home from the wood merchant in Kentish Town Road (bought with money handed out by Anthony before he left to go to a meeting one morning), and hauled each plank up with a rope, positioning it and hammering in the nails.

The twins were big and strong and clever with their hands. In no time the shell of the little house was ready – reached by a ladder set against the trunk of the old horse chestnut tree.

'Now we need to make it comfortable,' declared Vita. 'And we need food for our meals.'

'Can we sleep up here?' asked Florian.

'Girls only,' said Perdita firmly.

Once the tree house had been erected, the elder boys lost interest and disappeared to concentrate on some other project. Now the interesting part started for the girls. They had spent the morning swimming at the Lido on Parliament Hill, Lucy included, and then returned for an afternoon in the garden at home. With the older boys out of the way, the tree house was theirs.

They dashed in and out of the house, carrying cushions and dragging blankets and rugs from the playroom. They carted out orange crates to sit on and kitchen towels to hang across the windows as curtains.

Slowly the house in the tree took on a rough look of comfort. It was finished. The girls looked at each other, wondering what to do next.

'I'm hungry,' Celestria whined miserably, clutching her belly.

'Olwyn said she'd bring us out a snack.'

Within five minutes, while the girls were settling themselves cross-legged on the tree house floor, Olwyn came out of the house carrying a wicker basket. David trailed along behind her.

'David wants to join you,' Olwyn said, as Vita let down a rope to be tied around the handle of the basket.

Perdita grimaced, though Olwyn could not see her.

The basket was hoisted up into the tree house and David clambered up the ladder to join them.

Perdita was silent as she divided up between them the egg mayonnaise sandwiches and freshly baked butterfly cakes and chocolate fingers.

David sat down opposite Lucy. He did not say a word but tucked into his pile of food with a cheerful smile on his face. Lucy felt sorry for him. It was so obvious that he wanted to be included all the time, and it just wasn't that easy.

She watched him as he ate. He was stockily built and had floppy brown hair which fell over his eyes, and wide gaps between his teeth.

He rarely spoke but ate his sandwiches slowly, chewing each mouthful with deep concentration.

'I'm still hungry,' said Perdita, licking the crumbs off her lips and eyeing the empty basket. 'I wonder if we can get anything else.'

Vita looked doubtful. 'Olwyn said we couldn't have any more or we'd ruin our appetites for tea later on.'

Perdita rolled her eyes impatiently and pushed herself to her feet. 'We'll see about that,' she said. With the basket swinging on her arm, she climbed down the ladder and disappeared into the house.

It was cool in the tree house under the waving green leaves of the horse chestnut tree. Conkers were appearing between the leaves. The children did not say much as they waited for Perdita to return. Lucy watched a ladybird walking slowly up the side of the tree house, carefully negotiating the rough splinters in the wooden plank as though each one were a tricky hill. At one point she caught Vita's eye. Vita smiled at her, causing a warm rush of pleasure to flow through Lucy's veins. Lucy smiled back.

The younger children had started a clapping game and then they began to play scissors – 'One, two, three . . .' – each time, forming the shape of paper, stone, pencil or scissors with their hands.

At last Perdita ran from the house carrying the basket. She climbed breathlessly up the ladder.

'Great!' Vita began to unpack the basket to reveal apples and pears and a packet of biscuits.

'There's some cold chicken, too,' said Perdita with some pride. 'Probably enough for a bite for everyone.'

'It's a lot,' commented Vita, sharing out the biscuits. 'Did Olwyn give you all this?'

Perdita laughed. 'Of course not! She wouldn't give me anything more. I just took it from the larder. There's so much food in there, no one will know . . .'

She stopped abruptly. Lucy noticed Vita roll her eyes. Perdita turned to David who was looking intently at the biscuits in his hands. Her eyes narrowed. 'Don't you dare say anything, David. Do you hear? You'll get it if you do . . .'

David looked at her, his mouth working slowly at the biscuit crumbs inside his mouth. Raising his eyebrows in an expression of innocence, he shook his head. 'No, of course I won't tell,' he said simply.

After a while the tree house lost its appeal so they climbed down to do other things. The younger children cooled off with water from the hosepipe, chasing each other around the lawn and shrieking with laughter, while Lucy, Vita and Perdita played a game of *Monopoly* with the older boys.

Lucy left the Valentines' house in the early evening after high tea of fried sausages, chips and peas. She felt happy and content. To her irritation, when she was halfway down Lady Margaret Road, she realised that she had left her swimming bag behind. After their swim at the Lido, she had stuffed her wet towel and costume into the duffel bag which she now realised she had left behind in the Valentines' house. Her mother had already scolded her twice that week for coming home without her cardigan and for getting filthy dirty while playing in the Valentines' garden. Lucy was half-tempted to leave the bag at the house, to say nothing and to hope that her mother would not notice. But there was always the risk of her mother asking where her swimming things were (she had the habit of remembering things like that). Also, she had arranged to go back to the Valentines the next morning for another swim, and the thought of having to wear a cold, clammy swimming costume was intolerable.

No, she had to go back, even if it meant getting home a bit late. Her mother would be cross but it would be too bad. Her newfound bravado surprised her. She must have caught it off the Valentine girls, she thought with some pride.

At the Valentine house, she let herself in through the gate and walked round the side to the back of the house, the route she always took nowadays.

There was the sound of water upstairs as the bath was being run for the younger children. Shouts of youngsters running around wildly upstairs rang out into the evening air.

Lucy stepped in through the back door. In the small hall outside the kitchen, she was stopped by the sound of Olwyn's raised voice. It was angry and threatening.

'Don't you dare do that again,' she was saying.

Nobody answered. Lucy edged forward to peer through the gap between the door and the wall. She could see Perdita standing before Olwyn, her head held high, her arms hanging straight down her sides. Her hands were clenched in tight little fists of defiance. Her chin jutted out.

Over by the far wall, Lucy could see David leaning nonchalantly against the Aga, a smirk spread across his face.

Oh dear, thought Lucy, Perdita's in trouble for stealing that food. And now she's being told off . . .

She watched with horror as Olwyn's arm came up and, as if in slow motion, whacked Perdita hard across the side of her head. Perdita staggered several feet across the room, crashing into the kitchen table. Her hand flew up to her ear.

Lucy's hand flew up to her mouth as she stifled a gasp. Stepping back, she quickly retreated from the house. She could leave her bag until the morning, after all.

She let herself out of the garden and ran down Lady Margaret Road. Her heart was racing, not from exertion but from shock, from the image which now swirled in her head of Perdita standing there challenging Olwyn to hit her again, and from the startling fact that during the entire incident, Perdita never once uttered a sound.

Lucy did not say anything to her parents about Olwyn hitting Perdita. She wanted to but she was afraid that if she did her mother would immediately stop her going to play with the Valentines. She could not bear the thought of that happening, so she said nothing, neither that evening, nor ever.

CHAPTER 7

June, 1997

Family Life

Lucy was in a buoyant mood on the day she went down to the market in Hammersmith to buy food for supper. There was an unfamiliar spring in her step, her shoulders were squared, her head held high. It was a long time since she had felt so good. With a life inside her, she felt consciously alive. It was also true that the early panic about Andrew had subsided after he had recovered from his early attacks of pneumonia remarkably well.

Andrew had been out of hospital for ten days now. His first evening out, at the small house he shared with Patrick in Notting Hill Gate, Lucy, Andrew and Patrick had drunk the champagne to celebrate the existence of Lucy's unborn baby.

The celebration was slightly subdued by the unexpressed acknowledgement that much of Andrew's life from now on was likely to be taken up with visits to and from hospital.

Andrew was sanguine about it. 'We'll take it slowly,' he said.

Now Lucy was shopping because she had invited Andrew and Patrick to supper that evening, along with her parents.

Andrew was loath to invite his parents to his own home, afraid that they might turn down the invitation. So Lucy had taken the matter in hand and invited everyone to her house with her and Simon. 'Neutral ground for everyone,' she said.

Simon was not pleased about the arrangements. 'You can't be the peacemaker, Lucy,' he said. 'You mustn't try to make people be what they aren't. Your mother has rejected Andrew up until now and it's highly unlikely that she's suddenly going to change in any fundamental way.'

Lucy frowned and said nothing. She was annoyed to be ticked off but she knew that Simon was probably right. She just could not help herself, so desperate was she for everyone to get on without friction.

Ignoring Simon's criticism, she focused on her fear that Andrew might cancel at the last minute. He had been cancelling on her a lot recently. Since being discharged from hospital, he had called off two lunch dates with her because he had not felt well enough to drag himself out of the house. He could only make plans on a daily basis because he was so chronically tired that he could never anticipate how much energy he might have in any one hour. He had oral thrush, with nasty white curds in his mouth, and he felt nauseous for much of the time.

As she wandered around the market, she tried not to think about Andrew's physical condition and switched her thoughts to the busy life of the street market around her.

She had always liked the noise and bustle of the market and the chirpy veneer of rudeness from the stallholders. There was one in particular she liked, because he was happy to let her pick out her own fruit and vegetables, so she always gave him her custom. Today she examined the glossy green peppers, and blue-black aubergines, gently squeezing the courgettes, testing them for firmness.

As she paid and waited for her change, she found herself staring at the green grapes nestling in blue tissue paper on the fake grass matting underneath. She had once seen a photograph in a magazine (probably Rosie's rag) which showed the female reproductive organs as represented by various fruits and vegetables – grapes for the ovaries, a pear for the uterus, a courgette for the vagina.

She remembered it because it had been a striking image, and a warm one. It was unusual and rather pleasant to think of one's reproductive organs as familiar objects and not alien bits of flesh and tissue hidden inside her belly.

Now she was pregnant, Lucy felt able to like her body again and to feel affectionate towards her reproductive organs in a way that she had not before. For all the time she had been trying to conceive, she had perceived her body as alien and hostile, as something separate from her real self, month after month rejecting her and her deep longing to start a life inside her.

'There you are, darling.' The stallholder handed Lucy her change.

She smiled broadly. 'Thank you,' she said gaily. She did feel good today. It was still difficult to believe that she was truly pregnant. It made her feel like a different person, as if she were empowered with a special strength. Such fortitude made the prospect of an evening with her parents and Andrew together more bearable. Perhaps it would all go well. Perhaps everyone would make up and forget their years of differences and there would be love and reconciliation. Then Simon would see that Lucy's efforts were right, rather than foolish and naïve, after all.

At least she would enjoy cooking the meal, listening to the

radio as she chopped the vegetables and softened the onions in the frying pan. She felt omnipotent with this little life inside her. No, the evening was bound to be a success . . .

Lucy's parents arrived first, and flustered, after a traumatic journey from Dulwich up to Lucy and Simon's house. Hilda Butler hated having to drive into town at the best of times but this trip confirmed her view that living north of the Thames was a dire mistake on Lucy's part.

She and Gordon had set off with plenty of time, as always, and had made good progress until they reached Clapham, where road works had caused long traffic jams all along the road. Young men and women were walking up and down the lines of cars offering bunches of roses or the latest edition of the *Evening Standard* for frustrated commuters on their way home from work. A couple of young girls were waving wet sponges and occasionally washing the windscreens of those drivers who allowed them. They could not have been much older than seventeen. One, with bright orange hair which stuck straight up in the air, began to wash the windscreen of Dr Butler's car.

'No, thank you,' he called out of the window. Dr Butler washed his car every two weeks with water considerably cleaner than what was being splashed on to it at that moment. 'No, thank you,' he repeated.

The girl ignored him and reached across the windscreen with a rubber wiper, revealing a sinewy, unshaven armpit.

'Go away!' Dr Butler stuck his head out of the window. 'Go away, I said no!'

His wife shrank back into the back of her seat. She was frightened of young people.

The girl stepped back and stared at him with a hostile

expression. She chewed gum slowly. 'I'm just trying to earn a bob or two,' she hissed. 'You stupid old gits.'

Fortunately the traffic had started to move again. Dr Butler wound up his window and put his foot down on the accelerator. 'I suppose we are old,' he said quietly.

Hilda pursed her lips and sucked in air. 'I think you might have been a bit firmer with them,' she snapped. 'You didn't sound very authoritative.'

Gordon kept quiet. He was used to his wife's digs by now and knew better than to respond.

At last they were moving and escaped the worst of the jams. But then, going over Chelsea Bridge, a young boy in the car in front had stuck his head out of the window and let out a stream of vomit which flew straight back towards the Butlers' car and splattered all over the windscreen.

It took Dr Butler ten minutes to clean up the mess before they could set off again. As he wiped the vomit off the windscreen, his wife sat tensely in the front seat, her fingers twisting around each other, her lips tight.

Andrew and Patrick had not yet arrived. Dr Butler paced around the sitting room while his wife perched on the edge of the sofa, her knees pressed together, her neck taut.

Simon offered them drinks while Lucy put on the water for the pasta. Seven minutes later, the doorbell rang. Mrs Butler jumped, her nervousness apparent to everyone. Hilda and Gordon had seen Andrew several times in hospital, but this was the first time in four years that they had met socially.

Lucy opened the door, wondering, as always, what Andrew would look like now. She had not seen him for a week and he had mentioned over the telephone that he had lost a lot more weight.

Indeed, he had. Now the skin was taut over his face so

that the outline of his skull was becoming clear to see. His eyes were large and staring, giving off an expression of deep sorrow. His fingertips were bluish, as though he had come in from the cold.

Andrew and Patrick walked into the sitting room behind Lucy, who watched Patrick walk over to her mother and hold out his hand. Mrs Butler pushed herself off the sofa to her feet. She shook Patrick's hand and tried to smile as she mumbled a greeting. A look of confusion spread across her face as she turned to Andrew, who was standing behind Patrick, waiting for her to make the first move.

For a brief moment, Lucy's spirits rose as she thought her mother was moving towards him as if she were going to kiss him. But then Hilda hesitated, she held back and the opportunity was lost. She hesitated for another second. Andrew had been poised to respond. Now he stepped back and nodded. 'Hello, Mother,' he said. 'Hi, Dad.'

Lucy felt Simon's critical gaze on her face. She looked away; it was excruciating.

As the evening progressed, Lucy was filled with a growing sense of hopelessness. She watched her mother's nervous and undemonstrative greeting, and she saw Andrew, after an initial look of hope, back off, hurt by his mother's inability to gather him in her arms and hug him. Her father's inept attempts to humour everyone made her squirm, and she was annoyed by the way he talked too loudly about the cricket score with Simon. Every now and then Lucy tried in vain to shut Simon up by glaring at him. Dr Butler loved cricket and followed it enthusiastically at every opportunity. When he discovered that Simon was a fellow fan, he had been delighted. That made up for the fact that his own son had never shown any interest in sport of any kind, ever.

Dr Butler did, however, talk to Andrew, asking about his

health. As a doctor, he was genuinely interested in hearing the latest developments in treatment and what was being done by the doctors to help him, and this was a language he shared with Andrew.

Gordon also talked to Patrick, who was a personable young man, a solicitor, sociable and friendly, and easy company.

Lucy watched and listened. She watched her mother sitting anxiously in her place at table sipping at her soup and nibbling at her pasta. As the men talked, Hilda said nothing, retreating into a troubled silence at the end of the table. The whole situation clearly made her uncomfortable. Lucy's heart was thumping with frustration and anxiety. If her mother could not talk to Andrew, her own son, now, she thought, she never would.

Gripped by an urge to inject some life into the conversation, Lucy was keen to pump Andrew for more memories about the Valentine family. Placing a bowl of green salad on the table, she jumped in. 'What else can you remember, Andrew, about the Valentines? I want to know your impression of them.'

Andrew was looking uncomfortable but he managed a smile. 'I remember that you were besotted with them. You would do anything they asked you to do . . .'

Lucy was aware of her father's own discomfort at the other end of the table. He was frowning and fiddling with his napkin. Her mother, meanwhile, looked cross. Lucy was not going to be deterred from grabbing this opportunity to learn more from Andrew. Ignoring her parents, she pushed on. 'Like what? What sort of thing did I do for them?' She was excited that Andrew did seem to remember the Valentines so well. He would be able to help reconstruct that summer.

But Andrew's face had become twisted with pain. He winced as his body hunched over the table and he clutched at his chest.

'Are you all right?' Lucy stared at her brother.

Patrick was instantly solicitous. 'Is your chest hurting again?' He jumped to his feet and moved over to stand behind Andrew, whose eyes had filled with tears from the pain.

Perhaps it was more than the pain, which came and went in an erratic way, and the doctors never knew for sure what it was. Perhaps this time it was just the stress and strain of such an evening with his parents, but Andrew finally broke down. His attempt to hold back his feelings failed as his thirty-five-year-old face crumpled like a five-year-old's, and he dropped his head in his hands.

Patrick massaged Andrew's shoulders affectionately, rubbing them rhythmically and firmly.

Lucy watched her mother frown in embarrassed confusion as Patrick then bent down and kissed Andrew on the neck, murmuring reassurances into his ear. 'You're going to be all right, darling,' he whispered. 'Do you want to go home?'

Everyone else was silent. Dr Butler and Simon looked away, uneasy with this display of affection from one man to another.

Hilda sat rigid in her chair. The sinews of her neck were visibly taut. Was it disapproval she felt? Or was it disgust? She had always been too scared to imagine fully what homosexual men got up to when they were on their own, and this display simply confirmed that she was right not to think about it. She just knew it was wrong.

But as she watched her son crying, she remembered him as a little boy wailing because he had fallen over and hurt his knee. She saw her boy, her only son, who now, in his thinness, looked more like that little boy than a grown man.

Something inside her made her react now. She quietly reached out over the table and took Andrew's fingers in her hand. His fingers were cold and bluish, and she saw how skeletal they were. For a second she wondered if she was risking infection this way, even though she knew rationally that she could not. But just for that moment, her instincts as a mother were stronger than the prejudices and beliefs that normally ruled her life. As Andrew's fingers closed on hers, she took a sharp breath and tears filled the corners of her eyes.

Patrick took Andrew home before Lucy could serve up the chocolate mousse she had made for pudding. Andrew's pains had subsided but it was agreed that he was tired and that perhaps he should get a good night's sleep. Perhaps, too, he could go to the hospital again the next day, just for a quick check-up and reassurance, for what that was worth.

After they had left, Lucy's parents decided to leave, too. They had been traumatised enough by the evening and were anxious to get back to the safety of south London before it became too late. As they said their goodbyes, Lucy and her mother clung to each other for a second longer than usual, as if in recognition of what had happened that evening.

It was still quite early as Simon and Lucy washed the dishes in silence. The evening had been a sort of disaster but also a kind of triumph. And Lucy still felt relieved by the fact that her mother had been able to reach out and hold Andrew's hand. She was also intrigued by Andrew's remark about her being besotted with the Valentines and that she would do anything for them. Lucy hoped desperately that she was going to get the chance to ask Andrew more before it was too late. She was becoming very aware of how their time together was running out.

Lucy and Simon snuggled up together on the sofa to watch the news on television. Afterwards, Lucy took herself off to bed. She was exhausted. She had been feeling quite tired from the pregnancy anyway but as she undressed she was suddenly hit by a strong dragging feeling pulling her down.

That was the first sign.

The brown spots of blood on her pants were the second.

The pains, first nagging throbs and then what felt like deep stabbing period pains, began within half an hour.

Her own doctor was on call that night. Dr Kenny arrived at around midnight. By this time, Lucy knew that she was about to miscarry.

After a brief internal examination, Dr Kenny confirmed that the miscarriage could not be stopped. Lucy's cervix was dilating.

'I'll call an ambulance for you now.'

Lying in bed, her face pale, Lucy grimaced. 'What's the point of that? If I'm going to lose the baby, I don't need to go to hospital. It doesn't matter where I am.'

The doctor looked down at her for a moment and nodded. She reached over and squeezed her hand. 'That's true. But they could make you feel more comfortable in hospital.'

Lucy turned her face to the wall. 'I'd rather be in my own home,' she muttered.

The doctor left after Lucy had listlessly turned down her offer of an injection of pethidine. 'I'd rather feel the pain,' she murmured.

And feel the pain she did. She regretted turning down the doctor's offer of pain relief. The first few stabbing cramps seemed to come from a deep dark hole inside her.

They came in waves, each time preceding the expulsion of blood and foetal matter. An hour later, Lucy miscarried the ten-week-old foetus. It was two in the morning.

Simon held her hand throughout, and cried with her as they watched the tiny baby and livery placental tissue flush down the lavatory.

Lucy only managed to get a few hours' sleep that night. She was half-conscious throughout. She dreamed of a crowd of tiny children, their arms outstretched to the sky. 'Mama! Mama!' Their wail was high-pitched and sad. Lucy was walking towards them but they shied away from her with wide, frightened eyes. She stopped to stare at them and the children began to shrink in size and fade into the darkness that was creeping up behind them. Their images melted into the blackness, their wails lost in the wind. Then they were gone.

Dr Kenny telephoned the next morning and sounded genuinely sad for Lucy. 'I think it might be a good idea for you to come down to the surgery so that I can check that everything's all right. And we can have a chat,' she added.

'Yes,' replied Lucy in a flat voice. 'I shall.'

But she knew she would not. Why bother? The baby had gone. Nothing could be done to save it now, as it made its way down through London's sewerage system. What was the point of anything?

CHAPTER 8

July, 1968

Larking About

The day after Lucy had seen Olwyn swiping Perdita across the head, Lucy came up to play at the Valentine house. She had said nothing to her own parents about the incident she had witnessed the night before, but she was certainly expecting some comments from her friends. Indeed, she expected the house to be in an uproar about such a terrible event!

Oddly, when she arrived there was no reference to the previous evening from anyone. Odder still, she found Perdita sitting at the kitchen table using the old Singer sewing machine while Olwyn stood beside, guiding Perdita's fingers as she manipulated the soft fabric. 'Olwyn's been showing me how to make clothes with the machine. I've made a pair of shorts.' With obvious pride, she held up a pair of simple, red cotton shorts.

Perdita looked quite cheerful and happy, and acted as though nothing had happened between her and Olwyn the evening before. Lucy was puzzled and she even began to doubt her own memory. Perhaps that scene had not happened at all. Perhaps she had just had a vivid dream about it.

'You left your swimming things,' Olwyn said. 'I hung them out to dry for you.'

'Thank you,' whispered Lucy, feeling even more confused by Olwyn's apparent thoughtfulness. Lucy had to ask Vita about it. Surely she would have something to say about Olwyn's unkindness.

Waiting until they were alone in Vita's room, she said, 'When I was going home yesterday I saw Olwyn hit Perdita.'

She said it and stopped, watching the other girl, waiting for a reaction.

Vita looked up and stared at her, her face strangely blank. Lucy wondered if she had been listening. 'I saw Olwyn hit Perdita,' she repeated. 'On the head, hard.'

There was another moment's silence. Vita turned to look out of the window and up at the sky. Then she turned back and shrugged. 'Well,' she said casually, 'Perdita didn't say anything about it so it was probably nothing.'

So that was it. It was probably nothing. Vita's words wormed their way inside Lucy. Now she felt silly for even mentioning it. It was probably nothing. There was something wrong with her, Lucy, for making a fuss, for thinking that what happened was unusual.

From that moment she resolved never again to ask about anything that seemed out of the ordinary. Such naïveté would expose her as an outsider. When you were at the Valentines', you should never be surprised by anything, she told herself. Nothing was strange.

Lucy went up to play at the Valentines' house every day that week. While her mother was glad that Lucy was being entertained during the long summer holidays before they set off for their own family trip, she was not delighted when Lucy came home all grubby from her games with the Valentine children. Sometimes it was just her hands and fingernails that were dirty but occasionally, if the children had staged, say, a wrestling match in the garden, her clothes were muddy, wet or grass-stained, too.

'What does it matter, Mother?' Lucy asked one day as her mother pulled her T-shirt off over her head. 'You wash the clothes every day anyway.'

Her mother gave her an annoyed frown. 'That's not the point,' she said. 'I don't like you wandering home looking as if you haven't had a bath for weeks. What will people say? Anyone would think that you were from one of the estates . . .'

Lucy was too young to grasp the extent of her mother's snobbery but she did sense Hilda's continuing confusion about the Valentine family. They were rich enough for her to approve of her daughter's friendship but she was clearly upset that they did not act rich, or in the way she thought wealthy people should act.

In fact, the Valentine parents did not act like anyone Lucy had ever met before. They said rude things about the Queen (Mr Valentine once referred to her as 'an old trout'), and made jokes about God – things she would never have dared tell her mother about. They talked a lot about politics and books and art and every week another pile of new hardback books would appear on the hall table.

It seemed to Lucy that the Valentines approved of everything her mother disapproved of, and disapproved of everything her mother believed good and right. They approved of children arguing with them, stating their position and defending it, when her mother could not abide what she called 'back talk' in a child. They approved of student demonstrations and rock music and long hair on men, while Hilda thought that all such matters were disgraceful.

They liked spicy food and lots of garlic, and wine with their meals every night, a sharp contrast to Hilda's diet of plain food, meals of well-cooked meat and boiled vegetables, and total abstinence, except for a medium dry sherry on Christmas Day, which she never finished because it made her tiddly.

The Valentines allowed their children to read comics and Enid Blyton stories – what Mrs Butler called 'trashy' books. And they never criticised their children's choice of reading, for they believed, Vita explained, that children discover for themselves the difference between difficult and easy literature.

Lucy was deeply impressed and envious. At home she was never allowed to read comics and only allowed to read an Enid Blyton story after she had read ten 'good' books, chosen by her mother. The Valentines were also allowed to watch whatever they liked on television – though they were only allowed an hour a day. They could choose what they wanted. Lucy had no choice. The only thing she and Andrew were ever allowed to watch was *Blue Peter*. And they never watched commercial television. Her parents could only get the two BBC channels on their television.

The more she saw of the Valentine family, the more she wanted to be part of it. They despised all conventions and loathed any kind of conformism. They thought it was good to be different. How Lucy longed to have parents who encouraged her to question everything that the rest of the world took for granted. And how shocked her mother would be if she knew exactly how much the Valentine parents cocked a snook at everything in life!

One day, Lucy was invited to stay the night at the Valentines'. She had spent the whole day there, having arrived at nine in the morning. She and Vita had gone swimming at the Lido and then cycled all the way across Hampstead Heath to Whitestone Pond and back, ignoring the shouts of the occasional official who yelled that bikes were not allowed on the Heath. The girls just laughed cheekily and pedalled faster. They climbed trees and scratched their initials in the bark. They tried to catch some ducklings until a woman shouted at them to stop. Coming home, they left their footprints in the wet cement floor on a building site near Little Green Street, and threw thick blocks of wood on to the railway line.

In the afternoon the older boys were around, and they all played noisy games of rummy until tea time. By six o'clock, after tea, it was agreed that Lucy should stay the night. Since she had been there all day, she might as well stay the night, too. 'You can borrow my pyjamas,' Vita offered.

The Valentine parents were going out to a dinner party. The elder girls sat in their mother's room while Seraphina sat at her dressing table and made up her face. Dressed in a kingfisher blue silk kaftan, she combed her lustrous black hair until it gleamed in the evening light. Leaning forward, and with the tip of her tongue peeping between her lips as she concentrated, with extraordinary precision, she applied a black kohl pencil over the edge of her eyelids. Then she painted her lips with a beige lipstick.

The girls hovered behind her, fingering the black boxes of Mary Quant make-up and watching to see exactly how Seraphina ran the liner over her eyelids. 'You need a steady hand,' she said with a light laugh.

In the bathroom next door, Anthony Valentine was listening to Bob Dylan's latest album while he lay in the soapy water. There was a speaker from the stereo system placed in the room above the door. He lay down on his back, his long legs bent at the knees. He closed his eyes and sighed with satisfaction.

Directly above, in the children's bathroom on the top floor, Olwyn was bathing the younger children. She scrubbed their faces until they were bright pink and quickly and thoroughly soaped and rinsed their bodies. She yanked each child out of the bath and rubbed it dry with a towel. She pulled their night clothes on. 'Into bed, now!' And she turned to the next one.

Downstairs Lucy sat shyly on the edge of the large double bed and watched Vita and Perdita crowd around their mother. They chatted to each other in the playful banter that characterised the way the Valentines spoke to each other. It was teasing and clever and, most peculiar to Lucy's ears, it seemed equal. Her own mother would have been shocked to hear children speaking to their parents in such a way; to Hilda Butler, such informality would signify a certain lack of respect for their elders.

Anthony Valentine had finished his bath. He dried his large hirsute body with a wide red towel and wandered into the bedroom, unaware of the nine-year-old blushing on the bed.

Lucy had never seen a full-grown penis before. She felt a weird thrill run through her at the sight of this long thick piece of flesh emerging from a dense crop of curly blond hair and hanging down to swing like an elephant's trunk between Mr Valentine's legs. It was both attractive and repulsive.

She tried to avert her eyes but they kept wandering back to peep at this strange piece of anatomy, so different from her brother's hairless little specimen. She had never seen her father naked, ever. Modesty was encouraged in the Butler household. She had never imagined that a man's willy could get so big. It was scary. She felt a mix of awe and excitement every time she glanced at it.

Anthony Valentine moved about the room, picking up clean socks and underpants. At last he had covered up his lower half and Lucy could relax again. She felt oddly exhausted by what she had just seen, and hoped that no one had noticed her embarrassment.

Seraphina's dazzling blue kaftan clung pleasingly to her soft curves as she slipped her feet into flat gold sandals. Finally, she sprayed a blast of scent into the air and walked through it.

Anthony had slipped on a white cotton turtle-necked sweater and a pair of well-cut navy blue hipster bell-bottoms. Pulling in his stomach, he did up the belt and inspected himself in the mirror. Then, smoothing down his thick blond hair, he rubbed his jaw to check the smoothness of his shave and thought about the evening ahead.

He was looking forward to the evening, which entailed dinner with some nicely argumentative friends. They were going to eat in a Greek restaurant in Camden Town where they would no doubt tussle over political matters as they ate their taramasalata and kleftikon. Then afterwards they would go back to their friends' flat in Gloucester Crescent for coffee and a few joints.

Anthony enjoyed smoking dope, though he tried not to smoke it too often because it had a tendency to make him sleepy in the mornings. He did love it, though. He relished the slow onset and the feeling of wellbeing it brought with it. And he liked the way various types of hash or grass affected him in different ways – from the giggly mellowness he got from his American friends' grass, to the intense buzz from the more refined Lebanese Gold. What he enjoyed most of all, however, was the ritual of rolling the joint itself. He loved the plucking out of the three Rizla papers from the red packet, the gluing together of two and then the third across the top. He loved running the tip of his tongue along the length of a No. 6 cigarette and pulling it open to allow the dry line of tobacco to drop quietly on to the papers, slightly to the right. Then, if it was resin, the heating of a corner of the sticky block and then the careful crumbling of hash over the tobacco, spaced evenly and fairly, making sure it was all the way through. The skilled rolling, tight and clean, followed by a quick lick of the glue to seal it. The roach. Tearing up some thin card – a postcard, or the Rizla packet itself – to roll up and push into one end. A swift twist of the other end, and the joint was ready to smoke.

Rummaging around at the back of the sock drawer, he found the little packet wrapped in silver foil and slipped it into his pocket. It was Friday night. He had worked hard all week. He deserved a night of indulgence.

He caught Seraphina's eye and winked. Smoking marijuana made his wife delightfully lustful, and he looked forward to sex with her later that night. Her quick smile in return told him that she would be in the mood for some good loving when the time came. He almost shuddered with pleasure at the thought.

Seraphina and Anthony finally left after a noisy departure of kisses and hugs for all the children. From upstairs, Olwyn called the elder girls to have a bath.

Perdita groaned. 'Friday night is hair-wash night. Torture!'

'I'll do yours as well, Lucy, while you're here,' Olwyn said in her soft Welsh brogue. Watching Olwyn's thick-set frame and square face, Lucy realised that she had never seen the housekeeper smile.

The bath had been run again and was filled with deep, hot

water. Vita stripped off and climbed in. It was a particularly long bath, installed to accommodate Anthony Valentine's tall frame, and it was ideal for bathing several children at the same time.

Lucy waited for her turn.

The younger children were playing in their bedrooms. From down below, whoops of joy and shrill laughter could be heard as they bounced on the beds and threw pillows at each other.

David appeared in the doorway. 'Shall I tell them to be quiet, Mother?'

Olwyn glanced up at him as she sprayed water on Vita's head through the steel nozzle of the spray. 'No,' she said quietly. 'I'll sort them out in a minute.'

The noise grew louder and shriller as the children became more excited.

Olwyn poured shampoo on to Vita's scalp, scrubbed it hard and then rinsed out the soap.

Then she turned to Lucy.

Lucy was used to her mother washing her hair, which she did as a weekly ritual, with jugs of water in the bath. Unlike the Valentines, the Butlers did not have fitted spray attachments in their bath. Lucy was often irritated by her mother's slowness but at least Hilda was always gentle.

Lucy only realised this as she felt Olwyn's long nails dig into the skin of her scalp, clamping it like the claws of an eagle. Her head was manipulated roughly from side to side. She tried not to cry out as the nails felt as if they were ripping her skin. She shut her eyes as Olwyn began to rinse the shampoo out, allowing the water to fall over Lucy's face, regardless of whether the soap ran into Lucy's eyes. By the time the hair wash was finished, Lucy was on the verge of tears, her eyes were stinging from the sharpness of the shampoo and her scalp throbbed from the rough scrubbing. She felt quite dazed.

Olwyn turned off the tap and replaced the spray. Gripping Lucy's upper arm, she pulled her out of the water. 'That's you done,' she said with satisfaction. 'Perdita, now you get in!'

As Perdita slipped her naked body into the bath, the noise in the children's bedroom grew. There were bangs and shouts. Olwyn handed Lucy a towel, then she marched quickly down the corridor and disappeared into the little ones' bedroom.

Immediately there was silence. Lucy could hear the sound of scuffling and a muffled thump. David was standing in the corridor looking into the bedroom. Then there was no more sound, just a silence.

Two minutes later, Olwyn returned to the bathroom, pushing the sleeves of her cardigan up her plump forearms to finish the hair washing. Lucy tried to catch Vita's attention but Vita was busy drying her toes with great concentration, biting the corner of her upper lip.

Olwyn turned on the spray and began to scrub Perdita's head. Lucy missed the look between the two sisters, a look through narrowed eyes.

After the bath, Olwyn put the other children to bed while the older girls went downstairs to have mugs of hot milk. As they sat in the kitchen, the three older brothers arrived home, triumphant from a tennis tournament where they had been playing all week. They had won everything. 'We cleaned up,' said Achilles. The twins had won the doubles together, and Achilles and Constantine were singles winner and runner-up respectively in their age-group class. Byron had won his class, too, in straight sets. They carried silver-plated cups and medals which they dropped carelessly on the sideboard as they rummaged around in the kitchen for something to eat.

In his pyjamas, David slipped into the kitchen and sat at the table with them. Elbows on the table, he rested his chin in the palms of his hands and watched with darting eyes, a nervous smile on his lips.

Scrutinising him, Lucy was surprised to feel a soft tug of pity for the boy. He seemed to regard the older boys with some admiration, and she felt sad for him. David was always trying to be accepted, in his way, even though he also always behaved in such sneaky ways.

'I think I'd like something stronger,' laughed Achilles, squatting down to reach into the lower part of the sideboard. The boys' striking good looks were further enhanced by their tennis whites, which showed off their strong tanned limbs, glistening with golden hairs.

Constantine grinned. 'You mean the gin?'

'Yup.'

Achilles glanced at Vita. 'Where is she?' he asked quietly.

Vita smiled. 'Putting the babies to bed.'

Achilles pulled the large green bottle from the shelf and held it up to examine it in the light. 'It's half full now.'

He glanced over his shoulder at the girls and winked. Then, seeing David, he walked over and grasped his shoulder. 'See this?' he said, holding the bottle threateningly by the neck.

David looked up and nodded meekly.

'You say a word to anyone and you get this smashed on your head. Understand?'

David nodded earnestly.

'I mean it.'

Achilles unscrewed the cap on the bottle, grabbed two glass tumblers from the sideboard and poured an inch of gin into each one. Then he turned on the cold tap and carefully ran water into the bottle, measuring it up to the point where the level had been before.

He handed Constantine his glass and replaced the bottle in the cupboard. 'No one will ever know,' he said with satisfaction. He tipped back his head and drank the gin in one go.

'Mmm,' he murmured. 'God, I love the way it burns my throat.'

Constantine took a sip of his drink and grimaced. 'I'm not sure that I like it straight,' he said. 'I think I need some tonic in it.'

'You drip,' laughed Achilles. 'Can't take it, eh?'

Lucy slept on a camp bed on Vita's bedroom floor. For a while, the girls talked in the dark. Every now and then Vita would let out a sharp hiss. 'Ssssh!' She would listen carefully. 'We've got to keep our voices down,' she whispered.

Lucy wanted to ask why, and what would happen if Olwyn heard them but she sensed an unspoken warning coming from Vita's bed. It was better not to enquire.

She lay in the dark, aware of the delicious warmth of her bedding. An intense feeling of happiness built up inside her as she pretended that she was part of the Valentine family herself.

'You're my best friend, Vita,' she whispered shyly, praying as the words came out of her mouth that Vita would not laugh at her. Was it a foolish thing to say? Something made her feel it necessary to stake her claim, to let Vita know how she felt.

There was a pause in the darkness. Then she could hear Vita turn over in bed. 'That's nice,' Vita said at last. 'I suppose you're my best friend, too.' There was silence. Then Vita added, 'I've never really had any friends. Our mother always says that when you have so many brothers and sisters you don't need friends because you always have someone to play with.'

Lucy took in Vita's words and felt wounded that she meant so little to this girl. She knew that friends were more than simply people to play with. Surely Vita knew that too!

In her sleepiness, she vowed to make Vita need her as a friend. More than anything in the world, she wanted Vita to need her, and for her to acknowledge it.

Vita woke Lucy up at five o'clock the next morning. 'Quick,' she whispered. 'Get dressed but be very quiet. We don't want the Brat to wake up and see us . . .'

It was a clear morning with a cloudless pale blue sky and a weakly yellow but promising early sun.

Perdita was waiting downstairs in the kitchen. She held three buttered bagels in her hand. 'Breakfast,' she said, handing one each to Lucy and Vita. 'We need plenty of energy for the slalom.'

Dido, the dog, stood by the door wagging her tail excitedly in anticipation of a good run outside.

They let themselves out into the garden and went to the shed from which they pulled a long home-made go-cart constructed by the twins from some old pram wheels and planks of wood.

Lucy followed behind as Vita and Perdita pulled the contraption out to the front gate.

'The timing's perfect,' said Perdita, her eyes shining with excitement.

Outside in Lady Margaret Road, the day was quiet. The girls pulled the go-cart up to the top of the road just where it

turned into the steep, tree-lined avenue that led into Leighton
Road at the bottom.

Vita dragged the vehicle into the middle of the road
and positioned it over the white line. 'Get in, Lucy!' she
ordered. 'Put your arms around my waist. Perdita's got the
stop watch. She'll sit behind you and time it.'

Lucy looked around her. The streets were deserted but she
felt nervous standing poised in the middle of a road like this.
'Isn't it rather dangerous?' she stammered.

Vita laughed. 'That's why it's such fun. Now, jump in so
that we can get off.'

Lucy clambered into the wooden box. 'But what happens
if a car comes along?'

Vita and Perdita sprang nimbly into the box at the same
time. 'Then we die!' they shrieked, their reckless laughter
blowing away in the wind behind them as the go-cart shot
down the hill towards Leighton Road.

It was undoubtedly fun. With Dido running alongside
them, her tongue hanging out, Vita steered the go-cart with
great skill, cutting diagonally across the road from left to
right and then to the left again, like a skier doing the slalom
in the snow. With the fresh wind in their faces, they shot past
Ospringe Road, Countess Road and Ascham Street. As they
passed Falkland Road, and the enormous Gothic Wesleyan
Chapel on the corner, Lucy thought of her family asleep in
bed and the horror on her mother's face if she saw what her
daughter was up to just a few hundred yards away.

They zipped past the council flats at the end of the road,
and finally came to a graceful stop at the bottom of the hill.
The girls stepped out of their chariot, laughing and panting
in exhilaration.

'Two minutes and fifty-nine seconds!' shouted Perdita,
checking her stopwatch.

'Our best time ever. You must bring us luck,' Vita grinned at Lucy who blushed with pride.

Then just as they pulled the go-cart on to the pavement, a car driven by a young man with shoulder-length hair screeched around the corner and roared up Lady Margaret Road at about fifty miles an hour.

Vita smirked. 'Glad we didn't meet him on our way down . . .'

Lucy watched the car disappear up the road and wondered how close they had been to being hit by it.

Pulling the go-cart behind them, the girls ambled along the pavement towards Kentish Town Road.

'There're the twins!' Vita stopped and pointed across the road junction where Constantine and Achilles had leaned their bicycles against the iron railings.

Perdita scowled. 'Those pigs!' she said crossly.

The boys themselves were straddled across the top of the railing over the railway bridge.

'What are they doing?' Lucy was mystified.

'They're up to something,' said Vita. She let out a low shout: 'Hey!'

The boys looked up, startled. Seeing that it was only their little sisters and friend, they turned back to concentrate on what they were doing before. They glanced briefly around them. The road was still empty, not a soul in sight.

Achilles looked at his watch. 'Any minute now,' he said.

'I can hear it,' said Constantine. In the distance the rumbling of a train echoed along the tracks. 'It's coming!'

It was then that Lucy saw that the boys each held a large rock in their hands.

The train was close now. They could hear the loud clackety-clack on the line.

The boys turned to look at the railway track below.

'When I say,' whispered Achilles. As the train appeared from out of the tunnel, the boys raised their arms. 'Now!'

They dropped the rocks at the same time. The sound of their crashing on to the roof of the morning train resounded across the road.

'Now scram!' The boys jumped down from the wall, grabbed their bicycles and rode off up Fortess Road, leaving the three girls watching them from the junction.

'They think they're so clever,' grumbled Vita.

'Why did they do that?' Lucy was watching the boys disappearing up the hill.

'Because they're pigs,' snapped Perdita.

'They might hurt somebody or cause the train to crash.' Lucy was unnerved. It seemed so wrong, so *bad*.

But that was not Perdita's concern. 'Oh, it won't hurt anyone,' she said casually. 'They said they'd take me with them the next time they did it, and they didn't. They deliberately left me behind. They didn't wake me up. Pigs.'

'They never keep their word,' complained Vita. 'You can't trust them, ever. They're about as bad as the Brat sometimes,' she added, her voice loaded with scorn.

It was still only six o'clock. Kentish Town was quiet, though there were now a few more cars on the road and the occasional pedestrian walking by.

Lucy's stomach rumbled with hunger. She was pleased when Perdita suggested they get something to eat. 'Let's get some raspberries on the way home,' she said. 'The Wilsons have got a lot and I know they're away this weekend.'

Hauling the go-cart up the hill behind them, and with Dido padding quietly alongside, the girls walked up Leverton Street to the wall at the corner of Falkland Road. Perdita looked around her. 'I'll go over and get some. You be the lookouts. If you see someone, give me a low whistle and scram. Then I'll make my own way back.'

Perdita pulled herself up on the wall and dropped down over the other side. Lucy's heart pounded in her chest as she stood with Vita on the corner. The dog sat panting by her feet. Lucy was frightened. She felt like a criminal. They were stealing. Her heart jumped in her throat. It seemed that they were waiting an age before Perdita finally reappeared, jumping back over the wall with her cardigan crammed full of plump red raspberries. No one had seen them. Now they could get home quickly!

They walked slowly back up Leverton Street, along Ascham Street and Lady Margaret Road, gorging themselves on the ripe fruit. Wiping the juice from their chins, they arrived home to find the twins cooking up a fine breakfast of bacon, eggs, mushrooms and fried bread. 'There's enough for you girls, if you want some,' declared Achilles generously. 'I'll stick some in for you, too.'

All friends again, Lucy sat down with the elder Valentine children and ate the tasty food long before the rest of the household had woken up. Cooking and eating their own breakfast as if they were grown-ups!

CHAPTER 9

June, 1997

Mother Love

The day after Lucy's miscarriage, her doctor telephoned to see how she was. She suggested that Lucy come in for a check-up but she did not push her. 'Just come down to the surgery if you have any worries about it. It's normal to bleed quite heavily after a miscarriage, so you shouldn't worry needlessly about that. But you know I'm here if you need to talk.'

'Thank you,' replied Lucy, half touched by Dr Kenny's concern and half annoyed by the intrusion. She felt exhausted and defeated by the events of the night before. There was no knowing how she could survive any more blows.

'Wait a while before you try again,' continued the doctor. 'Three months is the recommended period.'

'Three months! I can't wait that long,' exclaimed Lucy. 'I'm thirty-seven, I'm running out of time.'

Dr Kenny paused. 'Well, wait until the bleeding has stopped. It probably doesn't really make much difference physiologically. But you shouldn't be downhearted. Looking on the bright side, you now know you can conceive . . . That's very important. Now that we know you have done it once, there's no reason why you shouldn't be able to do it again. Conceiving is the most difficult part.'

Lucy listened to the doctor's cheerful pep talk with mixed feelings. She wanted to be hopeful, to believe what the doctor said but she also wanted to protect herself, not to raise her hopes again for fear of having them dashed and of laying herself open to more wounds in the future. Although she could not put it into words, she felt that where her baby had been, an anger now raged inside her, a fury at the unfairness of what had happened, of losing the baby she had waited so long to conceive. She burned with a fury that frightened her. And at the same time she felt defeated. They were back to where they had started, back to fertile days and soul-destroying periods. Could she bear it? Lucy was not sure if she had the strength to go through it all again.

In fact, the issue of how long to wait until trying again was irrelevant. After the loss of their baby, Simon unexpectedly sank into his own kind of gloom. Lucy had not realised how affected he would be but she was surprised and shocked to see how badly he took it. He was short-tempered and grumpy for most of the time. He rarely shaved and he stayed late at work, only returning home after midnight, often stinking of beer.

Sex was out of the question. He and Lucy barely spoke to each other, each incapable of comforting the other. They saw each other occasionally at breakfast, before Simon dashed out to work.

Then, after a while, Simon appeared to cheer up. He began to shave properly again and wear freshly laundered clothes. While he still worked late at night, he did occasionally suggest that they go to the cinema or down to the pub for a drink. But Lucy did not feel they were together as they had been, they did not engage as they used to. Babies and conception were not mentioned. They did not touch each other in bed or out of it. Neither seemed to have a spark of passion inside them.

Lucy was not very bothered by this because for her there was another profound reason for not rushing into trying to get pregnant again.

Andrew was fading faster now. It seemed that almost every other day there was another development with his health – another part of his body had broken down or given up on him. She spoke to him or Patrick on the telephone most days. The conversation was exclusively about Andrew's health.

She knew she could not cope with trying to bring another person into the world while this one was about to leave it, and she realised that she did not want to get pregnant until Andrew had died. She knew that she had to wait until she had buried him, until she had stopped worrying about him, before she could concentrate on herself again. So she was not sorry that Simon seemed willing to avoid sexual contact with her in bed. The question of how long the wait would be remained unanswered.

Andrew's appearance was now quite disturbing. To any-one who had visited an AIDS ward it was fairly obvious that he was close to the final stage of his life. To an innocent onlooker he simply looked ill and very undernourished.

Today Lucy was meeting Andrew in a small café in Notting Hill Gate. He had just come from a check-up at the hospital. He looked tired as he walked in through the door. He wore a blue Yankees baseball cap on his short cropped hair. His jeans were baggy over his thin legs. Unsteady on his feet, he came across the room and sat down opposite her.

Lucy ordered a cappuccino for him and waited. She was hoping to ask him again about the Valentines, to see what else he could remember but it was difficult to get him to talk about anything other than himself nowadays, and it seemed selfish, if not cruel, to force other subjects on him when he was preoccupied with his own problems. First she had to judge his mood.

'How was the hospital?'

Her brother turned his face towards her and shrugged. 'I've got a virus in my eyes, something called CMV. I noticed something was wrong with my right eye recently. I've been getting tunnel vision in it. Apparently, both eyes are infected now, though the left seems okay at the moment.'

'What does that mean?'

Andrew gave a small shrug. 'It means that I'm going blind. If I'm not treated, I'll go blind very quickly. If I am treated, I'll retain my sight for a few more months. It's very serious.'

'What's the treatment?'

'I have to have a catheter put into my chest so they can give me antibiotics intravenously every day.'

'How many more months will that give you?'

'Nine. Then I'll be blind.'

Lucy nodded. 'That's what happened to Derek Jarman.'

'Yup.'

Andrew toyed with the milky froth on his cappuccino. 'Going blind is my greatest fear.' He corrected himself. 'One of my greatest fears – losing my mind is the other.' His voice had dropped to a forceful whisper. 'I'm not going to let that happen . . .'

They sat in silence and, not knowing what else to do, Lucy reached over and squeezed Andrew's hand. As she did so, he bit his lip. Then he could not hold himself together. He began to sob, his mouth pulled back in a grimace. He looked at her with his big blue damaged eyes. 'I'm frightened, Lucy,' he whispered. 'I'm scared . . .'

Lucy glanced around to see if anyone was watching, but the other customers were concentrating on their own thoughts and worries.

Suddenly Andrew pulled himself to his feet. 'I think I'm going to be sick.' He looked around for the sign for the lavatories and disappeared, stumbling against a table as he went.

He reappeared five minutes later. He was dry-eyed.

The manager of the café – a fashionable place with classical music and designer sandwiches – had been watching Andrew. As Andrew settled down in his chair again, the man came over. 'Is everything all right?' he asked, looking closely at Andrew.

'Yes, fine,' Lucy said sharply. She sensed that the manager guessed what was wrong with Andrew. She also guessed that he probably did not want a person with AIDS on his premises. 'Everything's fine, thank you,' she insisted, her chest tightening with protective aggression.

They stayed for another ten minutes, if only to prove to the beady-eyed manager that they would leave when they chose rather than he. As they left, Lucy glared at the manager. 'I shan't be coming back here in a hurry,' she said loudly.

But her thoughts were no longer on their treatment in the café. The words 'Nine months' circled in her head. Nine months. No more than nine months left. And probably not even that.

Hilda Butler had laid on a delicious lunch for her daughter, which they now ate on the terrace in the garden of her Dulwich home.

It was a hot day so they had to put up the sun umbrella,

which now cast plenty of welcome shade across Hilda and Lucy while they sipped elderflower cordial and ate chicken salad with cold rice, followed by summer pudding and cream.

'What a feast!' Lucy sat back in her chair feeling bloated.

'Well, I thought you needed a bit of cheering up.'

Lucy glanced up at her mother, surprised by her sudden thoughtfulness. For once her mother was sitting still. Usually by this time she would be clearing the plates and wiping the table.

Hilda continued. 'It must be hard for you to lose a baby, especially after trying for so long. That must have made it feel like a double blow.'

Lucy felt her throat constricting. 'Yes, but I'm okay now, Mother.' She did not want to cry in front of her mother; she did not want a heart-to-heart. 'We'll just try again soon.'

'Don't try too soon,' Hilda said in a quiet but earnest voice. 'Let yourself grieve first.'

Lucy shrugged. She was beginning to feel embarrassed.

Hilda was still talking. 'I've never told you this before but I lost a baby once, too.'

Lucy looked up in surprise. 'You did?'

'You were too young to remember. You were a toddler. I had a little boy but there were so many things wrong with him, he didn't have a chance. He died almost immediately.'

Her face had become distorted and twisted at the painful memory she had pushed deep inside her for so long. 'And I don't think I gave myself long enough to get over it properly at the time. I got pregnant with Andrew almost straight away.' She sighed softly. 'That was probably a mistake, though it seemed right at the time.'

Lucy stared at her mother. 'But why haven't you told

me before? Why did you keep it a secret for all this time?'

Hilda shook her head. Her eyes and the tips of her nose were red. 'It was too painful, I suppose. It was easier not to talk about it. You never saw the baby because he never came home from the hospital, and I don't think you were even aware that I was pregnant, or what that meant, anyway.

'Your father was terribly upset at the time. I think being a doctor, he felt a failure because he couldn't do anything to save him. But nothing could have saved him, no doctor could have helped. He wasn't even properly formed – he had the worst hare lip and cleft palate that the doctors had ever seen and he also had the most severe form of spina bifida. If he had lived, he would have been severely handicapped.'

Hilda's voice had dropped to a whisper as Lucy suddenly began to recall the photographs of damaged babies she used to pore over as a child in her father's surgery.

'They say that miscarriages can be Nature's way of making sure imperfect babies are not born. I'm very sad that you had a miscarriage but if there was something wrong with the baby, if that was why you lost it, then perhaps it was better to lose it then rather than later. They also say that sometimes the body has to have a practice run with pregnancy before being able to go ahead. Next time you'll conceive and hold the baby with no trouble at all.' She smiled.

Lucy looked at her mother and saw a woman trying her best to make contact with her for the first time in years. She smiled back.

'I hope you're right, Mother.'

Lucy got to her feet. 'Let's clear away this lot and go for a walk in the park.' She began to stack the dishes and cutlery.

Her mother sat still. 'Oh, let's stay here. It's so pleasant just sitting in the garden.'

'But it'd be good to stretch our legs, and it's not too hot now, there's a lovely breeze. And since it's a week day, the park won't be crowded.'

She looked up at her mother and frowned.

Hilda was sitting rigid on the edge of her chair. Her neck was tight and strained. 'I really don't want to go,' she said, her lower lip wobbling like a child's.

Lucy looked at her mother in dismay. Instead of the strong, directed, busy woman she had known all her life, she saw a person on the point of collapse. Her mother seemed to have shrunk in size as she looked up plaintively at her daughter with watery eyes. Lucy waited. She knew that her mother was going to say something, and make a link with her.

Hilda's strength had gone. Her lower lip dropped as she spoke, her voice cracked. 'I'm so frightened for Andrew,' she whispered. 'I lie awake every night thinking about him and what's going to happen to him.'

'He's going to die soon,' Lucy said firmly. 'And there's nothing we can do about it, except love him.'

'I do love him,' whispered Hilda. 'Of course I love him, he's my son.

'What I think about every night is how he's going to be punished. He's going to be going to Hell . . .'

Lucy looked down at her. 'Fortunately, I don't believe in an afterlife,' she snapped, suddenly struck by the brutal thought that her mother had only herself – and her beliefs – to blame for such fears. Underneath, she felt angry that her mother's religious faith was now making her concentrate on Andrew's death rather than his life.

Hilda cleared her throat and collected herself. Perhaps she

had sensed her daughter's lack of sympathy. She blew her nose and shook her head. 'I want to give you something while you're here.'

She got up and went into the house. A moment later she returned and handed Lucy a Jiffy bag. 'I want you to have these now,' she said. 'I find them too painful to look at, and I'd rather not have them in the house. I may want to see them again in years to come but, for the time being, I'd rather they were in your safe keeping.'

Lucy reached into the bag and pulled out four leather-bound volumes. She recognised them immediately. They were familiar from her childhood when she used to help her mother put in the carefully edited pictures her father had taken of the family.

Holding one in her lap, she opened it up and turned the pages with care. This covered the late Sixties. Most of the pictures were grainy black-and-white shots of herself and Andrew as young children running around the garden of their old house in Kentish Town. Flicking through, she stopped at one striking close-up of Andrew, aged about six, fast asleep in bed. He looked like an angel, with pure features and unblemished skin, his arm thrown behind him on the pillow, his mouth slightly open.

Noticing Lucy pause, Hilda looked over her shoulder. 'That's my favourite picture of Andrew,' she said. 'I used to sit on his bed and stroke the hair off his forehead as he slept. I used to sit there, as I did with you, looking at that innocent face and imagine his life ahead. I'd imagine him at school, at university, becoming a doctor, getting married and having children. I used to have his whole life in my head.' She sighed deeply. 'But it was not to be,' she said wearily. 'And it never will be . . . now.'

Lucy chewed her lip and nodded. 'No,' she said, closing the album and hugging it to her chest.

Hilda had not finished. Her eyes had a glazed look as she talked. 'That's been one of my faults in life,' she said, 'planning other people's careers for them. Then it doesn't work out. Something goes wrong and it all gets ruined.' Hilda turned to look at her daughter. 'I did it to your father,' she whispered, 'and in a terrible way . . .'

Lucy looked at her mother in discomfort. This unfamiliar openness was almost too much for her. She absorbed the words about her father but her thoughts were on Andrew. For as she hugged the photograph album to her chest, she was reminded of an odd occasion when she had been mean to her little brother. It had been completely out of character, really, for Lucy adored Andrew, who had returned her feelings. But for some reason she had decided to assert herself as his older sister.

She could remember it now. She came home from the Valentines' one afternoon and Andrew had asked her in his usual way if she would play *Snakes and Ladders* with him.

'Shove off!' Lucy snapped brutally at him.

She reddened with shame as she recalled the unkindness in her voice. It was an experiment, she remembered. She was trying something out, an attitude, a sense of power, that she had picked up at her friends' house.

Andrew had looked at her with bewildered eyes, his lower lip trembled with confusion. Lucy had never spoken sharply to him like that before. It made no sense of what he knew of his kind big sister.

'Why are you being horrid to me?' he wailed.

Lucy stared back at him, waiting to see what would happen.

Andrew looked at her for a second more, and then ran off crying, leaving Lucy to turn away with surprise at her power. But she felt uneasy about it, too.

Now Lucy smiled tearfully at her mother. 'Andrew's life hasn't been what you wanted, Mother, but it has been closer to what he wanted. No one would ask for this kind of ending but he has enjoyed himself, too. That's important.'

Hilda nodded ruefully. 'If you say so, Lucy. It gives me some comfort to hear that, I suppose, but I don't think one can say the same for your poor father. I've been very hard on him, I'm afraid.'

For a moment they were close. Mother and daughter hugged each other tight, joined in their sadness for lost lives.

That night Lucy dreamed that she and Simon were walking along a river bank, hand in hand. Then they saw a child floating by in the water. It stared up at them with pleading eyes. Lucy reached out to grab the baby, but just before she could touch its fingers, it sank with a soft gurgle down into the fast-flowing black water.

CHAPTER 10

August, 1968

Sussex

Lucy was thrilled to be invited to spend a week with Vita and her siblings at their grandmother's house in west Sussex. She could never have imagined such a place existed.

Daphne Valentine lived in Graffham, a small village which nestles snugly at the foot of the South Downs. It is on no main roads and the quiet lane through the village itself leads into the private track cutting through Lavington Stud to a boys' boarding school called Seaford College.

The village itself lacks charm, with the church and the school at one end at the top of a hill, and the rest of the village sprawling along the road, with the sports ground and the war memorial at least half a mile away from the village shop.

Farther down the road, towards Midhurst, two white stone cones mark the gravel entrance to Glasses, a large house built on the site of a medieval glass factory. Originally the house had been named Brook House by its wealthy and unimaginative owner. Years later, after the war, when Anthony Valentine's parents bought it, his lively and inventive mother renamed it Glasses.

Daphne Valentine was well known in the area as the woman who not only hunted with the hounds twice a week but also rode side-saddle, dressed in an elegant bottle-green habit. She was rich, generous and gregarious. Her parties were famous and she enjoyed all company – old and young. She loved nothing more than having her grandchildren to stay though, of course, when they did come, she employed extra help – usually a woman from the village – for her housekeeper, Mrs Peters. And when Anthony's children came down – goodness, there were so many of them – their nanny, Olwyn, had to come too, to feed and bath them, and to put them to bed.

Daphne had been widowed ten years before, when her husband died soon after a hunting accident. Tackling a massive gate on Lord Cowdray's estate, his big chestnut hunter just caught his back legs on the top bar. The horse twisted in mid-air, sending Jasper Valentine crashing to the ground. It then rolled over on to its rider, pulverising his ribcage and bursting his spleen. Jasper Valentine never really recovered. After six months he had two strokes in rapid succession and died.

Daphne was sad not to have Jasper around, for she had been fond of the old boy. But in some ways she was also quite relieved. Fifteen years her senior, as he had become older, his demands had become increasingly irritating to her. He insisted on having two cooked meals a day and since he never learned to drive, and refused to pay for a chauffeur, she had to ferry him around everywhere. In fact, although she would never have admitted it, her husband's death brought her an unexpected and delightful sense of liberation.

Daphne enjoyed her grandchildren's company. She loved the way they were so bright and amusing, brought up not to be afraid of adults. They were also rather unruly. 'Anthony has already instilled in them his utter lack of respect for authority,' she told her friend Margery as they rode across the South Downs together on their hacks. 'It's all very well, cocking a snook at the system, but you have to be very clever and talented to get away with that much of the time . . .' She laughed. 'Anthony's bolshiness used to drive Jasper mad.' She urged her horse into a trot. 'I've always rather admired it myself!'

Daphne was pleased that Vita had brought a little friend along. Lucy seemed a well-bred girl, polite and quiet. 'It's good to have someone from outside the family,' she said. 'It changes the way the children behave towards each other. Sometimes I think they are too close.'

Margery nodded and waved the fly swat above her horse's thick black mane. The flies were bad that morning on the Downs. 'Anthony and his wife are lucky to have you to take all their children for a whole week,' she said. 'I'd never do that for my grandchildren, and I've only got three of them!'

Daphne laughed. Her horse had slowed down to a walk again. It was pleasant up on the Downs, with nobody around for miles. 'I suppose I'd do anything for Anthony. Anthony is my weak spot. And of course, Olwyn comes along with the children. She's marvellous – so organised and efficient. I don't know how any of us would manage without her.'

With that, she kicked her horse into a gallop and set off up a vast green firebreak which cut through the pine woods. Margery followed along behind on her ancient bay cob.

Anthony and Seraphina had gone to the United States for a week, so it was convenient for them to send all the children down, as they often did in the summer. They hated the country and rarely came to Sussex for longer than a

day, but they were grateful enough to Daphne for having
the children whenever necessary.

Daphne Valentine's house offered everything a child
could want. Apart from the attics and nooks and crannies
for playing hide-and-seek in, there was also a large games
room with table tennis permanently set up in the middle, and
an exquisitely carved wooden rocking horse (bought from
Heal's for Anthony's third birthday), and cupboards bursting
with games – *Monopoly*, *Risk*, *Cluedo*, cards, jigsaws, chess.
Everything anyone could possibly want for a rainy day.

Outside, there was a huge, sprawling garden, with rockeries and lawns and long herbaceous borders, shrubberies,
bluebell woods and streams. Behind the house up the hill
was a large kitchen garden, a wide chicken run, and two
long greenhouses. To the side of the kitchen garden was
a large blue swimming pool with an uninterrupted view
of the South Downs, and beyond that a hard tennis court.
Beyond that still, there were the stables and twelve acres
of fields for the many horses and ponies Daphne had
collected over the years.

Quite apart from her two grey hunters there were her
daughters' two New Forest ponies, now ancient and sagging
in the middle but too well loved to let go anywhere, and
three reliable ponies for the grandchildren to ride, as well
as Tweety, the fat chestnut Shetland she had bought when
Anthony was two, and just old enough to sit in a saddle.

Daphne always cherished having her grandchildren. When
they were staying, every day began with the tiny ones piling
into her high four-poster bed at an early hour, carrying their
picture books for her to read as they snuggled up to her. They
all loved this practice and continued to do it even when they
could read perfectly well on their own.

Daphne did not devote all her time to the children,

however. She had her own commitments and timetables. In addition to riding with her friends every day, there was the committee for the village fête, as well as the hunt committee and the local pony club, with which she was still involved. She did not disrupt her schedule because of the children but she still had plenty of time to see them at breakfast and lunch, and to have wild games of racing demon after their high tea before they went off to bed. Once or twice she ate supper with the older boys if they weren't too busy watching something on TV. Everyone came and went, free to choose what they did without interference from anyone.

The week that Lucy went to stay with the Valentines would remain vivid in her head for a long time afterwards. The early August weather was hot and clear, with cloudless blue skies from the sharp early dawn to drowsy dusk.

The children spent their days outside, swimming in the pool, riding the ponies around the fields, running through the woods, climbing trees and playing hide-and-seek in the huge garden. The older boys often went rafting on the river, which the girls were not allowed to do, their grandmother had dictated, until they were twelve.

The girls did not mind. The sun was hot and there was always the pool to swim in, which they did five or six times a day. All the Valentine children could swim like fish – even little Celestria was nimble and confident without armbands. Lucy felt clumsy and nervous, and hovered around the shallow end practising her breaststroke, but it gave her some pleasure to see that David was even less accomplished than she.

One afternoon the older children decided to play a game of hide-and-seek while the very young ones were having a postprandial nap. There was a raised rockery near the drawing room with a curious wooden door at the bottom.

'The house was taken over by the army during the war,' explained Vita. 'We think they dug these corridors under the rockery but we're not sure why. Grandmother thinks it may have been for storing their wine.' She pulled the door open and the girls stepped into a cold dark corridor carved out of the sandy soil. Lucy shivered. The air was chilled. A short walk round brought them back to where they had started from. 'It's great, don't you think?' asked Vita.

The game began. Perdita was It, and stood in the front of the house, her hands over her eyes, counting up to a hundred. Vita and Lucy began to run.

'Oh no,' groaned Vita as she saw David coming up. 'Find your own hiding place,' she snapped.

David's face puckered. 'Why can't I come with you?' he complained. 'You're better at finding places to hide than me.'

Vita hesitated for a moment, then she relented. 'Okay, come with us this way. I know where you can hide.' She ran quickly round to the back of the house, with David and Lucy following.

'Quick! In here!' Vita pulled away the wooden door to the underground chamber. 'You hide in here, it's the best place ever!'

'Thanks!' David beamed and crept inside.

'You sit down and I'll shut the door,' Vita ordered. She pushed the heavy door firmly back into place, then turned to Lucy.

'Let's go up to the stables – she'll never find us there.'

The game went on for half an hour. Perdita found Lucy and Vita hiding in the hay barn, covered with newly cut hay from the garden and giggling uncontrollably. She also found

Celestria and Florian crouching down in the greenhouse. Then someone else was It and the hiding places shifted to another part of the garden.

At five o'clock the gong rang out across the garden, signalling that tea was ready. The children ran back to the house, washed their hands and settled themselves at the table, where Olwyn and fat, jolly Mrs Peters had laid out plates of steaming shepherd's pie and baked beans.

'Where's David?' Olwyn asked. 'Wasn't he playing with you?'

Lucy had forgotten about him completely. She looked at Vita, who was about to place a forkful of mince and potatoes in her mouth.

'Oh,' she said. 'I forgot.' Placing her napkin on the table, she said, 'I think I might know where he is.' She signalled to Lucy to follow. Lucy glanced at Olwyn, who was watching them keenly.

'We won't be a minute,' Vita called breezily as the girls ran outside towards the rockery. When they reached it they stopped outside.

'Ssh,' whispered Vita. 'Listen.' Vita placed her ear to the door with a light smile on her lips. Lucy could just hear a feeble banging and a faint cry from inside.

'David!' Vita called, pulling back the door. 'Are you still in there?'

David emerged from the darkness, his small face swollen from crying. His fingernails were broken and torn from his frantic scratching at the door.

'You left me here!' he sobbed. 'You left me here on purpose!'

'No I didn't, David. I swear.' Vita rubbed his back with a show of affection. 'I didn't do it on purpose, I swear. It was an accident, David, I promise,' she kept saying. 'I forgot all about you, I thought you'd be discovered. I didn't know you'd stay in there all this time, it's true, I promise.'

David had stopped crying and was staring at Vita with narrowed eyes. 'I don't believe you, and I'm going to tell Olwyn what you did. Then you'll be sorry . . .'

Vita put her arm around his shoulders. 'Please don't tell Olwyn,' she said. She was trying to sound cheerful. 'Because it wouldn't be true, you see, so it wouldn't be fair . . .'

But David started walking ahead, on his own. 'We'll see,' he said. 'I'll think about it.'

Later that evening, Olwyn called Vita into her room. Lucy hung around in the corridor outside and Perdita joined her, pressing her ear to the door. But Lucy could hear well enough the low, threatening voice, followed by Vita's bright voice answering back. Then there was silence, followed by footsteps coming to the door.

'Quick, run!' said Perdita. She grabbed Lucy's hand and ran down the corridor, down the back stairs to the kitchen where kind Mrs Peters was heating up a saucepan of milk so that everyone could have hot chocolate before going to bed.

As Lucy and Perdita sipped their steaming chocolate with the others, Vita appeared down the stairs. She seemed subdued. Her eyes had a dull, glazed look.

David toyed with his drink, commenting on the Peter Rabbit design on his china mug. The other children glanced at Vita but then looked away as Olwyn herself appeared in the door.

As Vita lowered her head to drink, Lucy saw a tear glittering in the corner of her eye. She also thought her left ear was glowing an angry red, though that might just be the warm light in the kitchen.

Later, after supper, Lucy tried to get Vita to tell her what happened. It seemed different from when Perdita was hit. After that, Lucy had decided not to comment on unusual things happening. But this was different. She had seen Vita in pain. It would be wrong not to mention it.

'Are you okay, Vita?' she asked gently as they walked outside in the evening dusk.

Vita scratched her head and squinted up at the Downs in the distance. 'I'm fine,' she said quickly. 'Look!' She pointed to the hill directly in front of them. 'They've started to bring in the harvest. You can see the combine harvesters.'

Lucy peered into the far distance. She could see the soft rounded hill, yellow on one side and a deep ochre colour on the other, where the corn had already been cut. At the side of the huge field were parked two machines, ready to finish the job the next day.

'I like to see that every year,' said Vita. 'It's a week earlier this year. I suppose the weather's been so good. It's funny I didn't notice them doing it earlier,' she added, more to herself than to Lucy.

As the girls walked on back to the house, Lucy realised that it was pointless trying to get Vita to talk about Olwyn, and nothing more was said.

The Valentine children were remarkably knowledgeable about nature and wildlife. They knew many of the different types of birds and flowers and butterflies. Taught by their grandmother, who was a great naturalist, their knowledge about the countryside made Lucy feel quite inadequate. Daphne had passed her enthusiasm on to her grandchildren, making sure that they could tell the difference between the song of a thrush and a blackbird, and the call of a nightingale and a nightjar.

One morning Achilles called Lucy. 'Quick! I've got something to show you,' he whispered.

Lucy was flattered that he wanted to show her something alone, without any of the others around.

Feeling a thrill of smug pleasure, she followed him down the garden, past the colourful herbaceous borders and rockeries, under the old yew hedge and down to the outbuildings near the end of the drive. These were the old stables, now converted into garages for the cars, storerooms with slatted shelves for housing the apple harvest, and a large room where logs from the woods could be stored to dry before being chopped for the open fires in the house.

Achilles guided Lucy into the wood store. 'Look!' He pointed up above the thick oak beams which stretched across the width of the building. The roof rose a good thirty feet above them. 'Do you see?'

He kept his voice low.

Lucy looked up into the grey darkness. She could see the sky through several of the red roof tiles. Scanning the space above them, she could just make out two small dark bags hanging from one of the beams in the corner.

'What are they?'

Achilles smiled. 'Bats – bats roosting in the beams. They sleep in the day and in the night they go out to catch insects. I think those are noctule bats – they're the largest and most common. You sometimes see them in the evening because they come out so early after sunset. People often think they're swifts.'

Lucy stood still and shuddered. A horrible clammy sweat crept down her back as Achilles continued to display his considerable knowledge about bats. He told her that there were fourteen species of bat in Britain, that all types were found on the south coast of England, where the warmer climate meant that there were plenty of insects, and fewer and fewer species found as you go north.

She nodded and smiled as he continued. 'They're really just flying mice. They feed on insects, from tiny gnats to large beetles. It's reckoned that they can eat up to three and a half thousand insects in one night . . .'

'That's a lot of insects,' murmured Lucy, anxious to escape. The very thought of mice, particularly flying mice, made her shudder. She was convinced that the ones up above her would be woken by their voices and fly down and get caught in her hair. It was too sickening to think about.

She did not dare say anything to Achilles who was staring up so fondly at his find, so she was relieved to hear Vita calling for her to go riding.

She backed out of the barn and into the bright sunshine.

Achilles followed her but was still talking enthusiastically. 'There's lots of folklore about bats. It's supposed to be lucky to see bats flying in daylight but it's bad luck to wake them up to make them fly – so you mustn't disturb them.

'There are also a lot of silly myths about bats,' Achilles continued. 'That saying "as blind as a bat" is daft because bats have very good eyesight. They also never get caught up in people's hair, in the way some idiots think, because they have a sort of radar system which helps them locate objects in the dark so they never bang into anything.'

Lucy backed away, smiling. Her face was red with shame and she prayed that Achilles would not know that she was one of those idiots who thought bats would get tangled up in her hair. She was afraid he could tell from her expression.

'I'll see you later,' she called. 'Thanks for showing me the bats.'

'Perhaps we'll see them flying later this evening. That'll be good . . .'

Lucy ran to join Vita as Achilles went back into the barn to study his flying rodents more closely.

Even though she could do without his bats, Lucy was aware that she was developing a crush on Achilles. He was so funny, and he made her laugh with his endless stream of irreverent jokes and remarks. She thought he liked her, too (why else might he have taken her to see his bats?), but she was worried that she might appear drippy to him.

There was an excruciating moment at breakfast one morning. Lucy was just beginning to dare to join in with the normal banter between the Valentine children with a confidence that impressed even herself. They were eating delicious salty kippers, fresh eggs from the hens, and crisp fried potatoes. Celestria was looking sleepy and she rubbed her eye slowly.

'I've got a crust on my eye,' she lisped, picking something out and holding it up between her thumb and forefinger.

Lucy laughed affectionately. She liked Celestria, whom she regarded like a cuddly puppy. 'Oh, that's sleep in your eye. We call it fairy dust at our house.'

As she said it, she knew it was a mistake. Perdita smirked and looked down into her plate.

'Hah!' Achilles waved his arms around. 'Well, in our house, we call it eye crap!' He threw back his head and laughed while his brothers and sisters giggled into their kippers and eggs.

Lucy tried to smile but her mouth refused to form the right shape. A pink blush crept up her neck and cheeks. How humiliated she felt, how feeble they must all think she was! Suddenly she wished she were not there, that she was back home with her little brother Andrew who never made fun of her or tried to catch her out.

Her shame did not last long, for later that day Achilles asked her if she wanted to come swimming with him and Constantine that afternoon in the swimming hole they had discovered the day before while out rafting. 'You have to walk across three fields to get there,' he said, 'but once you're there it's great.'

The boys assured their grandmother that the swimming hole was not on part of the main river and that there were no currents. 'It's very safe to swim,' Achilles said.

'I want to come,' said Perdita.

'And me,' added Vita.

Achilles rolled his eyes. 'Do you have to?' he asked with a groan.

Daphne heard this last remark and decided to intervene.

'You can all go, you older ones; the babies have to stay behind with Olwyn and Mrs Peters. But I want you older boys to be in charge. The currents in that river can be very strong, and the water can look deceptively calm.'

'All right,' grumbled Achilles. Looking at Lucy, he added, 'We have to go through the field with the bull in it, you know.'

Lucy was thrilled to be invited by the older boys and she decided not to mention the river or the bull in her daily letter home. Because it was Lucy's first time away from home for more than one night, her mother had made letter writing a condition of her going. The Valentines all knew she had to do it but she did it as surreptitiously as she could, handing the daily envelope to the postman when he arrived with the delivery to the house each morning.

The letters were bland and flat and contained nothing of the truth about Lucy's stay. She described the house and the grounds and the animals, and assured her mother that she was eating at least one hot meal a day (a requirement

Hilda insisted on in spite of Gordon's assurance that hot meals were not essential for good health), washing behind her ears and brushing her teeth.

What Lucy did not write about was the exciting bits – how they stole the plums from the trees and gorged themselves on strawberries straight from the kitchen garden, or chased the chickens around the run, or how they jumped on to the ponies without saddles or bridles and trotted around the field until the ponies bucked them off. Nor did she write about pinching food from the larder for picnics in their secret hiding places in hedges and the tree house in the old beech tree in the wood. And she certainly said nothing about the boys shooting the local farmer's white ducks with their air guns and then cooking them over a campfire by the stream.

How her mother would have been shocked by her daily activities. And how much fun she was having! Rivers and bulls would certainly not be mentioned in the next letter.

That afternoon the three boys and three girls set off for the river. They were halfway down the drive when Olwyn called after them. 'David's coming too!'

Vita groaned.

'Trust the Brat to get his own way. He has to spoil everything.'

Achilles shrugged. 'Just ignore him,' he muttered.

The group set off, with Lucy trying to walk as close to Achilles as possible. She liked the shape of his bare arms below the sleeves of his T-shirt and his tanned legs with their curly golden hairs below his shorts. Even though he and Constantine were identical twins, and equally handsome and tall, she saw tremendous differences between the two boys now: Constantine was abrasive and nervy while Achilles seemed wonderfully relaxed about everything. He took life in his stride.

When they reached the field with the bull, they stopped to hang over the gate for a few minutes. The heavy black beast was grazing in a far corner. Occasionally the sun glinted on the ring in its nose.

'If we head over that way,' said Vita, 'it probably won't see us.'

'It probably doesn't care much about us anyway,' replied Perdita.

They climbed over, one by one. Lucy was nervous but she stuck close to Achilles, reassured by his look of quiet calm. As long as Achilles was not afraid, she thought, she would not be either.

They were halfway across the field when the bull saw them. It lifted its head and studied them intently.

David panicked.

'It's seen us!' he screamed. 'It's going to charge!'

The boy began to run but Constantine grabbed the neck of his sweatshirt and yanked him back.

'Don't be so stupid, David! If you run, you make yourself the perfect target. Just walk slowly and calmly and it'll probably forget about us.'

The children continued their walk across the field, each keeping their eyes on the bull, which had raised its head higher and was scrutinising them with more interest now. It did look as if it were trying to decide whether it could muster up the energy to investigate this movement on its territory.

One hundred yards from the gate, David let out a little cry and started to run again. This time they all caught the panic and they all ran. David wailed and whimpered in fear, convinced that the bull had begun his charge.

They got to the gate and clambered over, puffing and panting as they looked back to see where the bull was.

The animal had not moved. The sun still glinted on the brass ring in his nose as he stood in that same far corner. He was not bothered by them at all.

'Can we go back a different way?' asked Vita.

There had been a fair bit of rain earlier in the month, so the river was swollen and flowing fast in places. The older boys quickly led the others down to the water hole they had found the day before. It was a pretty spot, in a clearing under beech trees. A kingfisher darted from the mossy bank as they approached the large round pool that was fed by the river.

'Last one in's a drip!' yelled Achilles, pulling off his clothes and plunging his strong naked body into the cold water.

Lucy was riveted by the sight of Achilles' long penis and bush of blond pubic hair. She was then alarmed to see the other boys stripping off in the same way. Then Vita and Perdita were doing the same. There was no time for hesitation. She took off her skirt and blouse, but modesty made her keep her pants on. David too had stripped off but kept on his underpants.

'Come on in!' called Achilles. 'The water's great!' He swam powerfully into the middle of the pool, then disappeared underwater with a great kick. Vita dived in, followed by Constantine and Perdita.

The Valentine children took to the water with the graceful ease of otters. Lucy did not feel so sure of herself. And she knew that David did not feel particularly confident either. Unlike the Valentine children, who had regular swimming tuition at their private schools, David didn't get lessons at the local primary and could barely swim at all.

Lucy sat on the bank and dipped her feet in the water. It

was cold, but the sun shining on her back was pleasantly warm. The Valentine children gradually emerged from the water, dripping wet and panting from the exertion, then flopped down on the grass. Lucy could not stop herself peering furtively at the twins' large penises nestling in thick beds of curly pubic hair.

David stood on the bank, chucking stones into the water. Lucy noticed Perdita sidling up to him.

'Look up there, David,' she said, 'there's a squirrel.' She pointed at the top of a massive beech tree which spread its boughs gracefully over the water.

As David looked up, Perdita stepped closer to him and shoved him sideways, sending him toppling into the water with a great splash.

David dropped without a sound under the surface of the pool, then emerged seconds later gasping for breath, his arms flailing.

'Help!' he shouted, gulping at the air. 'It's too deep, I can't swim!' His head disappeared under the water again, and then reappeared again, gasping and spluttering.

Lucy watched in horror as David started moving downstream with the current. She glanced at the other children, who all stood transfixed by the sight of the helpless boy moving slowly away from them. Lucy looked over at Perdita. No one moved; no one looked worried; in fact, it was as if they were thinking of something other than the danger the boy was in. Lucy heard the words bellowing from her lips: 'Do something! Quick! Save him!'

A moment later there was a loud splash as Achilles dived in and swam expertly to David. He grabbed him in the special way he had been taught in life-saving lessons at school, swam to the bank, and dragged the exhausted boy on to the grass.

David lay panting for a few moments, then he turned to Perdita. 'You did that on purpose, didn't you! You pushed me in.'

Perdita raised her head and smiled. 'No I didn't,' she said. 'I bumped into you by mistake and you lost your footing. It was an accident, anyone will tell you that. Won't they, Lucy?'

She stared hard at Lucy as she spoke the last words.

'And besides,' she added as she turned back to David, 'you were rescued. You're safe. And you haven't even said thank you to Achilles.'

As they set off home for their tea, the children once again crossed the field with the bull. This time they had no fear. The bull was too lazy to budge from its position, they knew that now.

The Valentine boys walked ahead, their long legs covering the ground with ease. Perdita and Vita ran along behind them, their eyes shining, their heads held high. Coming along behind, Lucy walked with David. She did not say anything to him but she felt she ought to stay close to him, to make him feel a little safer after his shock. He was a brat, she thought, but he did not deserve the treatment he had got that afternoon. Lucy was unsettled by what had happened. Watching Perdita's purposeful step and proud posture, she wondered about her. Nothing would ever be said about what had happened, of course, but Lucy had finally come to realise that Perdita's feelings about David were not simply those of irritation. They ran far deeper than that. Lucy felt she had had a glimpse of something terrible and ruthless about Perdita, about all the Valentines. And for a brief moment, it scared her.

CHAPTER 11

June, 1997

Betrayal

It was still June, and four weeks since Lucy's miscarriage. For several days now Lucy had been convinced that Simon was having an affair. She had been aware of a distance between them for some time. They used to be so close, so attuned to each other's thoughts and moods. Now she felt they were miles apart, and with this feeling came a profound sense of loneliness.

Several nights a week Simon had been coming home later than usual. The gloominess that he had shown immediately after the loss of the baby had been replaced by a cheery consideration towards Lucy that was not entirely convincing.

On the rare occasions they made love, it was initiated by him. And now that she was suspicious, she felt there was a difference in his technique, an urgent pushing, new ways of stimulating her, even more solicitude. Even the way he kissed had changed.

Lucy's own days were grim. Her baby was dead and her time was taken up with worrying about Andrew and the few bits of copy-editing she was doing for a publisher. There was nothing to look forward to; it seemed that life could not be worse. She felt enveloped by gloominess.

Despite her suspicions she knew she couldn't accuse Simon of having an affair on the basis of his kissing technique. It was only when she was clearing out his pockets before doing the weekly wash and found a receipt for a restaurant bill for two – on a night when he had told her he'd been working late – that she felt she had some concrete evidence to go on. She remembered that he had come home particularly late that night.

It terrified her to confront him about it; she was trembling with nervousness. But telling herself she had nothing to lose, she braced herself and accused him, presenting the restaurant bill as evidence.

Simon denied it at first. 'I just had a bite to eat with Tom Edwards, the Features Editor. His wife's away and we decided to eat together.'

But the bill was itemised. Lucy knew that Tom Edwards was a rugby playing beer drinker. 'I suppose it was Tom who ordered the spritzer,' Lucy said coldly.

Simon never drank white wine, and certainly never messed around with mineral water.

'Please don't lie to me, Simon. Things are bad enough without this happening.' She covered her eyes with her hands to hide her tears.

Simon got up and put his arms around her.

'I'm sorry, my darling. I'm really sorry.' He nuzzled her hair. 'I'm sorry I lied. I'm sorry I thought I could get away with it. I have had a little affair but it wasn't anything, hardly an affair even. It was with one of the subs, one who's leaving next week anyway. Perhaps because I knew she was leaving, I knew it wasn't important. I thought I could get away with it. You know, it's really not serious. I'm truly sorry this has happened. It was insensitive and cruel of me to do this to you at such a time . . .'

He ran his hand through his hair and then added, 'But I suppose it's probably why I did it, too.'

'Well I hope you bloody well used a condom,' Lucy snapped.

Simon pulled her to him tight. 'Of course I did, my darling. I'd never do anything that would put either of us at risk.'

It was unfortunate that Rosie was away that weekend. She was the only person Lucy felt she could (or wanted to) talk to about the situation in which she now found herself. She knew it was all typical – the five years of marriage, the strain of trying to start a family, the grieving for a child never born. She felt all these things but she could not say them out loud to anyone except Rosie. Only Rosie was allowed to see the defences let down.

But Rosie was up in Scotland with a new boyfriend. She would not be back for another two days. Lucy would have to endure her problems alone until Rosie got back.

A couple of days after her confrontation with Simon, Lucy had Andrew and Patrick coming to supper. It had been arranged for a while now, that if Andrew was well enough the two of them would come round for a Chinese takeaway.

Lucy felt so angry with Simon that she wanted someone else to mix up the dynamics of the group. Normally she would invite Rosie but she decided, in her friend's absence, to invite Vita instead. When she phoned her, Vita was delighted.

'I'd love to come,' she said. 'I should be able to organise a babysitter. See you then!'

Lucy had barely said a word to Simon and they stepped around each other politely. Andrew and Patrick arrived first. It was a warm summer evening, so they decided to eat outside.

They sat out on the terrace at the back of the house. The dwarf sunflowers in their pots looked bright and cheerful, so different from Lucy's mood.

Andrew was very keen to see the photograph albums that Lucy had been given by their mother.

'I haven't looked at them for years,' he said.

Patrick squeezed him and said in his campiest voice, 'And I can't wait to see you as a little boy in shorts.'

They pored over the albums – baby photos of Lucy first, then Andrew going through the stages of infancy, babyhood, little-childhood.

The photo albums had been lovingly cared for and carefully edited by Hilda over the years. They showed only happy, smiling children and laughing, doting adults. None of the tears and screams and tantrums of childhood had been allowed on to the pages. The out-takes had been discarded years before.

Looking at them now, Lucy was struck by how happy her father looked in those early photographs. Since her mother was the photographer, she rarely appeared in the pictures herself, but there were several shots of Gordon holding his children by the hand and smiling proudly at the camera. He looked like a happy man. What on earth happened to make him the downtrodden faded creature he now was? And what had her mother meant when she said she had been hard on him?

Andrew and Patrick bent over the album together and turned the pages with fascination. They kept laughing and pointing at a funny expression, a ridiculous outfit, a bizarre bit of cropping by an inexperienced or harried photographer. As Lucy watched them she realised she had not seen Andrew laugh like that, seemingly forgetting about himself and his condition, for a long time.

The doorbell rang and Lucy went to let in Vita, who was looking very attractive with her hair pulled back off her face and arranged in a loose bun at the nape of her neck. Her dark eyes were accentuated by subtle make-up which made them seem even bigger and sharper than usual. Her skin was smooth and clear and her lips were highlighted by a rich plum lipstick.

Vita stepped up and kissed Lucy on the cheek.

Simon came up behind and greeted Vita in a friendly fashion, too. 'We've just been looking at old family photos,' he said. 'Come and join the party.'

He led her into the garden and introduced her to Andrew and Patrick.

As Vita shook Andrew's hand, he smiled. 'Well, Vita Valentine,' he said, 'Lucy's been telling me about how you've met up again. I don't suppose you remember me. I was probably just Lucy's irritating little brother.'

Vita smiled broadly. 'Of course I remember you,' she replied. 'I always thought you were rather cute. You were such a serious little boy, very observant, always watching . . .'

Andrew nodded and smiled. 'That's true,' he said. 'I noticed a lot that went on,' he added cryptically.

Patrick hugged Andrew to him. 'He's still observant and he's still cute,' he laughed.

Lucy showed Vita one of the albums. 'We're looking at these pictures that were taken while we were still living in Kentish Town, and I think there may even be some of you in here, when you came on holiday to Norfolk,' said Lucy. 'Let's have a look.' She handed Vita a glass of wine and settled down beside her with the album marked '1967–68'.

There she was herself, a bright-eyed nine-year-old standing with seven-year-old Andrew. There she was on her skates outside their terraced house in Kentish Town. Here they were, feeding the ducks at Highgate Ponds, and here was Lucy skipping on Hampstead Heath.

'Yes, look! These were in Norfolk, on that holiday.'

There was a collection of photographs of the holiday home with Lucy, Andrew and Vita running around in swimsuits in the garden, or playing in the sand on the beach. There was one picture of Vita on her own, looking straight into the camera with a grave expression on her face.

Seeing this now, Lucy was struck by how adult Vita had looked, with that deep, penetrating gaze. It was not cold but there was something unnatural about it. Lucy gave a peculiar shudder.

She turned the page to another picture of herself dressed in her favourite summer frock and Clarks sandals. She was smiling cheerfully at the camera.

Patrick peered over her shoulder. 'You were a stunner even then,' he said. 'Look at that smile!'

Lucy laughed and kissed him on the cheek. 'You're so kind,' she said. 'You can come to supper any time.'

While the others continued looking at the edited history of the Butler family, Lucy went into the kitchen to get plates and cutlery for their Chinese food. It was a good spread – hot-and-sour soup, Singapore fried noodles, deep-fried squid, stuffed tofu, pork spare ribs, seasonal vegetables and steamed rice. There were cans of beer and a couple of bottles of cheap but decent Chilean white wine.

Vita came in behind her to help.

'How are you, Lucy?' she asked, taking the tops off the cups of soup. 'How've you been? I haven't seen you since the miscarriage, but I've been thinking about you.'

Lucy shrugged. 'I'm all right, thanks. And thank you for your card, by the way. I meant to write to thank you properly . . . It was kind of you, I appreciated the thought.'

Vita smiled. 'You don't need to thank me. I felt bad that I couldn't do anything more.'

Lucy had not been meaning to say anything about Simon's affair but the warmth in Vita's voice gave her an urge to spill it out, to tell her new friend about this devastating event in her hitherto happy marriage.

'Well, since you ask,' she said quietly, 'I'm not really very all right . . .'

Vita looked at her so quizzically that Lucy could not stop herself blurting out her thoughts.

'Simon's been having an affair. He told me the other night.'

There, she had said it.

Vita continued looking at her. 'Did he tell you whom with?'

'Someone at work. A temporary sub on the paper. He promised me it was over.'

She looked at Vita, waiting for some advice. 'I don't know what to do. I don't even know what to think.'

Lucy felt tears rising up inside her and quickly went back to placing the cartons of food on to trays to carry out.

Vita was silent for a few seconds. Then she dropped the meat and stepped over to put her arms around Lucy. She gave her a big hug. 'I wouldn't worry about it too much,' she said. 'Lots of men have affairs, and most mean nothing. Simon really loves you. I know that. It's obvious to everyone.'

Lucy looked up at her friend. She sniffed and quickly blew her nose. 'Do you really think so?'

'I'm sure of it,' replied Vita. 'I think your marriage is very solid and strong.'

Lucy tore a paper towel off the roll and blew her nose. 'I'm sorry for being silly. Thanks for being so understanding.' She wiped her eyes.

'Come on,' said Vita, 'let's get this food out. I'm starving.'

As the women began to carry out the trays, Patrick called out, 'Quick! Something's wrong! Something's happened to Andrew.'

They all turned to look at Andrew in the chair. He had dropped the album he'd been holding and was trying to speak, but couldn't. He mumbled and lifted one hand feebly; his eyes looked up at them, frightened.

'What's the matter?' asked Lucy. 'Can't you speak?'

Andrew shook his head. He tried to open his mouth but only a few clumsy grunts escaped from his throat.

There was silence for a few moments, then Simon said: 'We'd better call an ambulance, quick.'

Andrew raised an arm and shook his head again. He did not want an ambulance.

'Do you want us to wait?' Lucy almost shouted, panic rising quickly in her.

'You don't need to shout,' snapped Patrick. 'He's not deaf!'

Tears had filled Andrew's eyes as he nodded at his sister, a look of pathetic helplessness in his face. He was pleading to her to help him. With a sense of impotence, Lucy stared back at him, like him unable to move. She knew what he was thinking. He was thinking that it was too late. If they called the ambulance he would be whisked away into the clutches of the hospital, where he would never get the chance to do what he had planned.

'Wunh-wunh-*wait*.' He just managed to get the words out, sounding like someone who had just emerged from the dentist with a mouth paralysed by the local anaesthetic.

Everyone stood quietly, glancing at each other, waiting, not knowing what to do or say. Two minutes, three minutes, four . . . Finally, Simon broke the silence.

'Are you sure we should be leaving him this long? Surely it'd be best to get some medical help – and sooner rather than later.'

Lucy glared at him. 'I'll take him to the hospital if he *wants* to go, and not before then.'

Patrick nodded. 'We'll wait.'

About half an hour later the effects of the stroke were wearing off. Slowly Andrew began to be able to move his arm, and talk more easily. The sense of relief was palpable, and enormous. It was as if he had risen from the dead.

Patrick, who had not left Andrew's side, began speaking to him quietly, urging him now to go to the hospital. 'I'll make sure you don't stay under their control,' he assured Andrew. 'I promise.'

Lucy offered to drive them. She and Patrick helped Andrew into the back of her car. She drove as fast as she dared, looking constantly in her rear-view mirror at the two frightened young men in the back seat.

At the hospital she helped Patrick get Andrew out, then saw them in and drove off. As she left them she made Patrick promise to keep her informed about what was going on.

Lucy got home about an hour later, and let herself in quietly. Simon and Vita were sitting on the sofa together, laughing and talking in the sitting room, their backs to her. They

had eaten their supper. Half-empty cartons of Chinese
food and a drained bottle of wine stood on the table
in front of them. They had not heard Lucy come in,
and for a few minutes she stood in the kitchen watching
them in the semi-darkness. After all that had happened this
evening, it seemed strange to hear them laughing and talking
so gaily.

Lucy looked at them again, and then she knew. From
the way they leaned their dark heads close together so that
Vita's sleek hair almost touched Simon's wild curls, from
the way Simon's arm reached across the sofa behind Vita's
back, Lucy knew.

Putting her bag on the floor, she coughed.

'I'm back,' she announced loudly.

Vita and Simon rose simultaneously, turning to face her.
Their faces were bright and flushed from the alcohol. Lucy
knew for certain. Vita's face was expressionless but Simon's
was covered with guilt.

'What happened at the hospital? How's Andrew?' Simon
was talking unnaturally fast. He was red-faced.

'Patrick said he'd let me know what happens,' Lucy
replied wearily. Picking up her bag, she added: 'If you'll forgive me, I'm going up to bed. I'm terribly tired. Goodnight,
Vita.' Her voice was cold. They knew she knew.

Without giving either of the lovers a chance to say more,
she walked quickly upstairs to the bedroom, and pulled the
door shut with a loud bang.

That night Lucy slept badly, unable to find a comfortable
position in bed. When she did finally sleep for more than
an hour, she dreamed that she had given birth to a baby
boy. He had black curly hair and smiling red lips. She
was very happy, swinging him in her arms and dancing around the room. Then a woman, the district nurse,

came to see him. After examining the baby, she told Lucy that she was not looking after him properly. The nurse then placed the baby in a wicker basket and carried him away.

CHAPTER 12

August, 1968

Perdita's Problem

The summer weeks passed slowly. Looking back Lucy would remember those weeks as permanently sunny but of course there were cool and grey days when a fine drizzle settled on the surfaces of Kentish Town all day long, or when the rain pelted down endlessly all morning making outdoor play impossible until the skies brightened in the afternoon as the sun's rays pierced their way like arrows through the clouds to earth.

Whatever the weather, there was never a shortage of things to do at the Valentines' house. With so many people, there was always lively activity going on somewhere in the house or garden.

Soon after their return from their grandmother's house, the three older boys were preparing for their annual trip with Forest School Camps, where they pitched tents on the Welsh border and learned how to chop wood with an axe, make fires with two sticks, and catch crayfish in the cold mountain streams.

Later in the summer it had been arranged for Vita to join the Butlers on their seaside holiday in Norfolk, where they had rented a small house. They had taken the same house for three years running now. But that was not for a while yet. The summer was gloriously long.

The Valentines still regularly welcomed Lucy into their home. Lucy and Vita had become very close friends but Lucy was relieved that Achilles was no longer around. Her crush was shattered after what he did to her and Vita the night before he set off for camp.

Lucy, Vita and Achilles had had an active day on Hampstead Heath together, swimming in the ponds and watching a large group of hippies rolling a big, brightly coloured balloon up Parliament Hill and down again.

The children watched in wonder as these child-adults then all sat on the pretty balloon and performed an eerie, silent ballet before carefully packing up their toy and drifting out of the park.

Lucy and Achilles had had a good laugh at a couple of young women who had attached strings to the ground with little sticks.

'What are you doing?' asked Achilles with, Lucy thought, impressive boldness.

One of the women, a waif-like creature with thin white-blonde hair, smiled. 'We're talking to the worms,' she said in all seriousness.

Achilles nodded conspiratorially at Lucy and she could tell he was suppressing a laugh. How close she felt to him at that moment. So how betrayed she felt by his behaviour only a few hours later!

It happened that evening. Vita and Lucy were having a bath together in the children's bathroom. Seraphina had allowed the girls to use her expensive, intoxicating scented green bubble bath, which they had poured liberally into the water flowing out of the tap. White froth came up to the top of the bath, right to the curve of their soft pink shoulders.

The girls were squeezed into the bath together and rubbed their hot limbs with pleasure. Every now and then Vita turned on the hot tap to maintain the deliciously tropical atmosphere (something Lucy was never allowed to do at home where her mother did not believe that the bath was for anything other than getting clean).

They were in the top bathroom, which was built into the roof. There was no window, just a grate to let in the fresh air. Light shone from a pretty lamp set into the wall, casting a soft sheen on the William Morris willow pattern wallpaper.

'Look at you two, then!'

The girls turned and laughed to see Achilles standing in the doorway. Lucy blushed and hugged her knees to her chest under the white foam. She liked the look of this big blond boy, standing tough and brazen in the doorway as he looked down on the little mermaids.

Her smile froze as she noted the cruel teasing in his voice.

'Bet you're afraid of the dark.'

'No, we're not,' giggled Vita. 'Go away and leave us alone.' She picked up a soaking wet flannel and threw it at her brother. The flannel landed against the door with a loud slap and dropped heavily to the ground, spraying water everywhere.

Achilles switched off the light. With no window, the room was pitch-black.

'Stop it! Turn it back on.' Vita was laughing.

Lucy laughed too, but nervously.

The room was suddenly quiet. They could not see anything in the still blackout.

'Achilles?'

'Is he still there?' Lucy whispered.

Vita began to get cross. 'Achilles, stop being so stupid. Turn the light on now. You're being silly.'

Silence.

Lucy sat in the dark, huddled in the frothy bubbles. It was so quiet and dark. She rather liked it. She wondered whether she should get out and turn the light back on but she did not want to do that until she was sure Achilles had gone. She did not want him to suddenly switch on the light and see her naked.

'Oh, honestly,' Vita said crossly. She began to get to her feet.

Just at that moment, Lucy felt something. It felt like a stream of warm liquid running down her neck and shoulders. 'What's that?'

'What? What's going on?' Vita sounded annoyed. Then she shrieked. 'Oh, for Christ's sake, Achilles, you're disgusting! He's peeing on us. Get away, you horrible pig!'

Lucy opened her mouth to scream and a warm stream of urine hit her tongue, making her gag. 'Ugh, that's horrible!'

'Ha ha!' Achilles laughed into the dark room. 'Bye,' he called.

The girls heard the door click shut behind him and the sound of his heavy shoes clumping down the stairs.

Vita was furious. Dripping with water she got out of the bath and pulled the light cord. 'What a pig! We'll have to run the bath again and really scrub ourselves now.'

Lucy was shocked. She had the taste of human urine in her mouth. It revolted her. She grabbed the soap and began to scrub her neck and shoulders and arms, where the liquid had touched her.

She felt a combination of revulsion and fear. Why had he done it? What a horrid thing to do! And her mother would never let her come here again if she ever heard about it. Yet there was also something thrilling about such a naughty thing.

With the older boys no longer around to tease or trouble them, the girls developed an even stronger bond between them. The friendship was based on their common interests. Both girls were bookish and enjoyed the same writers – Noel Streatfield, E. Nesbit and Joan Aiken. They liked to walk around the streets of Kentish Town together in a pair, sometimes, to Lucy's thrill, holding hands, if Vita suggested it.

Lucy's infatuation with the Valentine family grew endlessly. She felt so at ease with them all, so free of adult supervision. And not very far below the surface (though she would never admit it to anyone), she preferred the big house in Lady Margaret Road to her own home. Secretly, and most shamefully, she wished that her name was Valentine, too.

Lucy was particularly close to Vita, though she also enjoyed Perdita's company. Perdita had a hard, caustic sense of humour and seemed to have no fear of anyone or anything. However, she could be cold and cruel, too, and got pleasure from showing people up.

This was never clearer than the day they were playing *Monopoly* in Vita's bedroom, and a pungent smell suddenly curled around Lucy's nostrils. She looked at Perdita, sure that it came from her direction, and Perdita's eyes flashed. 'Ugh,' she said, wrinkling her nose and waving her hand in front of her face. 'Someone's farted! I bet it's you, Lucy, it's coming from your part of the room.'

Lucy shook her head. 'No, it wasn't me,' she protested,

but the other children staring at her made her begin to blush. The heat crept up her neck and cheeks.

'Then why are you going red?' Perdita laughed unkindly with a toss of her head. 'It must have been those baked beans at lunch . . .' As she said it, Vita and Celestria started to chant:

> Beans, Beans,
> The musical fruit,
> The more you guzzle
> The more you toot.

They fell about on the floor, kicking their legs in the air and laughing.

Lucy tried to laugh, too, but she was embarrassed and annoyed at herself. She was pretty sure that it was Perdita who had made the smell and then openly accused Lucy to cover up. But she would never have dared suggest such a thing.

One week, Perdita began to act out of character. Her confident, cocksure manner had gone and she had become unusually snappish and irritable. Reluctant to play with the others, she spent much of her time in her own bedroom, reading or painting large gloomy paintings in dark colours.

'What's wrong with Perdita?' Lucy asked one day. She had been afraid to ask but she wondered if it had something to do with her friendship with Vita. Perhaps Perdita was jealous.

'Oh, nothing's wrong.'

Vita's voice was casual but Lucy could tell that the query had bothered her friend. She tentatively pursued it further.

'I sometimes get the feeling that she doesn't like me. She seems so cross all the time . . .'

Vita smiled and shook her head. 'It has nothing to do with you,' she said. 'Perdita likes you a lot.' She paused. 'No, she's upset because something's happening and she doesn't know what to do.'

'What's happening?'

Vita studied her carefully. 'Promise you won't say anything about it if I tell you?'

'Promise.'

Vita glanced around quickly and lowered her voice. 'She's started wetting her bed again. It's odd because Seraphina says she was dry at night when she was two. Anthony says there must be something she's upset about to make her wet her bed but whatever it is, Perdita is very embarrassed. It's horrid for her.'

Lucy was silent, imagining only too easily how embarrassing it must be for Perdita. 'Perhaps she drinks too much water before she goes to bed,' she offered.

Vita shrugged. 'I don't think so,' she said.

Secret or not, Perdita's problem was open for discussion at the children's tea that afternoon. The Valentine parents were out, having gone to an emergency meeting at the Camden Arts Centre. Lucy learned that because the Russians had invaded Czechoslovakia the week before, the exhibition of an East German artist called John Hartfield had been called off by the Conservative councillor, Geoffrey Finsburg. Along with many of their friends, Anthony and Seraphina were outraged, pointing out that Hartfield had been a wartime refugee who escaped from the Nazis, returning to East Germany in 1950. Much of his work was anti-Fascist in character and it was absurd to react to the Russian invasion in such a way.

Meanwhile, at tea, Perdita asked for a glass of milk and Olwyn shook her head. 'I'm sick of changing your sheets,' she said sharply. 'You're not to drink anything between now and bedtime. You've got to get over this problem.' Her voice was flat and firm, with no sense of concern.

David looked up with interest. 'What problem?' he asked in a loud voice. 'You mean, the bedwetting?' He looked at Perdita and grinned. 'I stopped wetting my bed when I was three,' he said.

Perdita was sitting at the end of the table, her shoulders hunched, her face stricken. She was biting her lips and fighting back tears. 'Please may I get down?' she asked quietly. 'I'm not hungry.'

Olwyn shot her a quick glance. 'You may get down but you won't be getting any tea later if you suddenly decide that you're hungry.'

Lucy stayed the night, at Vita's insistence. After the unpleasantness of tea time, the evening was blissful, when the Valentine parents returned from their emergency meeting about the art exhibition and sat down in the sitting room for drinks and to play with their children before going out to see *The Odd Couple* at the ABC cinema in Kentish Town Road. They laughed and teased and ruffled hair. Seraphina was so elegant and gentle. Lucy often scrutinised her from a distance. She just could not imagine having a mother like that, so clever, so perfect, so beautiful. And Anthony was wonderfully jovial and loud, his quick mind probing, provoking and stimulating his children so that they laughed and made him laugh, throwing back his head with carefree enthusiasm and pride at his clever offspring.

Even Perdita cheered up, especially after Vita had managed to sneak her a ham sandwich and apple from the kitchen while Olwyn was putting the babies to bed before settling down to watch *Coronation Street* on the television.

With the little ones out of the way, the atmosphere was calmer, and after a few rounds of *Beggar My Neighbour* and rummy, at which Anthony was fiendishly good, the girls were beginning to yawn.

'Goodnight, my darlings,' Seraphina said to them, embracing them with a kiss and a scented hug before they trooped off to bed.

Then she spoiled it.

'Perdita,' she called. 'Don't forget to go to the lavatory before you go to sleep. Olwyn says she thinks that may do the trick. Perhaps you just get too excited by your reading and forget to go.'

Perdita did not reply. She turned, her cheeks flushed a bright pink, her eyes watery.

After brushing her teeth, she went to her room and said no more.

Vita and Lucy lay in bed talking in the dark. 'I feel so sorry for Perdita,' said Vita. 'I just don't know what to do to help her.'

'No, me neither,' murmured Lucy, as sleep overwhelmed her.

Lucy was woken several hours later by pressure on her own bladder, pressure no doubt caused by the large mug of hot chocolate she had drunk at tea time.

The hall light was on, as it always was, and she slipped out of bed and walked down the landing to the lavatory at the end. She heard a noise and stopped by the doorway, stepping back into the darkness as she saw Olwyn walk past.

Olwyn's bedroom was on the next floor, yet she was heading for Perdita's room at the end of the landing. Lucy's heart pounded as she watched the housekeeper walk into Perdita's room. Olwyn bent briefly over the sleeping child's bed and then straightened up and came back out.

Lucy tried to hold her breath, praying that she would not be seen. The housekeeper walked past and continued up the stairs to her room.

Peering at the short dumpy figure going up the stairs, Lucy noticed that in her right hand, Olwyn was carrying a white enamel jug.

Lucy stood in the darkness for a few minutes, her heart still thumping. A decent time had elapsed. Now it was perfectly reasonable for her to go innocently to relieve her painfully full bladder. She was nervous, but she told herself that there was no reason to be afraid to cross the landing to go to the lavatory at two in the morning.

She scuttled across the hall to the small lavatory, where her urine poured out of her. The relief was enormous, the discomfort gone.

The exquisite pleasure of relieving herself had almost made her forget what she had just witnessed, but as she flushed the lavatory and emerged from the little room, she jumped in panic.

At the bottom of the stairs stood Olwyn, dressed as before. She nodded and looked at her with narrowed eyes. 'Oh, it's you, Lucy,' she said.

For a moment, Lucy thought she saw relief in Olwyn's expression. 'I heard a noise and I wondered who was wandering around.' She looked directly into Lucy's eyes. Her eyes were a pale icy blue. She smiled. 'And it's you.'

Lucy stared back at her. Her heart was pounding in her throat. 'I was up earlier,' she said simply. 'I got up earlier.'

Olwyn's eyes were boring into her.

Lucy stared back at the woman defiantly, half wanting to run away, half wanting to see what Olwyn would say.

Olwyn did not respond. She stared back at her, and turned back up the stairs. 'Good night, child,' she said.

Nothing more was ever said about the incident. Lucy did not mention it to anyone. She did not dare. There was something about the way Olwyn had looked at her that made her feel that she should not say a word to anyone, not even her friend Vita. After all, she did not know what she had seen. Olwyn may have had a perfectly good reason for being in Perdita's room at that hour of the morning. But why with a jug?

But she had to be careful. She had no proof. If she was wrong to think ill of Olwyn then an innocent person would be accused. If she was right then by telling the truth she might jeopardise her own position in the household. She might not be able to come any more.

Thus Lucy rationalised her decision to remain silent. And there the matter rested.

That night was the last time Perdita Valentine wet her bed.

Vita occasionally came to tea at Lucy's house. Hilda Butler was always anxious to ensure that the social contributions were equally balanced.

'Oh, the Valentines don't care,' said Lucy breezily. 'They don't keep a check on how many times I've been there.'

'Perhaps not,' replied her mother briskly, 'but it's important to return hospitality and kindness in whatever way we can.'

The truth was that Lucy still preferred going to the Valentines' house to her own because there was always more activity and excitement there.

It was evident that Vita thought that too.

There was not a great deal to do at the Butlers' house, apart from play cards or *Monopoly*. They were not allowed to do handstands and somersaults on the beds in case they ruined the mattresses. They were banned from playing ball in the garden in case they damaged the flowers. And inside the house, it was so pristine and neat that any idea of romping was out of the question. The very atmosphere inhibited such behaviour.

Andrew, being only seven, was not much fun, either, particularly since he was unusually self-contained for a boy of that age and preferred to sit in his room drawing pictures to taking part in any active games.

In Vita's presence, Lucy found herself becoming self-conscious about her home. Her mother kept it so clean, not a speck of dust, not a ball of fluff was to be seen lurking anywhere. Nothing was out of place. The family photographs were lined up on the mantelpiece at exactly the same angles year after year. Carefully paid bills were laid neatly on the hall table waiting to be posted the next day. Everything was under control, at all times. It could not have been more different from the warm chaos of the Valentine house.

Lucy became aware of things she had never noticed before – the way the lavatory paper matched the pink surround to the lavatory itself, and the bath mat and soap, too. Once she had put a roll of blue lavatory paper in there and her mother had been very cross. That was only for the blue lavatory on the top floor.

But most of the time it was simply boring being at home, and it seemed ridiculous to have Vita to tea simply for the sake of it when both girls knew that there was more fun to be had up the road.

On one such occasion, Vita was looking particularly bored. She sighed repeatedly and kept looking at her watch. In desperation, Lucy suddenly had an idea.

Her father was out on his rounds visiting patients at home and her mother was cooking tea in the kitchen. Now was the time.

'Come with me, I want to show you something,' she said, leading Vita downstairs to the ground floor and her father's surgery.

There was the sharp antiseptic smell in the room. Some patients' notes were lying on the large wooden desk.

'Now, look at these . . .'

Lucy pulled down some medical textbooks from the shelves and showed a wide-eyed Vita the grotesque photos of Nature's mistakes, the medical curiosities that made it to the text books. Vita was indeed impressed. She stared at the pictures of the Siamese twins and Down's syndrome babies, and children born with six toes on each foot. Then her eyes strayed along the shelves, and she walked beside them, running her fingers along the books and peering at their titles.

Lucy felt pleased. With growing confidence she went over to her father's desk and pulled out the lowest right-hand drawer. 'Look at these!' She watched her friend come over to look and felt a rush of pleasure as she saw Vita's eyes open with sudden interest at the jumbled stash of drugs.

'Hey, that's cool! Are they all medicines?'

Lucy nodded and began to pick out some of them. 'They're mostly old pills handed in by patients who don't need them any more, but lots are samples sent to my father by the drug companies. He's a bit careless with them, really. He says they should be locked up but I suppose since his surgery is in his own home, he never gets round to it.

The main drugs are locked up, in that cupboard there.' She pointed to the large cabinet behind the desk.

Vita knelt down by the drawer and looked through its contents, carefully picking up each metal container and reading the labels. 'Drinamyl, dexedrine, sodium amytal . . . There are so many of them,' she said. 'How on earth does a doctor know what all these drugs are, and what they're for?'

Lucy smiled. She was pleased that Vita had asked this question because she was able to give her the answer.

She reached over to the bookshelf and pulled out a red booklet. 'This is what they use. They look up the drugs in here. It tells them what to use them for and they can use it to check when they shouldn't give someone a certain drug. She repeated with care the lesson her father had taught her about looking up drugs and watching out for side effects.

'Mmmm.' Vita took the softback book and flicked through it, back and forth. Then she looked something up in the index and studied it for a few minutes. 'This is great,' she said, 'very interesting.'

Lucy felt a joyful pride spread through her at Vita's words. At least a doctor's surgery was one thing the Valentines were not able to offer her.

'It's really great,' said Vita, nodding her head thoughtfully as she fingered the book and looked back at the drawer. 'It's like a treasure trove . . .'

Lucy was puzzled but she laughed. 'Well, sort of, and we could play Doctors, or something.'

Suddenly they could hear Lucy's mother calling them from the kitchen upstairs. It was time for tea.

Making sure they put everything back in its place, the girls carefully closed the surgery door and went upstairs to enjoy a tasty tea of Lancashire hotpot and peas, followed by deliciously sweet caramel custard, a Hilda Butler special.

CHAPTER 13

June, 1997

Sex and Pleasure

Lucy woke up feeling numb. For a few moments she lay in bed trying to remember what bad thing had happened the night before to make her wake up with such a strong feeling of unease.

Slowly the events of the previous evening came back. She remembered the laughter as they looked over the photograph albums, then the shock of Andrew's stroke, watching him struggle to speak and move. But there was more than that. She recalled coming home after taking Andrew and Patrick to the hospital, exhausted and drained, to see Simon and Vita leaning against each other on the sofa and laughing the conspiratorial laugh of new lovers. Finally, she remembered stumbling into the bedroom and slamming the door, shutting out the world on her misery.

Lucy turned to look at Simon. His side of the bed was empty, but it was rumpled so he had obviously slept there, creeping into bed after Lucy had fallen asleep. But now he had already left for work, rising early as he always did, and for once not turning on the *Today* programme to listen to while he dressed. Presumably he had wanted to get out of the house without a confrontation with Lucy that morning.

That suited Lucy fine. She did not want to see Simon, either. She felt so angry about his lies and deceit that every time she thought about it her chest tightened as if someone were pulling a leather belt around it tighter and tighter.

She showered and dressed and ate a breakfast of toast and black coffee. Without concentrating much on the copy, she read the newspaper until it was time to settle down to finish editing the book she was working on. Her heart was not in it; her heart was not in anything.

Halfway through the morning, she had an urge to go through the drawers of her desk, to look at the old love letters Simon had written to her all those years before when he was pursuing her. Gingerly, she pulled out each letter from its envelope and read it, rebuilding their courtship in her head: 'I couldn't sleep last night after being with you . . .'; 'You looked so radiant when I saw you from across the road . . .'; 'Your laughter still rings in my head . . .'

It seemed astonishing to her now that Simon could once have been so besotted with her, had spent so much time thinking about her and writing to her. All these references to loving her stung her sharply. Turning the letters over in her hands, she felt a rage roar through her. How dare he make her fall in love with him and then betray her like this! She bit her lip and did not bother to hold back the tears as she read on, picking through the letters one by one. They revealed Simon as a sensitive man with powerful feelings, so different from the taciturn fellow he appeared to the world. 'I have never felt so obsessed with anyone before . . .'

Now Simon had left her, gone and slept with another woman, casually, as if Lucy did not exist, as if her feelings did not matter. And it was not just any woman either; it was Lucy's own friend.

As she sat clutching the letters in her hand and tears trickled down her cheeks, Lucy realised that Simon's behaviour had certainly made her angry (how could it not?), but it had also touched on something else, something more primitive than hurt pride. He had touched on the fear of all little children, that of being abandoned and alone. They feel it with their parents, they feel it at school.

But the hurt was complex. Lucy knew that she was not just upset about Simon abandoning her; she was upset about Vita, too. Vita had transferred her loyalty from Lucy to Simon, and this sense that she was losing Vita's friendship as well stirred up old feelings from the past. As a child she was desperate to be Vita's friend. And as an adult, nothing had changed.

Lucy sat on the sofa for a good hour, wallowing in her torment, her chest tight with anger and self-pity.

After a while, she calmed down. She was tempted to throw Simon's letters away but thinking (and hoping) that she might regret such an act in the future, she replaced them in her desk drawer. Thought of the future made her think about Andrew. She should ring the hospital to see how he was.

When she rang the ward, she was informed by a nurse with a soft Irish brogue that Andrew had fully recovered from the stroke but was now sleeping. Would she like to ring again later?

Rosie telephoned at about midday. She had got back from her Scottish trip late the night before and was now back at work. The new boyfriend had turned out to be rather uninteresting. 'He wasn't a complete bore but, let's put it this way, I spent much of the weekend reading novels,' Rosie said wearily.

'That's too bad,' said Lucy. 'I'm sorry he didn't turn out right for you.'

'You sound a bit gloomy.' Rosie could always pick up on Lucy's moods.

Lucy poured out her troubles to her friend, first about Andrew, and then about Simon and Vita.

Rosie listened in silence and then said, 'The little shit. And how dare she!'

'I haven't even begun to work out what I think about Vita,' said Lucy. 'I'm still fuming about Simon. At the moment I just don't even want to see him.'

She had a sudden longing to see Rosie, her dear loyal friend Rosie. 'What are you doing tonight? You're not by any chance free, are you? Do you fancy going to see a film?'

'I can't. I've got a ghastly awards dinner for the magazine industry at Grosvenor House. I have to go. The tickets cost ninety pounds each and it's a glitzy black-tie nonsense with everyone getting gongs for this and that. Last year we won the best women's magazine award but this year we're not even short-listed, so it's not very interesting. Still,' she added, 'it's actually always quite useful for networking . . .'

'Oh.' Lucy was disappointed.

'Actually, Lucy, maybe you'd like to come. I was meant to take this so-called boyfriend of mine but I don't feel like being in his company for another night. You could come along as my date, if you like. You might enjoy it as an outsider. The food's usually okay and there's always lots of wine.'

'But what about the boyfriend? Isn't he expecting to go?'

Rosie laughed. 'Ha, I'm sure he'll be relieved not to have

to spend another evening with me. I'll tell him he's off the hook.'

Lucy was surprised that she was interested in the invitation. 'Well, if it's really okay, I might rather like to come . . .'

'We're actually sharing a table with *Mate*, the men's magazine in our company. They're not a bad lot, in fact they're quite fun. Thinking about it, Lucy, you *must* come . . .'

It was not the sort of event Lucy normally liked but now she found the idea distinctly appealing.

'And one thing's for sure,' Rosie was saying, 'the awards dinner is always a pretty good occasion for getting laid . . .'

Lucy laughed. 'Well that settles it, then, doesn't it! Yes, I'd love to be your date for the evening.'

'By the way,' Rosie said, 'I don't know if you're interested in getting a full-time job, or whether you even want to work on a woman's magazine, but there is a sub-editor's job open here. I'm sure you could get it if you applied. My recommendation would go a long way.'

Lucy was taken aback by the suggestion. 'I'll have to think about that one,' she said. 'We can talk about it tonight . . . Now I have to make the agonising decision about what I'm going to wear.'

Lucy spent a lot of time dressing up for the evening, choosing a long Chinese jade silk dress and silver jacket. It was a long time since she had dressed up for any occasion, in the way she used to as a child. Whatever the event, in those days – staying up for supper, going to the theatre, visiting Granny, she was always dressed in her best.

Life was just not as formal any more now but she and Simon rarely, if ever, went anywhere that required such dressing up.

So it was fun to soak in deep bath water smelling of Floris limes and to wash and blow-dry her hair so that it stayed in a rather attractive sweep off her forehead. She did her face meticulously, using the make-up that usually sat untouched in the cupboard – light foundation, rouge tint, mascara. There seemed to be a lot of it for what was essentially a natural, no-make-up look.

Every now and then Lucy realised that her teeth were grinding as she set about her task, her jaw stiff with rage at Simon and a desire to get her own back at him. Rosie's support had galvanised her. She was going to have a good time tonight, whatever. And maybe she would get laid . . .

She left the house before Simon had returned from work. She left a note on the kitchen table telling him that she had gone out with Rosie for the evening. She signed it 'L', with no 'love' or 'x'. A cold, matter-of-fact note.

The awards dinner was held in a long room at the Grosvenor House Hotel in Park Lane. Rosie was already at the door waiting for her when she arrived. She had spent some time getting ready in a glamorous skin-tight black body and a crinkly plum-coloured silk skirt. Long silver earrings dangled from her ears. Her perpetually smiling lips were also a deep plum colour. 'Come and have some champagne,' she laughed. 'I'll introduce you to someone interesting.'

Hundreds of people – editors, designers and publishers – dressed in silks and sequins, unique Jacques Azagury outfits or demure Jean Muir, milled about in the anteroom, greeting each other with ostentatious kisses or gossiping more quietly in corners.

The excited buzz of conversation was broken every now and then by shrieked greetings as old friends and work colleagues met up again, not having seen each other since the year before. Glamorous, confident people, Lucy thought, successful in life, and pleased with it. So unlike her, she thought with wobbly confidence.

But Lucy kept her nerve. She was determined to enjoy herself. She knocked back several glasses of champagne and accepted a top-up every time the waiters came round. She smiled and laughed and thrust out her chest in the way she had seen Rosie do.

Rosie introduced Lucy to several of her colleagues from the magazine and many other people passing by. When the Master of Ceremonies announced the serving of dinner, they made their way to their table in the main room.

The dining room seated one thousand people, all from the magazine world, from the glossy women's monthlies to the specialist trade publications. They all sat at tables of twelve. There were six people from Rosie's magazine, including Lucy, all women, and six from *Mate*, all men.

Lucy was seated next to *Mate*'s Features Editor, a tall, good-looking blond man called Giles. He had a broad face, a pleasant smile and warm brown eyes.

'Don't you think we journalists are a ghastly lot?' he asked Lucy as he offered her the bread. 'So self-satisfied, as if we had any influence in the world at all. We don't matter one bit, not in magazines, anyway.'

Lucy smiled. She was feeling drunk already but did not stop Giles filling her wine glass again. 'Why don't you get out of magazines then and work on a newspaper if you feel that way?' She grinned charmingly at him.

Giles looked steadily at her and raised his glass to his lips. 'Who said I want to influence anyone? I'd be crazy to move. No, I like magazines, it's an easy life. Newspapers are too much like hard work.'

Giles was fun and good company. He asked Lucy about

herself and was interested without being intrusive. He informed her that his girlfriend was away on business but she never wanted to come to these things anyway. 'And I don't blame her,' he added. 'She's an economist. She works for the Treasury. She thinks I'm frivolous.' He drained his glass. 'Frankly, it's just as well that one of us is frivolous, don't you think?'

The wine was going to Lucy's head. She was not used to drinking very much and she was aware of a delicious tingling in her legs. Inside her chest she could feel a rising excitement at the conversation. The teasing tone in Giles's voice was clearly flirtatious, and Lucy, with her half-open mouth and her quick laughter, was flirtatious back.

Halfway through the meal, she realised that Giles's leg was pressing against her thigh under the table. Her heart beat fast. What was she to do about it? She knew she had a choice. She could withdraw it priggishly and make it clear that she was not available, that she was a married woman, and remind him that he had a girlfriend. Or she could allow it to continue and see how far it went. But how flattering, how exciting it was!

Did it really matter if she went off to sleep with this man? Would it be a bad thing to do? The fact that he was flirting with her gave her a boost, and if he fancied her enough to take her home to bed, then that would be a help, too. Simon had damaged her confidence at a time when she was already low. Surely she was allowed to make herself feel better in any way she could?

Lucy had only had a couple of boyfriends before she met Simon, and (unlike Rosie) she had been rather scared of going to bed with people she did not know well. She had always rather regretted this limited sexual experience, wondering if she had missed out in some way. Giles was clearly offering her an opportunity. Why should she not take this chance to get her own back at Simon and satisfy this secret need of hers to sleep with a stranger? She did not have to rub Simon's nose in it. It would be for her own sake, and satisfy her own curiosity.

Draining her glass, she decided to go for it . . .

After the chicken liver parfait, they ate their way through the roast lamb and baby vegetables, then an assortment of sorbets, coffee and chocolates. The awards were announced during coffee, and the winners trooped up to the stage to collect their prizes amidst loud clapping and cheers, or jeers from rival magazines.

Lucy was aware that the pressure of Giles's leg under the table was growing stronger. Now she gave in and allowed her foot to rub against his without protest. She hoped the economist girlfriend was a long way away.

'Let's get out of here,' Giles bent over and whispered into her ear. She could feel his breath on her neck. The final awards had been announced and now the raffle tickets – five-pound notes with people's names written on them – were being drawn from a black moleskin top hat.

Giles got to his feet and stood behind Lucy's chair to pull it out for her. Without a word, Lucy got up from the table, waved goodbye to a grinning Rosie, and followed Giles out of the room.

Giles hailed a taxi and took her to his flat, a comfortable place in Holland Park. They had kissed in the taxi and their hearts were pounding as he paid the driver and fumbled to find the keys in his pocket.

Once inside the flat, they fell on one another, pulling off their clothes and dropping them on the floor.

Lucy had not felt such excitement since the early days of

her courtship with Simon. She did not hold herself back; she wanted to enjoy every bit of it.

Giles was as skilled a lover as he was conversationalist. He removed Lucy's remaining garments and led her to his large double bed. 'Take off your jewellery,' he ordered.

Lucy took off her earrings.

'And all your rings.'

Her engagement and wedding rings lay on the bedside table beside the alarm clock as Giles began to massage her body, rubbing in baby lotion he had brought from the bathroom. His touch was light and skilful. He knew what he was doing; he had done it many times before and he evidently prided himself on his sensitivity and dexterity.

'Lie still,' he whispered. 'I don't want you to do anything.'

He rubbed Lucy's back and shoulders, her buttocks and legs. He rolled her over and rubbed her neck and breasts, and on down her belly.

His hands were firm and tender. Gradually Lucy felt the tension building up inside her. She let out a dreamy groan. Giles smiled and put his arms around her. He kissed her and held her tight as the exquisite spasm ran through her.

They lay quietly together for a few minutes. For a moment Lucy thought that that would be it. Perhaps this great lover was in fact impotent, capable of satisfying her but not himself. She was wrong.

Now Giles began to stroke her belly and thigh, and rose over her, kissing her hard.

She was just about to push him away and say something about safe sex (she was not so drunk as to be stupid), when he reached over to the bedside table drawer and pulled out a packet of condoms.

'Do you want to put it on for me?' He smiled lazily.

Thus it began again. He pushed hard inside her but his lovemaking was gentle and skilled. He varied the pace, always in control.

Lucy had never had more than one orgasm during a lovemaking session so she was surprised to feel the delicious tension building up again deep inside her pelvis.

Giles pushed and pulled back, he waited, he teased. He was very efficient, very effectual. He stroked her breasts and ran his hands around under her back.

Lucy arched her spine as she felt herself begin to rise again. As she let out another light groan, Giles pushed himself hard into her and let himself go. They collapsed in the warm groans of their synchronous orgasm.

Giles kissed her gently on the cheek and moved a tendril of damp hair off her forehead. 'Well done,' he murmured. 'That was good.' Lucy felt as though she had been given a gold star by the gym teacher, but she was pleased with herself all the same.

He rolled off and they lay together, she on his chest, his arm around her shoulder. Lucy felt eerily distanced from herself, as if she were taking part in a film and watching herself on the screen. This is the sex scene, the long naked intertwined limbs, the large double bed, the rumpled white sheets.

She began to doze. It was very late but Lucy did not care to know how late. She sighed happily. Whatever the consequences of this evening, she thought, she vowed that she would never regret these moments.

Sleep had almost overtaken her when she felt Giles's hand again running over her body. Was he really up to it again? More to the point, was she?

His touch ran over her upper arm again, rhythmically, then he shifted position and ran his fingers down her belly.

He did not seem at all tired as he kissed her again, softly, gently. Again, and again to her surprise, her body began to respond.

There was something different about his lead this time. His hands touched her thighs lightly, ran over her lower back and down between her buttocks.

She stiffened as she felt him press his finger against her.

'No!' she whispered, pulling away.

Giles kissed her. 'Have you never been buggered?'

She shook her head, embarrassed by his bluntness and by her own self-consciousness.

'Do you want to try?'

She looked up into his calm dark eyes.

'Won't it hurt?'

'I won't hurt you, I promise,' he said. 'It doesn't have to hurt.'

Lucy hesitated. She was tempted. It was something she had wondered about and now was surprised to feel an eagerness, almost an urge, in herself to try. Certainly it was not anything Simon would ever have suggested.

'Okay,' she said warily, 'I'll try. But you must stop if it hurts at all,' she added quickly.

She had to trust him.

Giles reached over to the drawer again. She had her face in the pillow but she heard the soft tearing of the condom packet. He was responsible. Then she heard him fiddling with something else, and then felt him rub the cold liquid jelly on her skin.

Positioning himself above her, he pushed against her gently and very slowly.

It did not hurt. It was strange, singularly exciting and sensuous. Giles was as careful as he said he would be. He came with a shuddering groan and then stayed inside her until he could slip out of her gently as their bodies relaxed.

Lucy smiled and kissed him. She felt almost proud of herself and she knew now why she had felt a need to try it. It was not just the erotic thrill of doing something that was a taboo but it was also that in some odd way it made her feel closer to Andrew. This must be what her homosexual brother did with his lovers, the act that was now killing him.

Giles climbed off her and rolled over on to his back beside her. 'Did you enjoy that?' he asked.

Lucy ran her hand over his strong chest. 'I did. I was surprised, but I did.'

Giles smiled. 'My girlfriend likes to be buggered,' he said. 'She says it's the only time she ever feels really vulnerable.'

Lucy swallowed hard. 'I suppose that says a lot about her,' she replied faintly.

'Yes, it does,' said Giles. 'But we get on fine. And don't you worry – she's at a conference in Washington until next week. Now, let's get some sleep. We have to go to work in the morning.'

Lucy's eyelids flickered. What an evening! She listened to Giles's breathing as he fell asleep. She knew that she would probably never sleep with him again. The likelihood was that she would never even see him again. And she would not care. It did not matter. That night had been enough.

Sex that night had been like playing a long and exciting game of tennis with a complete stranger. Sex with a stranger. What a boost! Rosie had been right. She sighed deeply. As she fell asleep she found herself wondering briefly if sex with economists was so varied. But before she could even think further about Giles's high-powered girlfriend, she was slipping into the mattress, slipping off into a deep and almost blissful sleep, without dreams.

CHAPTER 14

August, 1968

Norfolk

It had been Hilda Butler's idea to invite Vita Valentine to join the Butler family for a week in the house they were renting for a fortnight on the north coast of Norfolk.

'After all the time you've spent at the Valentines' house, being looked after and fed, it's the least we can do,' she told Lucy. 'And it'll be nice for you to have a companion for some of the time, too.'

Lucy was afraid that Vita would think a holiday with her family boring and would not want to come, so she was relieved and delighted when the invitation was accepted. It was wonderful to have Vita along, for as much as she loved her little brother, Andrew was no fun at all as a playmate. He spent all his time drawing pictures and reading books and had no interest in the seaside or the woods that Norfolk had to offer.

The small cottage they rented was on a farm, quite close to the seaside, and surrounded by fields and copses. The girls spent their time wandering bare-legged through the meadows and watching the animals and insects in the woods. Again, Vita revealed her extensive knowledge of the natural world, pointing out interesting beetles and butterflies, and identifying the songs of birds in the trees.

After all that time on the Valentine turf, it was interesting for Lucy to see Vita in a different setting. She was what her mother would describe as 'well brought up', always good about saying please and thank you, and greeting people with good mornings and good nights, and offering to help at appropriate moments.

But she also had opinions that shocked Hilda because they were about matters Hilda thought should not concern children. When Vita stated that the Vietnam War was morally wrong, Hilda reddened with annoyance and muttered to her husband that the child was simply mouthing what she had heard at home, which was probably true, thought Lucy. However, when on Saturday evening there was a discussion about going to church the next day, Hilda was truly shocked.

'Does your family normally go to church on Sundays, Vita?' she asked as innocently as she could sound. She did remember Lucy once telling her that the Valentines were atheists, but she could not quite believe it.

Vita shook her head vigorously. 'No, we never go to church.'

Hilda looked at her quizzically. 'What? Never? Not even at Christmas or Easter?'

Vita shrugged. 'My father said he might take us to Midnight Mass at Westminster Abbey one day.' She paused. 'But I don't think that really counts.'

'No,' agreed Hilda, her brow crossed in a vexed frown.

'Actually,' Vita continued, 'I'm not even christened. None of us is. My parents don't believe in God. And neither do I,' she added.

'Oh,' Hilda did not quite know what to say. She had

never heard of someone not being christened, unless they
were Jewish. She pressed her lips together and said, 'What,
none of you children?'

Vita smiled and shook her head. 'Nope. Not one. My
father said we could decide for ourselves when we were
older. He says the decision will be ours alone then.'

'I see.' The frown on Hilda's face continued to show
her disapproval. 'Well, what about tomorrow? We shall
be going to church and you are welcome to join us if you
would like.'

Lucy listened uneasily to the edge of sarcasm in her
mother's voice.

Vita shook her head. 'That's okay,' she said. 'I think
I'll stay here and try to finish my book. I'm enjoying it
so much, and I think it might be a bit hypocritical of me
to go to church.'

Hilda went off to make the tea, muttering as she went
that she doubted if Vita knew the meaning of the word
hypocritical.

There was a curious incident that day when Lucy and Vita
came into the house laughing and panting after racing each
other through the nearby woods.

As the girls sat down at the kitchen table, Hilda reached
over to Vita's head. 'You've got something in your hair,'
she said.

As she said it, her hand raised to pick out the brown twig
caught in Vita's thick black tresses, Vita jerked her head
away suddenly and cringed from Hilda's hand, her right
arm held up protectively before her face.

'Hey, I won't hurt you!' exclaimed Hilda. 'I'm just trying
to get this twig from your hair.'

Vita stood up straight and gave her an embarrassed smile.

She recovered her composure quickly and laughed as if her exaggerated gesture had been deliberate.

Lucy watched intently. She was pretty sure why her friend had ducked away like that. Later that afternoon, she asked Vita about it.

The girls were out in the garden where Vita had just taught Lucy to catch grasshoppers, sweeping their feet through the long grass to make the insects leap before them and reveal themselves. Then the girls crept up, crouching down, two hands cupped together, ready to pounce and capture the creatures in their closed palms.

Quicker and more agile, Vita was much better at catching the grasshoppers than Lucy, though Lucy did not mind. It was not a competitive activity for, once a grasshopper was caught, it was released. 'The fun's in the catching,' explained Vita.

After a while, they stopped and threw themselves in the grass, rolling over on their backs to chew sweet blades of grass and stare up at the blue sky. Small dark swallows swooped and darted above them.

Remembering the earlier incident, Lucy turned over on her belly. 'Why did you shy away when my mother took the twig out of your hair?'

Vita did not respond. She chewed her grass and shut her eyes.

Lucy waited but Vita continued to ignore her.

'Don't you want to talk about it?'

Vita rolled over and smiled at her. 'You know, Lucy, a long time ago we talked about friends. You are my friend, I can see the point of having a friend, and that's nice.' She pushed herself to her feet. 'Come on, let's catch some more grasshoppers.'

The change of subject caught Lucy off guard. She smiled.

Vita owned her, had claimed her as a friend at last. And in her flush of pleasure, she forgot entirely that Vita had not answered her question.

On Sunday afternoon, when church was over and Hilda had served up a real Sunday roast in the cramped cottage kitchen, complaining constantly about the inadequate utensils, the girls went for a walk with Dr Butler.

They left Hilda behind to listen to the radio and Andrew to read the new book he had just started.

Dr Butler liked Vita. He found her a bright and inquisitive child and he liked to linger behind the two girls and eavesdrop on their charming conversations. He was struck by how sophisticated the Valentine girl appeared to be. Lucy seemed protected and naïve by comparison.

As they walked through the beech woods, Vita displayed an impressive knowledge of nature. She knew a lot about birds. She could identify the chaffinches and woodpeckers they saw, and identify their songs if she listened carefully enough. Some she could even imitate. Dr Butler raised his eyebrows in admiration as Vita mimicked the Great Tit – 'Tea Cher! Tea Cher!' and called to the wood pigeons in the trees with a 'Coo-roo-coo-coo!'.

But Vita also knew that all birds moult every feather at least once a year, and to prevent interference with flight, most moult slowly, shedding the feathers in orderly rotation.

Vita also knew about plants. She pointed out the vivid red berries of the lords and ladies and the pretty purple flowers of the monkshood, the waxy berries of the yew and the hanging fruit of the woody nightshade.

'You seem to know a great deal about plant life, young

lady,' remarked Dr Butler with amusement. He always enjoyed talking to children.

Vita smiled. 'My grandmother is terrified that one of us might eat poisonous berries by mistake so we have all been drilled from an early age, and taught what they looked like so we knew we should never touch them.

'It's interesting to think about the olden days, before there were books, when people discovered what was poisonous and what wasn't,' she said. 'Do you think a child would eat a yew berry and be very ill and then they'd know? Before books and pictures, how could anyone know about the dangers of some plants in advance?'

Dr Butler was stimulated by the child's chain of thought. 'Well, of course, in a village there would have been someone who knew a lot about plants and their medicinal value and they'd pass it on.

'And I'm sure you know, of course,' he continued, enjoying his role as teacher, 'that many poisonous plants can also be put to good use. Such poisons are often used in modern medicine.'

Vita looked up at him with her large dark appealing eyes. 'Really? Like what?'

'Well, take deadly nightshade, or belladonna. It produces something that is essential for ophthalmology, the study of the eye. It produces something called hyoscyamine, which changes into something called atropine. There's no substitute for atropine in treatment of the diseases of the eye. It is also an important antidote to a number of poisons, including lead and digitalis, or foxglove. It relieves muscle cramps and so it's also given for asthma. It's also used for gallstones and even sea sickness.'

The girls both looked impressed, so he continued. 'So you see that although many of our plants have great power to do harm, they also possess important medicinal properties that can do a great deal of good.'

Vita was pensive. Looking up, she asked, 'But how would a doctor know how much of a poison to give? How would he know how not to poison someone?'

'For a dangerous plant to become a remedy depends on the dosage, and it is then made weaker as a substance by dilution.'

'That's interesting,' murmured Vita, and she fell silent with her own thoughts.

They walked on. The only sound came from the little brook to their left and the occasional soft cooing of a wood pigeon in the trees.

Vita looked thoughtful, then a worried frown appeared between her eyes. 'Dr Butler,' she said quietly, 'can you tell me a little about leukaemia.'

Dr Butler smiled and looked quizzically at her. 'Of course! What do you want to know about leukaemia?'

'Well, what is it exactly and how do you know if you have it?'

'Leukaemia is a cancer of the blood. There are several types, and the symptoms vary but you would know if you had it. The symptoms are quite obvious and debilitating.'

They walked along side by side. Lucy trailed along behind.

'Why?' asked Dr Butler. 'Why do you ask? You don't think you have leukaemia, do you?'

Vita did not answer. She kicked the leaf mould with the toe of her brown sandal.

Dr Butler laughed gently. He did not want to mock her for her worries. 'I can assure you,' he said, 'If you are worried that you have leukaemia, that your worries are unfounded. You're as fit as a fiddle . . .'

Vita bit her lip and nodded but she said nothing.

Later that night, as the girls lay in their bunk beds in the dark, they referred back to that conversation.

'I like your father,' said Vita, staring up at the ceiling. There was a pause.

'Yes, I do, too,' replied Lucy. She would never actually admit to anyone except herself that she liked her father more than she liked her mother. But she knew it was true and Vita's remark confirmed that for her.

Vita turned over on her side. 'He made me feel much better about leukaemia.' She stopped and then started again. 'You see, I did think I had leukaemia but now he's made me think I probably haven't. I've been thinking about it a lot.'

Lucy smiled. 'I'm glad he's made you believe him. But why did you think you had leukaemia in the first place?'

She waited for her friend to reply but there was just silence in the room and the sound of a barn owl hooting outside. After a few minutes she stopped expecting an answer. Her breathing became steady and deep as she sank into sleep.

Vita lay awake in the dark, her eyes wide open, her mind ever-active as she thought about her life back home in the big house in Kentish Town.

Vita went home to London on the train. Seraphina Valentine had assured Hilda on the telephone that Vita would be perfectly safe on the train.

'She'll be met at the station in London. She's quite used to travelling on her own. She's often been on the train to Sussex by herself.

Hilda Butler was clearly surprised that Vita's parents should not drive up to collect their eldest daughter but she was not one to argue, and certainly not with intellectuals who did not baptise their children. Wherever could one start?

She did a final check with the child herself. 'Wouldn't you like someone to drive up and collect you from here?' she asked Vita.

Vita had shrugged. 'Not particularly,' she stated simply. 'I get to read a lot on the train and I like the peace and quiet. My home is very noisy most of the time,' she added with a spontaneous grin.

With her characteristic politeness, Vita thanked Mrs Butler for having her. 'I've had a wonderful time,' she said.

And on the train home she composed a beautifully written letter that would arrive a few days later.

'Well,' said Mrs Butler, reading it with approval. 'Whatever else those Valentine parents do, at least they've drummed some basic good manners into their children, which is more than you can say about a lot of people these days.'

CHAPTER 15

June, 1997

Reconciliation

Lucy paid her fare and got out of the cab around the corner from home. She did not want the whole street to see her returning at seven thirty in the morning dressed in her evening gown and high heels from the night before. It might have been something to flaunt and laugh about as a student, but she did not want the tongues wagging too much in their quiet west London street. She was particularly worried in case Mehmet, the friendly grocer, had seen her as he opened up his shop.

Lucy let herself into the house quietly and, taking a deep breath, braced herself for a confrontation with Simon. She squared her shoulders and held her head high. Although exhausted, she was still glowing inside from her adventure. Fired up, she was ready to meet Simon head on.

Having anticipated anger and recriminations, she was not at all prepared for what happened.

Simon was sitting in the kitchen, slumped miserably over a cup of coffee. His rumpled clothes and unshaven face made it clear that he had not been to bed at all. He had probably had even less sleep than Lucy.

He leaped up when Lucy came in. 'There you are! I've been so worried about you. Why didn't you ring and let me know where you were? I've been trying to get hold of Rosie. I assumed you'd have gone home with her but there was no answer, or only her answering machine. She never rang back.'

Simon's tired, bleary eyes looked pleadingly at her. 'I'm so sorry, Lucy.' Taking a step towards her, he held out a hesitant hand, unsure of how she was going to respond.

Looking at him standing there, so big and tall but so vulnerable and unhappy, Lucy gave in to the warm rush of affection which flowed through her.

'Oh, Simon,' she cried, moving towards him and placing her arms around his waist. She laid her head against his chest while Simon buried his face on her shoulder.

'I'm sorry,' he mumbled, giving way to his exhaustion. 'I'm sorry about what I did. I'm sorry about being unfaithful to you, and I'm sorry, so sorry, about lying to you.'

He paused and then stood back, his hands grasping her shoulders. 'I spent the whole night thinking about what was happening – what has happened and why. And then you didn't come home so I began to imagine all sorts of things – that you had left me, or something terrible had happened to you. I imagined that you had been murdered and I'd never know and it'd be all my fault.'

He was talking, gabbling so fast that he was almost incomprehensible. Lucy let out a sigh and reached for the kettle. 'I need some coffee,' she said. 'And then we should talk.'

They made a large pot of coffee and Simon rang his office to tell them he would be late. Then the two of them sat on opposite sides of the kitchen table and talked.

They talked about the strain of trying to have a baby and the pressure that had put on their relationship. They talked about how they had focused so much on that that they had forgotten about each other in their isolated obsessions. They talked about the miscarriage and what it had meant to them to lose the baby. They talked a lot about Andrew and the misery of watching him die while they were hoping to start a new life. And they talked about the strain of supporting Andrew and trying to bring about some sort of convincing reconciliation between Andrew and his parents. Finally, they talked about Vita.

'She means nothing to me,' said Simon.

Lucy was silent.

'And I know that I don't mean anything to her,' Simon continued. 'You shouldn't really blame her, either, Lucy. I initiated it and she responded. I asked her to come and see me at the paper to discuss the possibility of her doing a story for us. Then I invited her out for a drink. It went from there. She never once took the lead. It was all my doing and my fault.'

He promised never to see Vita again. 'At least, not without you knowing,' he added sheepishly.

Simon never once asked Lucy where she had been and she knew that he probably never would, either. That suited her fine.

After they had talked for three hours, they went to bed. Simon began to kiss her. 'I haven't even showered,' murmured Lucy.

But Simon was undeterred. It was as if he had to put his mark on his woman again. There was an urgency to his lovemaking that spread to Lucy. As they tussled and rolled on the bed, Lucy was fleetingly reminded of the time when Rosie had slept with three men in one day. But she knew that she was meant to be with Simon, that she loved him, and would continue to do so for a long time.

Exhausted, they finally dozed in each other's arms.

In the afternoon, refreshed and showered, Simon went in to work and Lucy went out for a walk.

Thinking about what had happened over the past few days, she realised that she was genuinely sanguine about Simon, and she knew that her relationship with him was solid and safe. When he promised that he would not see Vita again, she believed him.

She thought a lot, too, about Vita. Her feelings about Vita were much more complicated and she appreciated the fresh air to clear her thoughts.

She was surprised by what she thought about Vita Valentine. In spite of her rage and hurt, and her sense of betrayal, she was reluctant to sever all ties with her old-new friend Vita.

What Vita had done was wrong and certainly not the sort of behaviour you expect from a friend but, for some reason, Lucy knew that this whole affair was not really a moral issue. It was not even a serious matter. For some reason (and she did not know why) she knew that Vita, like the rest of her family, lacked a common sense of morality. She knew that Vita would not regard sleeping with Simon as particularly wrong. It just happened.

After all, Lucy herself had just slept with another woman's man the night before. She may not know Giles's girlfriend but she knew of her existence, and that had not stopped her sleeping with Giles. That was not very moral behaviour, either.

She walked into Holland Park and, as she walked, feeling the warm summer breeze on her face, Lucy was very aware of a primitive tug inside her for Vita's friendship. She valued her relationship with Vita, which stemmed from that long summer when they were nine. She valued it more than she was bothered by these recent events. She did not know why but she knew that Vita could not help herself, that in some odd way, she was not responsible for her actions.

Something had happened all those years ago that had made her understand this about Vita. Something linked them and bound them together. Lucy could not remember what it was; it was buried too deep inside her. But she knew that she had to forgive Vita, just as she had to forgive Simon.

The sun warmed her cheeks. Everything would be all right between her and Simon. They would go on holiday and get rejuvenated and start to try and have another baby.

They would not rush it. Even in her optimism, she had not forgotten that she had to wait for Andrew to die first. On holiday they would just try to relax and forget about trying.

As she turned for home, she decided that she would apply for the sub-editor's job on Rosie's magazine, after all. She needed a proper structure to her life, and some way to keep her thoughts off her own condition.

And it would tempt fate. If she was offered the job, she was bound to find herself pregnant!

The next morning the telephone rang at five o'clock. Lucy woke with an uncomfortable start and grabbed the phone, certain that something terrible had happened.

It was Andrew. His voice was rambling, almost incoherent. 'I just wanted to tell you, in case I suddenly don't get the opportunity, how much I love you,' he said. 'It's hard to get the opportunity to say important things any more, and I just wanted to let you know how I feel.'

Lucy was suddenly wide awake. Tears flooded her eyes.

She sniffed into the receiver. 'You know I feel the same about you, Andrew,' she said. 'I love you, too.'

Lucy and Simon went away to Provence for a week. The trip served its purpose. They went back to the place they were staying when they decided to get married. The weather was not too hot and they saw the sights of Orange, Avignon, Arles and Nîmes, and they ate and drank until they were bloated. They stayed in a small hotel in Beaumes de Venise and made love every night. It seemed like a new beginning to their relationship. Even Lucy's childmares seemed to subside.

'Perhaps we just needed this crisis to remind us of why we like each other,' Simon said one night after a particularly delicious and filling meal of crudités, chicken, and *marquise au chocolat*.

Lucy laughed and gave him a playful push. 'You sound like a therapist,' she teased.

'It's reading that magazine of Rosie's – according to that, if everyone "got in touch with their feelings" they'd all be a lot happier.'

Lucy poked him in the ribs. 'You laugh,' she joked, 'but even I think there's something to be said for that!'

They returned home several pounds heavier and much happier. Lucy had not felt so close to Simon since the early days of their courtship. It gave her strength to tackle what was awaiting her back in London.

She had interviewed for the job on Rosie's magazine and she had more or less been offered it on the spot. She knew the job was hers if she wanted it but she was beginning to wonder how wise it would be to work in the same place as Rosie. Much as she loved her as a friend, she was not sure what she would be like as a colleague.

But her uncertainty had more to do with her concern about Andrew, whose health was steadily deteriorating. He had had a couple more strokes since the last one, and although he had recovered completely each time, the gaps between them were shortening. In addition, the different drugs he took for his various conditions had debilitating side effects which were almost more unbearable than the condition they were meant to treat.

His eyesight was now failing. Although he was taking intravenous antibiotics every day, a recent examination had revealed that the blindness was advancing as the *cytomegalovirus* took hold.

Two days after Lucy returned from holiday, she had a call from Patrick to say that Andrew had been whisked into hospital again with suspected pneumonia.

'He's very down,' said Patrick. 'If you can manage to see him this evening, I know it'll mean a lot to him.'

Lucy cancelled her supper date with Rosie and took the underground to visit Andrew in the now familiar AIDS ward at the Middlesex Hospital.

Andrew was in the same bed he had occupied during his very first admission to hospital. He looked so thin and pale. His head looked too heavy to be held up by his thin neck.

Lucy took his hand and squeezed it gently. His fingers were just bones. She noticed that the purple-blue blotches of Kaposi's sarcoma were now on his chest and upper arms.

'This is it,' he said. His voice was cracked and tired. 'I've had enough.'

Lucy sat quietly next to his bed, not moving, not knowing how to respond.

A cheerful male nurse with a noticeably camp manner came round with the tea trolley. Lucy accepted his offer of a cup of tea but Andrew declined miserably.

'They're all so decent in here,' he said, 'but really I'm just a medical specimen. The doctors keep wanting to try out all sorts of tests and experimental drugs on me and they don't see that perhaps I don't want to fight for my life to the bitter end, regardless.'

He turned to Lucy and looked at her with his huge sunken eyes. He looked so sad a lump rose in her throat.

'The time has come now, Lucy, and you've got to help me.'

'Yes.' Lucy squeezed his hand again but she was puzzled. 'What do you want me to do?'

'I've got to do it.' Andrew was talking through his teeth with a frightening urgency. 'I've got to do it before it's too late, before I get too weak to carry it out. You must get me the pills, Lucy. You've got to get them to me quickly!'

Lucy frowned. 'But how, and where from?'

Andrew lay back on the pillow and closed his eyes. 'From Dad's drawer in his surgery. You know it's full of sleeping pills, all sorts of drugs. You have to get a large supply of sodium amytal . . .'

Lucy was puzzled. 'Surely you could write a prescription for yourself. You're a qualified doctor.'

Andrew shook his head. 'I'm not registered. I can't write prescriptions.'

Lucy stared at her brother. 'I don't know if I can do that. I'm not sure that I would even get the opportunity.'

Andrew frowned and looked annoyed. 'Of course you can,' he snapped back with a sudden strength to his voice.

Lucy looked quickly around her to see if anyone was listening. 'Look, Andrew.' She chose her words carefully. 'I have always been happy to support you and encourage you in every way I can but I never imagined that you expected me to provide you with the means to do away with yourself.

The very idea scares me for all sorts of reasons. It's illegal, for one thing.'

As she voiced her fears she could see Andrew growing angry. 'I've been banking on you helping me, Lucy. You're the only person I know with access to an untraceable supply of drugs – enough to make it work. I need your help now.'

His voice sounded bitter. 'I've been counting on you, Lucy.'

Lucy grimaced. 'I just feel a bit funny about stealing drugs from Dad.'

'Well, you didn't worry about that before,' he snapped impatiently.

Lucy stared at him in puzzlement. 'What are you talking about? What do you mean?'

'You must remember,' said Andrew, 'a long time ago. You got drugs out for those friends of yours. You didn't seem to be sorry about anything then. I'm your brother, Lucy, your only sibling, and I need your help.'

'I don't remember anything about getting any drugs, ever . . .'

'Well, you must have deliberately forgotten about what happened. Do you really not remember what you did? And what happened afterwards?

'I saw you. I came into Dad's surgery just as you were getting the drugs for your friends. You told me what you were doing. I was only seven but I remember the sequence of events. I remember those days as vividly as I remember yesterday.

'You are as responsible for what happened as your friends were. You may not have been in on the plans but you were instrumental to the plot.'

He laughed bitterly. 'I'm not surprised you've forgotten

about it. Your conscience would find it hard to tolerate something as bad as that.'

He raised himself on his elbow. 'Look, you got the drugs when you were asked to get them. Now you must do it for me. If you care about me, you'll do it.' He paused and looked at her, fixing her eyes with his gaze. 'Please . . .'

Lucy stumbled home with her head swimming with memories. Flashes of the past kept coming before her eyes, of the Valentine house, of a small boy in grey shorts. She could hear the tinkling sounds of children's voices, laughter and talking, and orders.

Gradually, something emerged, rising up from the dark caverns inside her, something she had forgotten long ago. Something that now was as familiar to her as the smell of her mother's shepherd's pie in the oven or Simon's warm body when he lay close to her.

Slowly the scenes unfolded. A massive piece of the jigsaw puzzle of her life slipped into place. She had completely forgotten that Andrew had known what she was up to. She knew he had been telling the truth and that she had to help him now.

She was shaking when she got home, shaking with dismay at the memories that now flooded her head, and with dread of the task which lay ahead of her.

CHAPTER 16

August, 1968

Right and Wrong

Home from their Norfolk holiday, Lucy went back to visiting the Valentine house every day. She was beginning to see something new in the family, something she had not noticed before. Lucy was beginning to realise that one of the things that made the Valentine children so different was their very odd idea of what was right and wrong. In fact, at times she thought that they did not think that anything was necessarily wrong at all; it merely depended on the circumstances. They thought nothing of cheating at games, of pinching from someone's stash of play money, for instance, when they went out of the room to go to the lavatory in the middle of a game of *Monopoly*. And she remembered being surprised by how often Achilles used to cheat when playing tennis on Parliament Hill. It seemed so unnecessary to lie about whether a ball was inside the court or out, when he was by far the best tennis player of the lot anyway. He had no qualms about it at all.

The first time Lucy became properly aware of this was when she found the five-pound note in the road.

One fine morning, Lucy was walking down Fortess Road with Vita and Perdita on the way to the public library, when she spotted a piece of grubby paper fluttering in the gutter. Something about it made her look again. She bent down and picked it up.

It was a five-pound note, crumpled and dirty.

'Five pounds! Look what I've just found.'

Vita and Perdita turned to look. Vita smiled. 'Let's spend it, quick!'

Lucy looked at her companions and stepped back, clutching the note in her raised fist. 'But we can't . . . it's not ours.'

For a moment, the Valentine sisters stared at her quizzically.

Lucy frowned. 'Surely we should hand it in . . .'

Perdita squared her shoulders. 'Hand it in? Where?' Her voice was sharp with disbelief.

Lucy could feel her neck reddening. Something was going wrong here. 'Well, the police station . . .'

Vita snorted, and tossed her head back dismissively. 'What's the point of that?'

Lucy's blush was creeping rapidly over her face. 'But if you hand something in and nobody claims it after three months, it gets given to the person who handed it in.'

Perdita was standing with her weight on one leg, a hand on her hip. 'Oh, yeah? Who told you that? The fairy godmother?'

Lucy bristled defensively. 'No, my mother . . .' Her voice tailed off.

'I think finders are keepers,' Vita said firmly.

'No, they're not.' Lucy was sure of her ground here. 'What if it belongs to an old lady who needs it? It's not finders keepers at all.' Her throat was tight and her voice came out rather squeaky.

Perdita took her hand off her hip and stood in front of Lucy. 'Look, even if you want to wait three months, if you go and hand that note in at the police station, the chances are the policeman will keep it for himself.'

Lucy was shocked. 'A policeman would never do that!' Again she felt she was on steady ground.

Perdita rolled her eyes impatiently. 'Oh, for goodness' sake, grow up. My father says a lot of policemen are worse than the criminals . . .'

The girls looked at each other for a long time, each one standing her ground on the corner of Leighton and Kentish Town Roads.

Finally Vita broke the silence. 'So, what are you going to do?' It was a direct challenge.

Lucy looked away and watched the cars crossing at the lights. Her heart was thumping uncomfortably. 'I suppose . . .' She started to speak and then she stopped. She swallowed back the hard lump in her throat. She tried again. 'I suppose . . .'

The Valentine girls were staring hard at her, their mouths set in identical straight lines.

Then Lucy knew she had to give in. She sighed. 'All right, we'll keep it,' she said quietly.

The moment she said the words, Perdita smiled and put her arm around her shoulders. She hugged her tight while Vita grinned and nodded approvingly.

'Good,' said Vita, 'that's settled, then. Now, let's go and buy a Wimpy. Then we'll have some money left over and we can buy some sweets.'

So the trio set off up the road to buy hamburgers and chips.

Lucy was quiet as they sat on the grass by the railway track and ate their food. She ate very little of it. What she did consume of the greasy chips left the bitter taste of guilt in her mouth.

A similar incident happened closer to the end of the summer holidays.

Lucy had gone up, as usual, to play with the Valentines. It was a hot day and Seraphina was sitting in a deckchair in the garden, reading a book. She was wearing a flowery ankle-length dress and a broad-brimmed hat to shield her face from the sun. She had beautiful white skin, which she carefully protected from the sun's rays.

The younger children were playing in the sandpit. Lucy played a skipping game with Vita and Perdita for a while, then the girls wandered into the house. It was quiet inside. Olwyn was out shopping and the older twins had gone off fishing somewhere. Anthony had driven a pile of books over to Arnold and Dusky Wesker's house in Highgate. The Weskers were collecting books to send to Cuba where, because of the American blockade of the island, Vita explained to Lucy, there was a terrible shortage of books. Even the famous playwright John Osborne had sent a complete collection of his works, Vita said.

The three girls went into the house. It was cool in the hall and Perdita looked hurriedly around, as if to check that no one was nearby. Then she turned to Vita and said, 'Let's go see if Anthony's forgotten his change.'

Vita smiled and nodded, and the two Valentine girls ran up the stairs. Lucy followed, taking the stairs at a slower pace till she reached Anthony Valentine's book-lined study. It was at the back of the house, overlooking the garden. Perdita was already inside.

'Yes!' she exclaimed as Lucy entered the room. She sounded triumphant. On the large wooden desk before her was a pile of coins – pennies, threepenny pieces, sixpences and a few shillings. Anthony Valentine had a habit of emptying his pockets every night before hanging up his trousers but he often forgot to put the change back the next day.

Lucy watched in amazement as Perdita's quick fingers picked up a couple of sixpences, three threepenny pieces, and one shilling.

'Do you think that's enough?' whispered Vita.

'I don't want to take too much,' replied Perdita. 'We don't want him to notice.'

Vita smirked. 'We usually get quite a bit,' she explained to Lucy.

Lucy looked at her tentatively, unsure of how she ought to respond.

Perdita laughed. 'Yes, we have to supplement our pocket money somehow. Come on, let's go and spend it.'

As they left the room they saw David dart across the corridor. Perdita sighed with irritation.

'Damn,' she spat. 'The Brat's been spying on us again.'

'Or trying to,' replied Vita. 'I don't think he could've seen us.' Nonetheless she glared at the sight of David scuttling down the hall.

The sisters looked at each other for a moment, clearly communicating something in that brief glance. It was as if they were confirming something that they had discussed and agreed earlier.

'Hey, David!' called Perdita.

The small boy stopped at the bottom of the stairs and turned around. 'What?' he asked in a small, frightened voice.

'Were you spying on us?'

'No, no I wasn't.'

'Well what's that you've got there in your hand?'

'Nothing.'

'Yes you have!' Perdita ran down to him and grabbed his arm. She twisted it hard to make him open his palm.

'Let go! Let go!' His voice was a terrified squeal, like the cry of a cornered animal.

'He's stolen something from Vita's room! He's taken your pear drops. You brat!' She grabbed at David's hand just as the boy threw the sweets on to the floor and ran off down the hall.

The girls picked up the scattered boiled sweets and stuffed them into their pockets. 'God, he's such a pain,' grumbled Vita.

'Come on,' said Perdita. 'Let's go spend the money before Olwyn comes back and goes through our pockets.'

Without telling anyone they ran out of the front door and down to the sweet shop round the corner. There they bought copies of *Bunty* and *Judy*, a couple of Kit-Kats and some sherbet lemons. Strolling to a nearby wall, they sat down and ate the chocolate wafers and sweets, swinging their legs and leafing through their comics.

Lucy felt troubled by what they had done. The chocolate tasted sour.

'It's not very good to take money like that, really,' she suggested in a quiet voice.

Perdita eyed her with raised eyebrows. 'What do you mean?' Her voice was both astonished and threatening.

Lucy began to stutter. 'Well . . . it's st-stealing, really. Isn't it?'

Vita shook her head. 'Not really. It's family money. And we're family.'

'But your father wouldn't like it if he knew, would he?'

Perdita shrugged. 'Probably not. But the point is, he *doesn't* know.'

'Don't you get enough pocket money?' asked Lucy.

Vita laughed. 'We get lots of pocket money.'

'Then why do you take more from your father?'

The sisters hesitated, Perdita rolling her eyes in exasperation.

'Because it's *fun*,' she said finally. 'Because it's not allowed.'

'Anyway,' added Vita, 'it's Anthony's own fault. He promised to take us up to the riding school in Barnet this morning, and then he couldn't. He had to take those stupid books over to go to Cuba. He's always saying he'll do something with us and then not doing it.' She paused. 'Taking his money somehow makes up for it. A bit.'

Vita leaned over and poked Lucy gently in the ribs. 'You're really quite the goody-goody, aren't you? I began to think it when you wanted to hand in that five-pound note to the police station, but now I know for sure.'

Lucy looked down at her shoes. She was hurt. Vita's remark had hurt her so much, she reddened with pain. 'No I'm not!' she protested.

Perdita jumped down from the wall. She squinted over at Parliament Hill where they could see people flying kites and sunbathing on the grass. 'You are a goody-goody, Lucy,' she said firmly. 'There's no getting around it, I'm afraid.'

Lucy went home that night feeling deeply wounded. She was angry with her parents for being so conventional, always sticking to the rules.

'Whatever's wrong with you?' her father asked, noticing his daughter's silent mood at supper.

'Nothing,' Lucy shrugged. 'I'm just tired.'

'Too much running around with those Valentine girls, if you ask me,' said Hilda.

But when Hilda chided Lucy for putting the milk bottle on the table instead of pouring the milk into a jug first, Lucy let out a cry of exasperation, and stormed out of the room, leaving her astonished parents open-mouthed and baffled by her uncharacteristic behaviour.

Only Andrew could guess what had triggered Lucy's rage. He did not know why his sister was in such a bad mood but he knew that it was stupid to care about whether milk was in a jug or a milk bottle.

The next day, Vita rang the doorbell at Falkland Road and asked if Lucy could come swimming with her and Perdita. Hilda was glad to let Lucy go, especially seeing how her gloomy daughter had lit up at the sight of the Valentine girl.

The girls went to the Lido where they swam and dived in the cold water. Lucy's swimming had improved a lot that summer. She had studied the way Vita and Perdita swam, and tried, with some success, to imitate them.

They went back for tea at the Valentines' house. And it was then, after tea, that Perdita came up with the challenge. They were in Perdita's room, playing rummy.

The top of the sash window was open. The curtains fluttered in the cool breeze. Lucy had been aware of the angry buzzing sound on the window as a fly tried to escape, banging pitifully against the glass.

Looking up from her hand of cards, Perdita frowned. 'That fly has been annoying me since early this morning.'

She placed her cards down on the floor and stood up. She stepped over to the window, crouched for a moment and then pounced. 'Got it!'

Under her cupped hands, the fly buzzed angrily.

Perdita rubbed her fingers together and manipulated the fly until it was held between her forefinger and thumb. Holding it against the sky, she pulled off one of its wings. Lucy flinched and watched with distaste as Perdita dropped the fly on the windowsill where it started buzzing furiously, turning round and round in circles like a stranded rower with one oar.

Lucy grimaced.

Perdita looked at her and grinned. 'I know what you're thinking, Lucy,' she said. 'You're thinking it's not nice to pull wings off flies.'

Lucy remained silent, afraid to agree. She was scared.

Perdita poked the fly which buzzed more angrily. 'Do you know what kind of fly this is?' She poked it again.

Lucy looked at the insect's large metallic-blue body. 'It's a bluebottle, I think,' she replied. She could feel both the sisters staring at her; the tension in the room frightened her even more.

Perdita nodded. 'That's right, it's a bluebottle. It's also called a blowfly.'

'Do you know what the dictionary says about the blowfly, Lucy?' Vita's voice was piercing. Vita reached up to the shelf and pulled down a dictionary. 'Let's see what it says.' She leafed through it nimbly. 'I'll read it to you: "blowfly: any of various flies (family *Calliphoridae*) that deposit their eggs or maggots especially on meat or wounds; especially a bluebottle . . ."' She laughed. 'The bluebottle's Latin name is *Calliphora vomitoria* – how appropriate! "Commonly found in houses and often carriers of disease."'

The iridescent blue fly was still moving in circles but the angry buzzing was no longer continuous; it stopped for a second or two before resuming.

Perdita studied it and then turned to Lucy with a laugh.

'I know it's cruel. I should put this household pest out of its misery.'

Crouching down, she positioned her forefinger above the fly and slowly brought it down to squash it on the woodensill.

The buzzing stopped.

'There!' Perdita smiled at Lucy. 'It's not suffering any more.'

Lucy looked away, perplexed. Vita shut the dictionary and replaced it on the shelf. She said nothing.

Perdita picked up the dead fly by the remaining wing and dropped it out of the window. She glanced at Vita, who gave her a quick nod.

'We wanted to talk to you about something, Lucy,' said Perdita. 'We like you a lot but we want to give you the chance to prove that you're not a goody-goody.'

Lucy looked at them both, from one sister to the other, puzzled. Her throat ached with fear and her heart was pounding.

Perdita was staring at her with a concentrated look in her eyes.

'Whatever do you mean?' asked Lucy in a faint voice.

Vita came up close and leaned towards her. Lucy could see her own reflection in her friend's dark eyes.

'We want you to do something for us,' she said. 'To get something we need.'

Lucy frowned, torn between relief that she could do something for her friends, that they needed her in some way, and a deep fear of what it was she was expected to do.

Perdita looked around as if to make sure that no one could hear her, then leaned forward to position her face just inches from Lucy's.

'We want you to get something from your father's surgery. You can prove you're not a goody-goody by bringing it to us tomorrow. At noon.'

'But I can't do that!' cried Lucy.

Perdita tossed her hair disdainfully. 'You don't even know what it is yet. Told you,' she mocked. 'We said you were a goody-goody.'

Lucy's heart was racing. She could not believe that this was happening. Suddenly her best friends were challenging her to prove to them that she was one of them.

Lucy hesitated. The trouble was that she *did* desperately want to be one of them. She felt a hardening inside her as she felt that she could do it. Narrowing her eyes, she turned to the sisters and faced Perdita defiantly.

'All right,' she said, looking Perdita straight in the eye. 'Tell me what I have to get, and I'll get it.'

Vita and Perdita glanced at each other again, smiling. Vita pulled a piece of paper from her pocket and said, 'It's a kind of medicine. I've written the name down here. Your dad has some in that drugs drawer of his, I've seen it. I'm sure I saw it when you were showing me round that day.'

Lucy took the paper in her hand but did not read what was written on it, even though she could see the blue ink in Vita's neat, confident writing.

As Lucy stood there, waiting, Perdita smiled sweetly. 'If you want to stay friends with us,' she said quietly, 'you'd better get this.'

'What's it for?' asked Lucy. Her voice sounded faint to her through the drumming of blood in her ears.

Vita frowned and snapped, 'It doesn't matter what it's for. Just get it. That's all you have to do, it's no big deal.'

Lucy bit her lip. 'Okay,' she said. 'I'll try and get it tomorrow.'

Vita put her arm around Lucy's shoulder and hugged her.
'That's the spirit,' she said. 'It'll be really easy for you,
I'm sure.'

Lucy went home that evening feeling shaken. What the
Valentine girls wanted her to do, to raid her father's surgery,
was wrong, but her desire to remain their friend was too
strong; she couldn't resist them. She did not know why she
wanted to remain friends with them when they tormented
her in these cruel and demanding ways. Even Vita, with
whom she shared so many interests, could be unpredictable
and suddenly turn on her savagely after a period of acting
like a best friend. What was the attraction that pulled her
back to them again and again?

Lucy did not know why she felt as she did. It was all
confusing. Yet she knew that even though the girls did not
always treat her in the way she would like, she would still
forgive them for it, in the hope, perhaps, that some day they
would accept her without question.

The Valentines were not like other people, and she would
do anything for them.

Lucy started to whistle as she walked down the road
thinking about the best way to slip into her father's surgery
and find the medicine for her friends.

CHAPTER 17

June, 1997

Criminal Acts

Her parents would be out shopping. They always were on Saturday mornings. Every week they climbed into their blue Ford Fiesta and drove to Sainsbury's in Streatham to do their shopping for the week. Dr Butler would drive his tense wife, stand next to her while she chose what she wanted, and wearily carry the shopping bags to the car for her. Then they would stop for lunch in the pub with the non-smoking area at Crystal Palace before returning home to unpack.

Letting herself into the house with her key, Lucy went straight to her father's surgery. It was almost identical to the one in Kentish Town she remembered from her childhood, with photos of her grandfather and great-grandfather on the wall, the huge bookcase with spellbinding medical textbooks down one side, the large mahogany desk and the locked cabinet behind it full of boxes and bottles of drugs.

As she sat down at the desk and opened the bottom right-hand drawer, a strange feeling came over her. She had done this before. She felt as though she were nine again, she could feel herself as a child, bending down like this to open her father's drawer. Indeed, the inside of the drawer was just as she remembered it, an untidy mess of letters and phials, boxes of samples and supplies handed in by patients or their families. It was her father's drug bin, that he was always meaning to clear out or lock up but never got round to doing.

Lucy walked over to the bookcase and pulled out a red catalogue. After a quick glance at the table of contents under INSOMNIA, she knew where to look for sleeping pills. Flicking through the pages she studied one page for a few minutes, then walked over to the drawer.

'Sodium amytal,' she murmured. 'Intractable insomnia. Blue capsule.' She knelt down and rummaged around in the drawer, picking up the plastic containers and reading their labels. *Norinyl. Buscopan monodral, Provera, Gestone* . . . They were all names that meant nothing to her.

'There must be some,' she murmured. Again a weird feeling of *déjà vu* enveloped her. She stood up to clear her head. She was all right; the peculiar feeling had gone.

Kneeling down again, she rummaged some more. 'Someone must use this stuff,' she murmured. Then she spotted a large grey plastic container with the name she was looking for.

'Yes!' she said aloud. Shaking the container she sensed that it was quite full, and opened it up. Blue capsules filled it nearly to the brim. She poured out a handful and counted roughly – there must be fifty in all, she thought. Lucy returned them to the container and carefully read the label: 'SODIUM AMYTAL 200 mg. One at night. Avoid alcohol.'

Lucy didn't know how many were needed, but surely there were enough there.

Her heart was thumping uncomfortably in her chest as she left the house, the container of pills tucked safely in one of the pockets of her handbag. She felt shifty as she left, fearful that the neighbours had seen her. If they did, would they report her presence to her parents when they came back? Not that it mattered any more. She had what Andrew needed now. But as she put her car into gear and drove off, she was troubled again by the old feeling of familiarity, of having behaved like this before, a long long time ago. Pushing these haunting feelings aside, she tried to concentrate on what Andrew was going to do with these pills. The events of the next few days were impossible to imagine.

Lucy drove straight to the hospital. Andrew lay listless in bed, his eyes half closed. Lucy smiled at him, proud that she could deliver what he wanted. She leaned over his bed and whispered to him, as quietly as she could, 'I've got them.' He opened his eyes and she spoke again.

'I've got what you wanted.'

Andrew's eyes lit up. He pushed himself painfully into a sitting position.

'Thank God,' he croaked. 'Thank God.' His eyes ran searchingly over Lucy's bag, as if seeking confirmation that she was telling the truth. Lucy reached into the bag and dug out the grey container, slipping it into Andrew's hand as casually as she could.

'There must be enough there,' she said. 'But you must make sure you get rid of the container, otherwise they may be able to trace them.'

Andrew nodded. 'Don't worry,' he said. 'No one's going to get into trouble for this.'

'I hope not,' replied Lucy. But she knew that the fear in her chest had nothing to do with being implicated in a crime. It had to do with what she knew the next step would be. She paused and then said, 'You will say goodbye, won't you? You won't just – just do it . . .'

Andrew looked down at his hands and picked at a fingernail. 'I don't know, Lucy.' His voice was very quiet, almost a whisper. 'I don't know if it'll be possible. I have to do what's easiest for me.'

'Yes.' Lucy could not argue with him.

Her head was still spinning with thoughts and memories stirred up by what she had just done. She longed to quiz Andrew, to ask him what he meant when he had talked about the Valentines and their father's surgery, but it seemed cruel to make him use up his precious energy thinking about something he was not concerned with. She would ask him one thing. She spoke softly.

'If you remember what happened, Andrew, years ago, why haven't you ever mentioned it?'

Andrew turned towards her with a look of surprise. 'Because I assumed you also knew what happened. You never spoke about it, so I assumed that you did not want to talk about it, and that it wasn't very important.'

Andrew reached over and took her hand. 'There's something else I need to talk to you about now, while I have the chance. I've been wanting to ask if you and Simon will organise my funeral. Patrick will be in too much of a state. Will you do that? I've chosen some tapes I want played and I've given Patrick five hundred pounds to be spent on a party afterwards. Loads of booze. I want my friends to have a spectacular time.'

Lucy fought back tears as she nodded. 'Yes.' Her voice came out as a croak. The opportunity had gone. She still did not know what Andrew knew, and she could not push him to spell it out. Now he was talking about life after his death.

'I know you'd do a really nice funeral: it won't be

impersonal like most of the ones I go to, where a priest who didn't even know "the deceased" pronounces his name wrong, and talks only in vague platitudes. And I've been to rather a lot of funerals like that in the last few years,' he added sadly. He sighed. 'But I've been to some good ones, and I want mine to be good.'

His head dropped back on the pillows. His eyes closed. 'By the way,' he said without opening his eyes, 'I've written my will. I've left almost everything to Patrick but the rest is left to you.'

'Thank you,' Lucy whispered faintly.

Brother and sister stayed in silence for a few minutes, hand in hand. Lucy knew it was time to go now, and she gave Andrew a kiss on the cheek before standing up and reaching for her bag. Impulsively, she knelt down again and gathered Andrew's thin shoulders in her arms.

'Please don't go without saying goodbye.'

Andrew pulled away, his head sagging when the emaciated neck muscles could support it no longer. He looked at Lucy with his huge, starving eyes and shook his head.

'I can't promise you that. Sorry. I'm really sorry.' He paused and smiled wryly. 'Look at it this way: George Eliot wrote somewhere that in every parting scene there is an image of death. So what difference does it make if it's real or imaginary?'

Lucy nodded, her eyes filling again with tears. There was nothing she could say.

'How long will you stay here in hospital?' she asked.

Andrew shrugged. 'It's Saturday today. I'll probably discharge myself tomorrow morning. I'm not sure . . .'

      *   *   *

Lucy travelled home on the tube without noticing anything around her. She bought her ticket, took the escalator, boarded the train and sat in a seat all the way to Shepherd's Bush station staring blindly ahead of her, all thought shocked out of her. Was what she was living now real or imaginary? Were her feelings real or imaginary? What was real, if anything, ever?

When she got home, she found Simon lying on the sofa watching the cricket on television, his long legs stretched out and crossed in front of him.

Lucy slumped down next to him and stared at the television screen.

'What's up?' Simon looked over and saw Lucy's tear-swollen face. He sat up and reached over to hug her.

'I don't think I'll ever see Andrew again,' she said quietly.

She blew her nose noisily on the handkerchief she'd been clutching all the way home, then leaned wearily on Simon's broad chest and sobbed with a deep sadness.

Later that afternoon, Lucy felt she had to talk to Andrew again. Just one more time. She might never have another chance. She telephoned the hospital and asked for Andrew's ward. When she asked to speak to him, she had to identify herself as always: in the AIDS ward, every patient had a list of people from whom they would (and would not) accept calls. After the nurse checked his list, she was put through to Andrew on the ward's mobile phone.

'Andrew, hi. It's me. I was wondering . . . if you'd thought more about your plans.'

Andrew hesitated for a moment, then said: 'I've just discharged myself. I'm just on my way home now.'

'I thought you were going to wait till tomorrow,' replied Lucy with dismay. 'Tomorrow morning, you said.'

'I decided not to hang around. There's no point.'

Lucy sat in silence, shocked by the suddenness and inevitability of it all. Then Andrew spoke again, his voice weak but clear.

'Goodbye, Lucy.'

Lucy's voice cracked as she started to cry.

'Goodbye, Andrew. I love you.' She said the final words loudly, so he couldn't fail to hear them. Then the line clicked dead and she slammed down the phone, rising at once to run into her bedroom. Throwing herself on to the bed, she hugged the pillow, screwed herself into a foetal position, and sobbed.

Lucy and Simon went out to dinner that evening, to a new local restaurant off Shepherd's Bush Road. They ordered half a bottle of white wine to start with, and toasted Andrew. When that went, they ordered another half; then a full bottle of red with their main courses; then a glass of dessert wine with their puddings. Even as drunkenness came over her in slow waves, Lucy felt acutely self-conscious. She felt as if she were acting a part in a film and being watched by millions of people. 'I am someone whose brother is at this moment killing himself. He's swallowing pills I got for him. He is killing himself while I sit here eating rack of lamb like any other customer.' She imagined Andrew swallowing the capsules, one by one. Where was he doing it? What would he be washing them down with? What was he thinking? How did it feel? Would he know what was happening, or would he just go to sleep?

And at this time tomorrow, she thought, he will be dead. My little brother will be dead.

'And just think,' she said, slurring her words as she knocked back some more wine, 'what it must be like for poor Patrick . . . It's even worse for him.'

Back home, in bed, she and Simon made love in a fumbling, drunken sort of way. Though hardly up to it, they both felt – without discussing it – an urgency that was rare for them. They wanted to affirm that they were alive, while Andrew was dying.

Lucy woke up early the next day with a throbbing headache. It took a few moments for her head to clear, for her to remember what had happened the night before. When she did, a slow pain spread through her. Now she was wide awake. She wanted to ring Patrick immediately, but it was only seven o'clock. She had to make herself wait.

First she took a long, hot shower, then she put on the kettle and made a pot of coffee. She went out to Mehmet's shop to buy croissants and the newspapers, both of which the thoughtful shopkeeper sold on Sundays. She exchanged greetings with Mehmet, trying to sound as normal as she could. Mehmet could tell from the dazed look in her eyes that something was wrong, but it was not for him to comment.

Back home, Simon was still sleeping heavily. She flicked through the papers without registering any of their contents, and folded them up for Simon.

She noticed that the cooker needed cleaning, so she went at it with a Brillo pad and warm water. When that was done, she cleared out some clothes she'd been meaning for months to give to Oxfam. Anything to make herself busy, and to keep her hands away from the telephone.

Finally, at eleven thirty, just as Simon hauled himself out of bed and started to take a shower, she thought it was time. She could wait no longer. With her heart racing, she dialled

Andrew's number. The machine was on, his voice singing out as usual. Lucy hung up without leaving a message.

Two hours later she tried again. This time she left a message.

'Patrick, I, it's Lucy. I'm just . . .'

She was broken off in mid-sentence by a click, then by Patrick's voice on the line.

'Lucy,' he said. His voice was grave and heavy.

'He's dead, isn't he? Andrew's dead . . .'

'No he's not,' replied Patrick. He sounded worried. 'He took the pills last night, around eight o'clock. We had a wonderful evening together. We put candles all around the bedroom and put on some music. Then we drank some champagne and said our goodbyes. Then he took the pills. He took them all, one by one. I sat with him till he fell asleep, then I snuggled up beside him and fell asleep myself.

'But I don't think they've worked. When I woke up this morning, I expected to find him dead beside me, but he seemed the same. He just seems to be in a very deep sleep . . .'

'It probably takes a long time,' replied Lucy. But her words sounded false even to her. She could hardly believe that she was trying to act calm in these circumstances.

'I just don't understand it,' said Patrick. 'He took *thirty pills* – enough to kill a bloody horse! This is terrible, just terrible. He was so brave . . .'

'I don't think you should be there, Patrick. Just think what would happen if people knew you were with him after he'd taken the pills, and had done nothing about calling an ambulance or a doctor or anything. You could get into terrible trouble.'

'I don't care,' replied Patrick. 'What could be more

terrible than what we've been through already? I want to
be with him. I can't leave him.'

'But I really think you should,' said Lucy. 'At least go
out for a while. Go for a walk, stay away for a few hours.
Maybe when you come back, maybe then it will all be over.
Then you'll be able to say you found him like that. You
must, Patrick. Andrew doesn't want you to be in trouble.
And what you're doing now is definitely illegal.'

Patrick suddenly seemed worried. 'Do you think so?'

'I really do. Just go out for a few hours. Please. Then give
me a ring when you get back. It's bound to be over by then.'

At eight that evening, the phone rang again. When she
heard Patrick's voice, Lucy was frightened but relieved at
the same time. Now, she thought, she could collapse.

But the worry in Patrick's voice made her realise that
something was still wrong.

'I've just come in,' he said. 'Andrew's still breathing.
And I think, I think he's waking up. He's moving about
now, his legs and arms. Those fucking pills didn't work. I
can't believe it.'

'We're coming over,' said Lucy. She hung up the phone
and told Simon what was happening, and they got into the
car. Simon's hands were trembling as he steered through
the twilit streets.

Patrick answered the bell almost instantly, his face white
and drawn. They followed Patrick up the stairs to the
bedroom.

Andrew was lying on the bed, naked under a sheet. He
was in a deep sleep but breathing loudly, in great gasps.
His legs and arms twitched and his body and face were in
constant movement.

'Oh my God,' whispered Lucy. 'He's surfacing.'

Patrick started to cry. 'What shall we do?' he moaned.

'What if he's brain-damaged? Oh, what a cock-up. Oh, he was so brave. Jesus, what can we do? Perhaps we should stick a plastic bag over his head, before it's too late. He doesn't want to wake up. He doesn't want to live!' He was panicking.

Simon stepped forward. 'No, that would just make things worse. That would be murder.'

Lucy was relieved to see how readily Simon took charge, to make decisions, for she certainly could not. 'I think we should call the doctor,' continued Simon, 'just to cover ourselves. Otherwise we could all find ourselves in trouble.'

'But the doctor will want him back in hospital!' said Patrick. 'He'll want his stomach pumped. And we'll still get into trouble!'

'That's probably a risk we just have to take,' replied Simon. 'We'll just have to make something up.'

The doctor came out straightaway. He was a young GP who knew Patrick and Andrew well. At first they told him they had just discovered Andrew like this when they returned home after a drink in the pub, but then, after the doctor had given Andrew a brief examination, and picked up the telephone to call an ambulance, Patrick could not restrain himself.

'Oh, please don't call the ambulance,' he begged. 'He wants to die. He's taken a whole load of sleeping pills. He's in constant misery. He's going blind, he's got chronic diarrhoea, he's covered with KS, and he's had enough. It'd be cruel to send him back to hospital – he's just discharged himself, and he did this so he wouldn't have to die there. He wants to die before it gets any worse . . .'

The trio looked pleadingly at the doctor.

'Please,' Patrick begged. 'Please don't make him have to suffer any more.'

To their relief, the doctor relented. He had seen too many of his young patients die of AIDS to be unaware of how horrible the end could be.

'Well,' he said, 'let's make him as comfortable as we can. And hope there's no damage done as a result of the overdose. It looks as if he's close to surfacing anyway. I suspect that his body just didn't absorb the drug.'

Lucy and Simon stayed the night, dozing next door through the early hours of the morning as Andrew's body fought off the effects of the sodium amytal, attended to by the gentle doctor and Patrick. His soiled sheets confirmed the doctor's quiet guess that Andrew's chronic intestinal condition had caused the capsules to shoot through his body, giving it no chance to absorb toxic levels of the drug.

At six o'clock, Andrew became conscious. At first he was confused about where he was and what had happened, but gradually his head cleared and by eight o'clock, he had worked out what had happened. His suicide attempt had failed. He was overwhelmed by the thought, and deeply distraught. He wept uncontrollably.

Lucy felt so ashamed she could hardly bear to look at Andrew. She had let him down. He had put his life in her hands with the unquestioning faith of a little brother. And she had failed him.

Once the doctor had checked all Andrew's reflexes and made sure the drugs had caused no damage, he gave him a sedative to make him sleep.

Lucy went down to the kitchen. She stood at the counter making a pot of coffee, tears streaming down her face. On the kitchen table were three CDs and a scrap of paper with her name on it. She picked up the CDs – Mozart's *Requiem*, a Cat Stevens collection, and a band called the Gypsy Kings which she had heard once or twice. The note told her which tracks Andrew wanted played at his funeral, and which of his friends had said they would read poetry. He had written their telephone numbers next to the names but there was no other message.

Patrick sat on a chair by the window with his head in his hands. He was crying and kept shaking his head. 'I can't believe this has happened. Oh, God, we should have finished him off, for his own sake. Now he's got to go through it all again . . .

CHAPTER 18

August, 1968

The Task

By the time Lucy reached home, the words on the piece of paper Vita had handed her were ringing in her head like a chant: minims atropine, minims atropine, minims atropine.

She had no idea what kind of drug it was or what the girls could possibly want it for but she had the uncomfortable feeling that their purpose was not what their father would have called noble.

In spite of her concern and her hurt feelings at being doubted, she still so much wanted to prove that she was one of them, that she was as brave, as naughty, as fearless as any Valentine. She would find this drug and get it to them. She would show that they were wrong, that she could do it.

It had to be done that evening, too. Lucy knew she had to do it soon or she might miss the opportunity, and she had to do it fast because she could not bear even the thought of failure.

After supper her parents settled down to listen to a play on the radio in the sitting room upstairs. Confident that they would not be moving from their armchairs for at least half an hour, Lucy crept downstairs and let herself into her father's surgery.

It smelled, as it always did, of surgical spirit. The sharp smell made her nostrils curl. The door shut behind her with a soft click, and she walked straight over to her father's large desk.

'Minims atropine,' she muttered, pulling open the bottom drawer on the right.

The drawer was packed, as ever, with containers of all shapes and sizes. Many of them were unused pills handed in by patients, and many samples of amphetamines, sleeping pills, the contraceptive pill, anything and everything, sent to GPs by the drugs companies in the hope that they would prescribe them instead of the competition.

Lucy picked each one up, scrutinised the label, dropped it. She rummaged some more, looking, reading, scanning the labels, dropping and rummaging. Her heart was beating fast and she could feel a frightening panic rising up inside her. Time was running out. She could not find anything with the words 'minims atropine' on it. Her fingers moved with increasing urgency.

She was sweating. Her hands were clammy with perspiration as she became aware of the loud ticking of the clock on the mantelpiece. The ticking seemed to bore into her head. She tried to control the panic rising in her at the thought of the radio play drawing to an end. She had ten minutes left. This was ridiculous! Where was this drug? It had to be here somewhere. Vita said it was here, and her father could not have used it since Vita had looked inside the drawer. He never actually used any of the drugs in this drawer; the drugs he did administer, he kept in his black doctor's bag or in the locked drugs cabinet behind the desk. Perhaps she could find some there! The drugs were not in the bag. She had to look in the cabinet.

She knew where the key was. Pulling open the middle drawer of the desk, she lifted out a small key on a red cord.

Her fingers trembled as she slipped the key into the lock and opened the cupboard. In contrast to the muddle of the drugs in his drawer, the cupboard was, thanks to Hilda Butler, methodically organised, with all the drugs placed in alphabetical order with neat labels on the shelf beneath.

It took just a moment for her eyes to run along the names. She let out a gasp of relief as her gaze settled on the now familiar words, minims atropine. 'Yes!' she exclaimed. 'There it is!'

There were four bottles. One would not be missed. She grabbed one bottle and placed it on the desk while she swiftly shut and locked the doors to the cabinet.

As she turned the key in the lock, she gave a jump of fright as she heard the surgery door click open. She turned, and her heart thumped as the door began to open. Surely she was in big trouble now! The blood drained from her head as she stood, terrified, waiting to see who it was.

Then she dropped her shoulders and sniffed. 'Oh, it's you,' she said with annoyed relief as her little brother's tousled brown curls appeared around the door.

'What are you doing?' Andrew asked. 'What are you doing here, Lucy?'

Lucy turned her back on him. 'Never you mind. It's none of your business,' she snapped, in the sort of tone that Vita used when talking to the Brat. She dropped the key back into the middle drawer of the desk.

'I don't want you here,' she said bossily. 'Get out, quickly.

You know we're not allowed in here. You'll get us both into trouble.'

But Andrew was not going to be deterred. 'What are you doing?' He had spotted the bottle on the desk. He walked over to her. 'What's that? Why are you taking that?'

Lucy was feeling extremely agitated and annoyed. 'Stop asking questions!'

But Andrew persisted. 'Tell me what you're doing and I'll stop asking,' he said quietly. 'What are you going to do with this medicine?' He picked up the bottle and held it up to his face to examine the label.

Lucy snatched it from him. 'Stop it!' She hissed the words at him. 'Get out of here!'

'Just tell me what it's for.' Andrew paused and lowered his voice. 'Or I'll tell Mum and Dad what you're doing.'

He had trapped her.

Lucy hesitated as Andrew continued to stare at her through determined narrowed eyes. She could tell that he meant it. He would tell, not really out of malice but just to show that he would not tolerate being excluded from an interesting secret.

'Okay,' she said, giving in. 'I don't know what it's for. I've just been told to get it for Vita and Perdita.'

Andrew nodded. 'Oh,' he said. 'Okay.' He grinned and turned on his heels. 'I wonder what they want it for,' he mused.

He walked to the door and peered out. 'Okay, you're in the clear,' he whispered. As he walked out, he stopped and turned again. 'I won't say anything,' he said. 'Promise.'

Lucy forced a smile. She did trust her little brother to keep his word but she would rather that he had not caught her in the first place.

'Thanks, Andrew,' she said softly. 'I'll do the same for you someday.'

He nodded. 'I'll remember.' He pointed to the piece of paper lying on the desk. 'By the way,' he said with a conspiratorial grin, 'don't forget to destroy that note.'

Lucy quickly picked up the note and stuffed it into her pocket. Giving the room a quick check to see that everything was as it had been before, she followed Andrew out of the surgery and shut the door quietly.

Later, upstairs in her room, she tore the note into tiny pieces which she threw into the wastepaper basket.

The next morning, immediately after breakfast, Lucy ran as fast as she could up Lady Margaret Road to the Valentines'. Letting herself in through the side gate, she ran through to the back garden.

Vita was doing handstands on the grass.

Lucy laughed with proud glee as she announced her success to Vita. 'I've got it! I've got it!'

Vita landed gracefully on her feet and looked around warily. 'Good.' She spoke softly. 'But don't take it out now. We'll go inside. You can give it to me then.

'We're going to visit our aunt this morning, so you can't stay. Maybe you'd like to come and play tomorrow.'

Upstairs in Vita's bedroom, Lucy handed over the booty. She could hear Olwyn calling the children to hurry up and get ready as the taxis would be arriving at any moment to whisk them all off to Hampstead to see their aunt.

Lucy knew that she had to leave. She was not welcome in that chaotic frenzy. She saw Perdita run by excitedly. Perdita raised a thumb at Lucy as if to congratulate her on succeeding with her mission, but she did not stop to talk.

She was too busy brushing her sleek black hair while at the same time looking for a clean pair of socks.

Lucy let herself out of the house and walked slowly down the hill. She felt unwanted in that atmosphere and a sudden sadness dragged her down. If she could admit it, she was hurt that Vita and Perdita had not praised her more for her daring feat. They had barely thanked her, let alone congratulated her properly.

She frowned. Trying to push back the feelings of disappointment, she focused on her achievement. Tomorrow, when she went up to play, Vita and Perdita would praise her and thank her, and tell her that she was not, after all, a goody-goody. In their rush to visit their aunt, they just did not have the time today.

Lucy did not go to play at the Valentines' house the next day. The death in the night prevented that.

The Butlers were eating their supper. Dr Butler was entertaining his family telling them about an emergency call he had received that afternoon. A worried father, left on his own with his three-year-old while his wife was still in hospital after giving birth to a second child, had called Dr Butler out at tea time.

'He said his daughter had suddenly started to stagger about and fall over for no obvious reason. When I examined the little girl, I discovered that she had both legs through only one hole in her pants! The poor child could barely move. She'd been dressing and undressing herself all afternoon, and ended up behaving as if she had cerebral palsy.'

As he chuckled at the story, the telephone rang. It was for him. There was an emergency at the Valentine house.

'What's happened?' Lucy frowned anxiously at her father.

'I don't know yet.' Dr Butler pulled on his jacket. 'Someone's ill. A child. I have to leave immediately.'

Lucy tried to stay awake that night but at ten thirty, when her father had still not returned, her eyelids closed and she gave way to sleep.

The next morning Dr Butler was already up at breakfast when Lucy came downstairs. Her mother was clearing up. Andrew sat at the table reading the back of the cereal packets.

'What happened?' She was terrified that something bad had happened to her friends. 'Who's ill?'

Dr Butler buttered his toast and spread his wife's home-made marmalade on top.

'Everything's all right,' he said calmly. 'It's young David, the housekeeper's boy. He's had a nasty dose of scarlet fever. I thought he'd be all right at home but after a while I thought it safer to send him to hospital. I called an ambulance at about midnight.

'I'm about to telephone the hospital now to find out how he is.'

Lucy spread marmalade on her toast and took a bite. She heard her father in the hall, talking to someone at the hospital. The confident tone of his voice suddenly changed to one of alarm. The murmuring stopped. Lucy then heard a click as her father replaced the receiver on the hook. Then there was silence.

A few seconds later, her father walked back into the kitchen. His face was ashen.

Hilda dried her hands and ran over to him. 'Whatever's wrong? Has something happened?'

Dr Butler shook his head and sat down heavily at the table. He slumped down, his head in his hands.

'The boy's dead,' he said quietly, his voice cracking. 'He died on his way to hospital. He was dead on arrival.'

He stared at the table. His hands gripped his head. 'It seems that I made the wrong diagnosis. The boy probably did not have scarlet fever at all. They're doing a postmortem.'

'What's a postmortem?' Andrew sounded bright and cheerful in the gloomy atmosphere.

'It's when they look at a dead body to find out exactly why that person died,' Hilda replied impatiently.

Dr Butler's face was still white. He kept shaking his head in disbelief, and in his mind he went over and over the symptoms he had seen – the hot dry skin, the rash, the temperature, the quickened pulse, the reddened fauces. They were all the symptoms of scarlet fever. 'This can't be happening, it can't be . . .'

He turned to his wife. Lucy was shocked to see tears in her father's eyes. Never in her life had she seen a man cry.

'What's worse is that my diagnosis delayed matters. I should have sent him to hospital straight away instead of waiting. They might have been able to save him. I thought he had scarlet fever, I was sure of it. My delay made matters worse.'

Lucy's toast had formed a hard lump in her mouth. She was unable to swallow but she did not dare spit it out.

The next day, Vita Valentine rang Lucy. She sounded very cheerful on the telephone and did not say anything about David. 'Would you like to come to play this afternoon?' she chirruped. 'We've got some delicious biscuits for tea. Perdita and I made them this morning while Olwyn was out.'

The Valentine house was unusually quiet when Lucy got there.

'What's happened?' Lucy asked. 'What happened to David?'

Perdita looked at her with her large cool eyes. 'He died,' she said flatly.

'Yes, but do you know how?' Lucy was desperate for knowledge.

Perdita shrugged. 'No one seems to know,' she said airily. 'He was a pest, anyway.'

'Yes,' agreed Vita. 'A real brat.'

The Valentine girls made it clear to Lucy that even if they did know more than they let on, they would not divulge it to her. She did not feel at home and she did not stay long enough to eat the freshly baked biscuits. Her throat felt hot and dry. She felt a headache coming on and left the house feeling unhappy and excluded.

Her throat was getting more sore by the minute. She walked down the hill towards her house with her head down. The Valentine girls had not included her. In spite of what she had done for them, they would not share their secrets with her. She felt painfully shut out and used.

A postmortem a few days later revealed that David had died of atropine sulphate poisoning. There are few characteristics of atropine sulphate poisoning but what confirmed the diagnosis was the continued dilatation of the boy's pupils.

Dr Butler was required to attend the inquest. The coroner was told that the Valentine children had informed the police that David had been boasting of stealing medicine from the doctor's black bag when he had paid a home visit to Mrs Valentine a few weeks before. It seems that for several days the boy was experimenting with the eye drops to make his pupils dilate. Then somehow, the child managed to swallow a fatal dose of the drug and inadvertently poisoned himself.

It was a terrible tragedy that people spoke about in the pubs and shops of Kentish Town for weeks afterwards. Some talked with sympathy about the doctor's mistake, he was not to be blamed. Apparently, the symptoms of atropine poisoning are not dissimilar to those of scarlet fever. Others were not so generous. They changed their doctor and did not talk to Mrs Butler when they met in the butcher's.

Hilda was mortified. She knew that they had to move and urged her husband to look for another practice elsewhere. Dr Butler was glad to have a project to work on, to keep his thoughts away from the terrible thing he had done. But every now and then, at night as he lay in bed, trying to fight off the guilt and remorse, there would be something nagging him, something that made him know that the tragedy was linked to something else in his life. He had had a conversation at some point with someone, about atropine but he could not for the life of him remember when.

It would be many years before he did.

Lucy missed all these happenings. Her sore throat developed into tonsillitis which kept her in bed for a week. Then it was the end of the holidays and suddenly her parents were planning to move to south London. Lucy was taken for an interview at a school in Dulwich which took her on as a pupil that September.

When she rang up Vita to say goodbye, her friend was out. In spite of Lucy's message, Vita did not return the call. Lucy did not see the Valentine girls again.

CHAPTER 19

July, 1997

Paradise Lost

Slowly patches of memory filtered up to the surface. They were like dreams, uncontrollable thoughts, but they came in the day. They came while Lucy was lying in the bath or walking down the high street to do her shopping. They came as she cooked supper or watched the news or read the newspaper. Something would trigger the memories, new ones each time, and gradually a clear picture emerged.

Lucy began to remember details she had forgotten for years. She recalled the telephone ringing while they were sitting down to their supper that night, and her father being called out on an emergency at the Valentines'. She remembered trying to stay awake until her father came home but finally giving way to sleep, only to be told in the morning that it was the housekeeper's boy, David, who was ill. She remembered the sense of calm, of feeling proud that once again her father, the doctor, had made someone better.

Then there was a shift, a change in the atmosphere. It was all going wrong. Her father was talking in the hall. His face was ashen as he came back into the kitchen where they were having breakfast. Lucy was eating her toast and marmalade.

Andrew was reading the back of the Rice Krispies packet. Dr Butler appeared in the doorway and said that David was dead.

Lucy could see it all now, as if it were yesterday – her mother's look of alarm, the frightened eyes, the dropped jaw. Something terrible had happened. Something had gone wrong. Then there was the hushed conversation between the adults, her parents talking in tense voices behind closed doors.

There was also the silence in the Valentines' house the last time she went there, and the unhappy sense of exclusion she felt from the girls who were supposed to be her friends.

There was more that she remembered from a distance but which she would never be able to put into words. She recalled being ill with a high temperature and burning tonsils, and lying in bed for a week.

She was aware that what had happened to David was her father's mistake. It was his misdiagnosis that was the cause of David's death. And she recalled now that it was soon afterwards that the Butlers moved away from Kentish Town to what seemed a new life in Dulwich, south of the river. She could not remember talking to the Valentine girls again. The holidays were over, school took precedence, and the Butlers moved.

While his daughter could recall certain details about that incident, she did not, could not, know the true extent of Dr Butler's shame and mortification at his fatal misdiagnosis. He was crushed by a decision of his that had resulted in a child's death.

For her part, his wife was even more ashamed of her husband's failing. Until then she had idealised him, believing that his status as a doctor – and, consequently, her status too – would enjoy a relentless and splendid growth, like the march of progress through history. Then his error, his stupid error, had brought gossip and glances from the very people whose respect she craved.

Lucy did not know that that incident had changed for ever the balance within her parents' marriage. Hilda Butler had always been the stronger personality but she had admired her husband for the respect he commanded and for his medical knowledge. After David's death, she continued to be the dominant one in the relationship but she no longer felt admiration: she only felt shame and despair. And deep down, though she did not know it, she despised her husband.

For his part, Dr Butler accepted his wife's scorn and whipped himself with it. He was happy to go along with her decision to move away. He was lucky to be able to take over a small practice in Dulwich and start afresh, with patients who knew nothing about what had happened. He withdrew from family life and allowed Hilda to take over. He did not have any friends who could slap him on the back and say that everyone makes mistakes, that all doctors have memories of decisions they regret. He did not have anyone like that. All he had to go on was his wife's response and the curious looks from his patients for those strained weeks after the boy's death and the postmortem. It was not surprising that he was relieved to move away.

Lucy did not know then the extent of the damage done to her father and to her parents' marriage but she was aware of some of it now. She could see the link, she could see now what Andrew had always seen, she could see that she was responsible.

She could always remember that David had died – she had been reminded of that when she first met Perdita again – but it had never occurred to her that the drugs she had delivered so faithfully to her friends had been used to kill the child. She, Lucy, had thus been responsible for that boy's death. She had also been responsible for ruining her father's life.

Lucy did not say anything to Simon about these revelations and memories that haunted her. On their visits to Andrew, whose condition was deteriorating fast, they talked only about her brother.

Lucy wanted to talk about what she had done, and the consequences of her actions. She felt an urgent need to talk it all out, but it was not to be with Simon. She had to meet the memory head on, and the only way to do that was to talk about it with Vita herself. It was Vita who had caused Lucy to act as she did, Vita and her sister. Lucy had to pick up from where she had left their conversation all those years ago to confirm these terrible recollections.

Lucy telephoned a surprised and wary Vita and arranged to meet her that weekend.

They met on Hampstead Heath where, Vita said, her daughters liked to ride their bicycles. It was a blustery day and the wind whipped their hair around their faces as the women walked side by side along the tarmac path that cut across the green expanse.

The two girls rode ahead on their brightly coloured bicycles, laughing and shouting at each other.

Vita looked unworried. Her dark eyes gazed steadily off into the distance.

'I'm not here to talk about Simon,' Lucy said finally.

Vita looked at her quickly. 'I'm not interested in taking him from you,' she said hastily. 'You have to believe that.'

'I do,' replied Lucy. She stuck her hands in her pockets. Her jeans felt uncomfortably tight, as if she had put on weight recently. All this stress must be making her eat

more than usual, she thought. And so preoccupied she had
not even noticed.

'But I don't want to talk about that,' she repeated. 'It was
a cruel and disloyal thing to do, particularly since you knew
that we've been having trouble starting a family. But I'm
prepared to believe that it wasn't a serious thing for you. I
think that it was a one-off and I'm prepared to forget about
it. Honestly.

'What I *do* want to talk about,' she went on, 'is David.
Olwyn's son. The Brat, the boy who died. I want to talk to
you about what happened to him.'

Vita nodded. What looked like a whimsical smile appeared
on her lips, as if she had been expecting this to come up
one day.

'I see.' They took a few more steps together, then Vita
stopped and faced Lucy. 'What do you want to know?'

'I want to know what happened to him,' repeated Lucy.
'I want the truth. I think you and Perdita poisoned him.
You made me get the drugs and then you poisoned him
with them. Please tell me exactly how you did it. And—'
she paused and drew a deep breath, 'I want to know why.'
She looked at Vita challengingly, her heart beating hard in
her chest. Was this going to work?

To Lucy's relief, after staring back at her for a moment or
two, Vita dropped her gaze and nodded assent. She seemed
happy to talk, and Lucy knew that she was going to tell
the truth.

'I don't know if we really meant to kill him,' she said. 'It
started out as kind of a joke, really. We thought we could
play a good trick on him, just make him a bit ill. Then,
somehow, it got serious . . .'

Lucy stared at her, her heart beating fast with anticipation.
Vita was happy to talk about it.

'Once when I came round to tea,' Vita continued, 'you showed me your father's drawer where all the drugs were kept. It gave me an idea about something I had been thinking about anyway.

'Then another time I came over, I saw a copy of that drugs directory – what's it called – that your father had thrown away. Presumably he'd got a new copy and didn't need the old one any more. So I picked it up out of the bin and slipped it in my pocket while no one was looking.'

'You mean MIMS.'

'That's right. The Monthly Index for Medical Specialties, the prescribing guide for doctors. It was sent free to doctors once a month.

'Well, I took it home and we studied it, Perdita and I. Then one afternoon, we went down to Foyle's bookshop with Anthony. He often liked to spend Saturday afternoons browsing through bookshops. While he was looking at the history books, Perdita and I nipped downstairs to the medical books department, the toxicology section, to read some proper medical texts about poisons and their effects. It was a usefully spent two hours.

'Then, back home, with the MIMS, we were able to pick out a drug that contained atropine sulphate. It's a derivative of deadly nightshade – belladonna. All portions of the plant – the roots, seeds, leaves and fruit – are toxic. If put on the skin, atropine gets absorbed into the body very quickly. The best drug containing atropine, we decided, was one called minims atropine, which is used in drops to treat various eye conditions. If you take it on your eye it's harmless but if it gets into a cut, say, enough can be absorbed to cause death. So we knew that if it was swallowed in large doses, it could kill you. Not that we meant to kill the Brat. We just wanted to make him good and ill. Give him a shock.

'Anyway, we guessed that your father, being a family doctor, would probably have the eye drops in his surgery – possibly even in his drugs drawer. We didn't know for sure, but we thought it'd be worth trying to ask you to get it for us. We could hardly believe our luck when you actually turned up with it.

'That same evening we gave it to him. Olwyn was out. I can't remember what she was doing. Probably collecting one of the younger ones from a friend's house, or something. While she was out, we tricked the Brat into swallowing the whole lot in a glass of chocolate Nesquik – he was always drinking that stuff. We dared him to drink a huge glass, and made a joke that it was poisoned. But he wouldn't believe us. He drank the whole lot in about three gulps. And then,' she paused for a moment, 'he began to have convulsions, within minutes. It was weird. I'll never forget it, seeing the effects work so quickly. At first, he became cheerful and lively – I can still see all this so vividly in my head. He kept dancing around my bedroom and laughing hysterically. He got more and more excited until it was obvious that he was out of control. He was desperately thirsty and kept drinking out of the bath tap and falling about in uncontrollable fits of laughter. He had a sort of ghost-like energy which took him over.

'It was very frightening. Perdita and I did not know what to do. He began to hallucinate. He kept saying that the shape of the bed was changing and the colours were different. He seemed to go completely mad. We had no idea of what to do or what was going to happen, and at that point we were scared, really scared about what we had done.

'Luckily, by the time Olwyn came home, the Brat had calmed down and become quieter. But by then also he had a raging temperature and his skin had gone all red.

'We decided to run and tell Olwyn that David was ill, and she took one look at him and immediately telephoned for your father to come to the house. Olwyn hadn't seen David being delirious and we didn't say anything about it, so she had no idea about how serious it was. We thought the worst of it was over and that he'd recover.

'Your father didn't know about the delirium either, and we didn't tell him. By the time your father had arrived, the Brat was very calm. He had a bright red rash, his skin was hot and dry and his pulse rate had quickened. Not unreasonably, I gather – and luckily for us – your father decided that the boy was having an attack of scarlet fever. The symptoms are not dissimilar to what he was seeing. He made the fatal mistake of waiting to see what happened. He waited an hour, sitting downstairs having a cup of tea with Olwyn. When he saw him again, the Brat was beginning to get drowsy. Your father was uncertain at first but then he decided it would be safer to have him admitted to hospital. He called an ambulance and went home.

'Olwyn went in the ambulance with him. She said that it was on the way to hospital that it was obvious that David was dangerously ill. His temperature dropped and he slipped into a coma. By the time he got to hospital, he was dead.

'The cause of death came out in the postmortem afterwards. Your father had got it wrong, and the doctors knew that the Brat had died from poisoning.

'At first Perdita and I thought we'd be found out but we made up a story and stuck to it: we told everyone that the Brat had stolen the drugs from the doctor's black bag. We told them that he'd been experimenting with it and that he'd swallowed the stuff himself.'

Vita's children had reached the top of Parliament Hill. They stopped and waved to their mother. Vita waved back.

The two women climbed on up the steep hill after the girls. There was silence between them but Vita's words were ringing in Lucy's ears. The children turned and began to cycle off towards the green copse beyond. The women were puffing from the climb.

Lucy turned to Vita. 'You didn't have to tell me the whole truth, did you?'

Vita shrugged. 'No, I didn't.'

'So why did you, if you're incriminating yourself like this?'

Vita turned to look at her. 'Because you wanted to know the truth and I happen to know that you won't spill the beans. At least, that's what Perdita reckons.'

Lucy's thoughts were racing back all those years. She struggled to think straight as the underlying meaning of that last remark became clear. 'You didn't actually know if that particular drug was in my father's drawer, did you?'

'No.' Vita rubbed her eyes. 'That was just a lucky guess.' She paused and then added, 'If that's the right word.'

Lucy fell silent once again. She could not say now that she had not, in fact, found them in the drawer at all. She could not bring herself to say that she had opened up her father's locked drugs cupboard and taken the supply from there.

Now she felt even more implicated; she was as guilty as Vita and Perdita. This was what Andrew meant.

'You talk about it in a very matter-of-fact way,' she commented. 'The boy died. You and your sister killed him. Don't you think it was wrong? Don't you feel guilty?'

Vita turned to look at her. Her eyes were clear and steady. 'We didn't mean to kill him, I told you that. It just happened that way.' Her voice was flat and expressionless, as if she were describing a soufflé that had failed to rise or a business deal that had fallen through. 'Perhaps it was unfortunate that he died, I don't know. But I do know that I wasn't sorry then and I'm not sorry now. And neither is Perdita.

'I suppose,' she went on, 'the difference now is that I can see we weren't really angry with the Brat. It was Olwyn we hated. But we didn't dare admit that at the time, not even to ourselves. I suppose you could say that the Brat died for his mother's sins.

'But whether it was wrong – I don't know. Deep down, I feel that we did the right thing. After all, it had the right effect: we got rid of the Brat and of Olwyn, in the end. She left soon after the Brat died. Went back to Wales, and good riddance! She hated us and we hated her.'

Expression came into Vita's voice only as she spoke those final words.

'Why?' wailed Lucy. 'What did you do to make her hate you so much?'

Vita let out a scornful laugh, full of bitterness.

'What did *we* do? Christ, you don't know anything about what happened to us. Not a single goddamned thing.'

'Then tell me,' pleaded Lucy. 'Help me understand this.'

Vita looked straight at her and said, 'It's not what *we* did, it's what *she* did. That bitch Olwyn. What *didn't* she do to us? But you wouldn't believe it if I told you.' Her voice went soft for a moment but then she thrust out her chin and looked straight at Lucy. 'But it did happen,' she went on. 'Every bit of it.'

'Tell me,' Lucy ordered. 'What happened? Tell me now.'

Vita stared at her, her eyes wild, and shook her head fiercely. 'I can't tell you, I'm sorry. It's impossible for me to tell you.'

To her surprise, as Lucy looked at Vita she felt a great surge of rage build up inside her. Gritting her teeth, she gripped Vita by the arm and shook her. 'You *have* to tell me!' She shouted the words. 'You've ruined a lot of lives. You owe it to me to tell me, you bitch!'

Startled by her own outburst, Lucy let go of Vita's arm and stepped back. 'I'm sorry,' she said, dropping her voice. 'I didn't mean to be vicious.'

But to her surprise, Vita nodded her head. 'You're right, Lucy,' she said, 'I do owe it to you even if it's difficult for me. I shall suffer for weeks for stirring up the memories again, just when I had them under control.' Her voice was soft and sad. 'But I want you to understand everything now, so I don't have a choice.'

Vita turned away towards her children, waving to them cheerily. But Lucy could see that her shoulders were shaking, and the hand by her side was closed into a tight fist. She was silent for a moment, her mind swarming with questions and confusions. Finally she turned to Vita and put a hand gently on her shoulder.

'Tell me,' she said quietly. 'Tell me what happened. I'll believe you, I promise I will.'

They had reached the brow of the hill. Vita quickened her pace and strode on. They could see the girls in the distance, two small dots of colour against the grey-green of the wood.

'Only my siblings know about this. They all know it from their own perspectives, but the outside world is ignorant. We don't even talk about it among ourselves very much because it's so difficult to deal with the memories and to think about what they all mean.'

Then Vita began to talk about her childhood and, as she talked, in her low husky voice, Lucy felt a clammy chill settle over her skin. It was what she had known and what she had not known. It was what had a silent presence in that big Victorian villa all that time ago. Lucy had always been aware of it but did not know what it was until now.

The child is dreaming, unsettled dreams but not frightening. Then someone is shaking her.

'*Wake up! Wake up!*'

The child surfaces from her deep sleep. She can feel strong fingers clutching her upper arm, pulling her up from the bed.

'*What's the matter? What's happened?*' *The child blinks in the bright light of the overhead bulb.*

The voice is matter-of-fact. Sharp.

'*The police are here. They've taken fingerprints on the boiler. They have discovered that they're yours. They know now that you keep turning up the boiler to a dangerous level. They've come to arrest you before you set fire to the house.*'

The child shrinks back into the pillow. Her face crumples as she begins to cry. She clutches the woman's arm. '*I didn't do anything. Oh, please don't let them take me away . . .*'

The woman shakes her head. '*It's no good. They know it's you. They've taken fingerprints.*'

The child is panicking. She sobs and clutches the woman's clothes. '*Please, please don't let them take me away,*' *she begs.*

The woman pauses. She disengages the child's hands and steps back.

'*Let me go and talk to them. Wait a minute. I'll be back.*'

The child sinks down under the covers and squeezes her eyes shut as she prays.

The woman is gone for ages. The child waits and waits. She can feel her heart thumping rapidly in her chest. Any minute now, she will know if she's going to prison or not.

Then the woman returns. She is smiling. The child sits up, anxious, hopeful.

'I've persuaded them to go away. They say they'll forget it this time. But if it happens again, they'll be back.'

The child leaps to her feet and cries with relief. 'Oh, thank you,' she cries, kissing the woman's hand in desperate gratitude. 'Thank you so much!'

The woman strokes the child's hair. 'That's all right, now,' she croons gently. 'Now get into bed or you'll be too tired for school tomorrow.'

The child snuggles down in bed. 'Good night,' she calls. 'And thank you for ever.'

'Olwyn had complete control over us,' Vita began. 'You see, our parents were too wrapped up in themselves and their work and their causes to notice what was going on behind the scenes at home. As far as they were concerned, so long as we didn't disturb their work we could do what we liked. What they didn't realise was that Olwyn came to control us so much that she did whatever she wanted. And she terrorised us.'

The child lies in the dark, unable to sleep. She thinks about her spelling test the next day and wonders whether the weather will be good enough for tennis. She listens to the sounds of the house. Her parents are out, as usual. The television is on downstairs in the den. Outside she hears a car door slam and a motorbike roar up the road. From her bed she can see the occasional flicker of her sister's torch as she reads her book under the bedclothes. It is an hour past lights-out. The house hums with familiar noises, the comforting screech of the water in the pipes, the gentle rattle of the wind against the windowpanes.

Then there is something else! The child holds her breath. Now she does hear the creak of the stairs. Is it the woman? The child tries to hold her breath more. She's trying to listen but all she can hear is the rush of blood in her ears.

Another creak. Silence. A long pause. There is nothing there. No, she always has time to warn her sister. The noises are something else.

But now she does hear quick steps on the stairs.

The child sits up in bed, startled. It is the woman. It's too late to call out a whispered warning. Too late . . .

She listens to the hurried steps, the sharp warnings, the thump, thump of a hard object on the bed. A hard object landing on bony knees under the covers.

Shrinking down under her own bedcovers, the child lays her head on the pillow and watches the woman pass her doorway, the brass poker glinting in her hand. Now she is gone. The child lies still, her open eyes sparkling with fear in the dark. No sound comes from her sister's room. The house is silent.

Vita's voice had dropped to a whisper. 'I can see now how Olwyn got so much power and how she abused that power. I can understand it as an adult, and be appalled, but at the time it just seemed normal for us children to be looked after by someone like that. This is the most awful thing about it – we thought everyone must be treated like that. It was nothing to make a fuss about.'

The child has a large piggy bank made of blue glass. She is saving up to buy a wicker basket for the bright red bicycle her parents gave her for Christmas. She has nearly got enough. She has three and sixpence saved up over the weeks from the pocket money she has not spent on sweets. It is made up of pennies and halfpennies, thrupences and sixpences, and sixpences collected from the tooth fairy. She likes having the money but she likes her piggy bank even more. It was given to her by her grandmother, who had had it as a child, so it's very old. She was given it because she is the eldest granddaughter.

The child comes home from school ready to count her money as she does every Friday. The piggy bank lies in shattered blue glass pieces on the floor of her room. The money is scattered about on the carpet.

She runs in tears to tell the woman, who is making pastry in the kitchen, sprinkling flour over the rolling pin which she pushes skilfully backwards and forwards across the table. The woman has no sympathy. She looks down at the crying child. 'It serves you right for leaving it in a place where it might get broken,' she says, and sprinkles more flour on the table.

Vita's eyes were dull with the pain of memory but she continued.

'Olwyn hit us regularly, with the back of the hairbrush, with wooden coat hangers, even the poker, if it happened to be nearby. If she couldn't find anything, she'd just use her hands and nails. She would creep up to our rooms at night, after the lights were supposed to be out, and if she caught one of us reading she would rush in and whack us on the knees – hard.'

'Surely there were bruises,' interrupted Lucy. 'Didn't anyone say something about the bruises?'

Vita made a snorting sound. 'Well, since Olwyn was the only person who gave us baths and put us to bed, no one else would have had the opportunity to see them. Besides, we were always climbing trees and mucking about, so it was not unusual for us to have bruises anyway.'

'But what about school? Didn't the teachers notice the bruises at school?'

'They may have noticed them but they certainly didn't comment. We were sent to middle-class schools. It would never have occurred to anyone that some of the pupils were being hit with pokers at home. All their pupils came from nice families,' Vita said in a voice loaded with sarcasm.

She smoothed her hair back on her scalp and continued. 'Olwyn particularly liked to hit me on my hands with the hairbrush. She used to hold it over my face as if to hit me there, so I'd hold my hands up to protect myself. Then she brought the brush down in short, sharp whacks on the tips of my fingers and my palms.'

The child is in a deep sleep and dreaming. She fell asleep as soon as she put her head on the pillow. The netball match after school has worn her out. She dreams of her mother and father, and of her brothers and sisters. They are laughing, first with her, then at her. But she is enjoying herself. She is at peace.

Suddenly the light is turned on, the harsh overhead light. The woman is standing by her bed, talking sharply to her in angry tones. Her face is twisted in a scowl.

The child sits up, confused. The woman pulls back the bedcovers and grabs the child by the wrist. She yanks the child off the mattress. 'I've got a crow to pluck with you . . . Get up and clear up that mess you left in the bathroom. How dare you leave your clothes like that, just lying on the floor!'

Blinking in the harsh light, the child crawls out of bed.

Unsteady on her feet, she stumbles to the bathroom and gathers up the piles of clothes in her arms. Her eyes are half closed. She says nothing.

'I'm not your servant, you know,' snarls the woman as she leans against the wall, her arms akimbo. 'Don't you dare do that again or I'll knock you into the middle of next week.'

The child's eyes are half closed as she walks slowly back to her room. She drops the clothes on to the chair in the corner and turns off the light. The child climbs back into the soft warm bed, and as she hears the woman's footsteps going down the landing, she hopes that she will be able to return to that nice dream which had engulfed her just before she was woken up.

As Vita talked, Lucy had to ask herself more than once whether she was dreaming. Vita's words were too unbelievable.

'I used to think that compared with the others, I had it easy,' said Vita. 'Olwyn would yank my little brothers and sisters across the room by the ear. She would literally bang our heads together if we were arguing. She was forever kicking the dog and breaking our belongings, and punishing us severely for the smallest misdemeanours. She killed our pets and told lies about us to our parents. She particularly liked throwing Perdita in the coat cupboard and leaving her there in the dark for half an hour or so. I think she had it in for Perdita more than the rest of us, probably because Perdita stood up to her more than the rest of us did, and Olwyn didn't like that. She wanted to break our spirits completely.'

The child is concentrating hard on her colouring in. She has made the clown's trousers and shirt red. She has given him yellow hair and blue shoes, a lovely deep blue like the sea.

The child smiles at her work. She is working very hard, like a grown-up.

Suddenly, the door opens. The woman walks in and marches straight to the child.

The child shrinks away. The woman is scowling at her.

'Don't take what isn't yours,' she yells. She reaches down to the child and yanks her by the ear to her feet.

The child yelps in pain, her feet barely touching the ground as the woman twists her ear and pulls her out of the playroom and into the hall.

'Oh, please, don't!'

The child cries out but the woman does not listen. She pulls open the door of the coat cupboard and pushes the child inside. Then she shuts the door fast.

The child breathes deeply. She has been in this darkness before. She knows she must fight the panic that creeps up inside her. Her big sister told her how. She is only six but she already knows that she must lie down on the pile of coats and try to think of wonderful things until the woman opens the door again to let in the light of the world.

Vita shuddered and wrapped her arms around herself. 'It gives me goose pimples even now to think about her hands on me. I can still feel her fingernails digging into the flesh of my upper arm.'

Lucy listened as goose pimples prickled on her own back.

'But how on earth could she do all this and get away with it? Where were your parents? Didn't you tell them what she was doing?'

Vita turned her head. The expression on her face was one of unbearable bitterness.

'I did try to tell them, very early on, when I was about

five. I complained to my mother that Olwyn had hurt me. She didn't do anything about it. I waited for things to get better but they didn't. Nothing changed, and I deduced, as only a five-year-old can, that my parents approved of what Olwyn did. I don't know if they really knew what was going on, but I do know that nobody believes the things that children say. They don't want to believe the word of a child.

'Whatever the case, I think my mother did not want to act on the word of a five-year-old, and perhaps waited to witness something herself, I don't know. All I do know is that pretty soon, being treated roughly and unkindly became so much the norm that we all thought there was nothing odd in it. I suppose I grew up believing that was how all adults treated children. We didn't talk about it ever, even among ourselves, because it was normal. There was nothing interesting about it.

The child runs home from school, eager to get back to the picture she has been working on with her new crayons. They are special crayons that become like paint when you dip them in water. She has been doing the picture for two days. It's of a special rainforest with lions and tigers and monkeys and goats, and colourful exotic birds among the green leaves on the trees. The picture is for her mother's birthday. Her mother is going to love it.

The child runs into the house and up to her room. The picture is on the bed. The paper is wrinkled and curling at the edges and the colours have run into each other so that you can hardly make out the animals any more.

The child is staring at it as the woman appears in the doorway.

'It was an accident,' says the woman. 'The flower jug was spilled on it.'

The child's eyes are filling with tears and her throat hurts. She turns away, partly to avoid seeing the light smile on the woman's face, but mainly to prevent the woman seeing how much she cares.

'And it wasn't just the physical side of things that was awful,' continued Vita. 'What Olwyn said did even more damage than her wallops with the hairbrush. Once I was looking at myself in the mirror and asked her about the veins I saw across my chest. She told me they were so big because I had leukaemia. I didn't know what that meant, so I asked her.

'"It means you'll be dead in five years," she told me.

'At first I didn't believe her and told her I was going to ask my parents. She smiled slyly, I can see her face now, and said: "There's no point in asking them. They don't want to upset you by telling you you're dying. So they'll just lie to you. They want you to enjoy the few years you have left without knowing that you're going to die young."'

'But that's incredible!' murmured Lucy.

'Incredible? I believed her for a few years. I used to look at myself in the mirror before bedtime and wonder if I would die that night in my sleep. It was your father who made me think that maybe I didn't have leukaemia, but even when I had the chance, I didn't dare ask him outright.

'She did the same to Perdita, too. Perdita had a hernia in her groin, a small bulge. She asked Olwyn what it was and Olwyn said it was cancer and that Perdita would be dead within a year. I didn't discover this until years later. Nice, eh.'

Lucy listened in horror. 'That's dreadful,' she said. 'I

don't believe that anyone could treat little children that way.'

Vita sniffed.

'Yes, that's the problem. It's really inconceivable. Unless you were there. And you know, the most ridiculous thing is that we deluded ourselves into thinking that we liked Olwyn – even loved her. I used to say that when I had children I would have Olwyn looking after them, just as my parents' nannies had looked after two generations of children. That's how deluded I was. For Christ's sake, when Olwyn left, after the Brat died, we all *cried*. I suppose that even though she was so cruel, she was all we had ever known. And we were afraid of who might replace her. We had lived with her long enough to judge her moods as far as possible. So we knew when to duck and dodge, and how to get around her as much as we could. For in the end, getting on with Olwyn became crucial for our survival. How could we break away and denounce her? It was dangerous, it could backfire, but it would also mean threatening the only solid base we had, however cruel it was. We could not denounce her because as children you don't know what's really right and wrong. And you cling to what you know, however bad.

'No, it was the Brat we all hated. I see now, of course, that we hated him because we couldn't risk hating Olwyn, since our survival depended on getting on with her. He was such a pain, such a sneak – always getting us into trouble. And he was incredibly lazy, never doing anything he was supposed to do while we all had to do our jobs in the rota. And he was a thief, always stealing our things.' She stopped and took a deep breath. 'And, of course, Olwyn never laid a hand on him. He would stand back and smirk while she walloped us.'

Vita paused, her eyes shut tight.

Then she opened them. 'But now . . . now that I'm a parent myself, I can see that he was just a sad, mixed-up eight-year-old who was desperate for attention. His only sense of worth stemmed from the fact that his mother had complete control over the rest of us.

'I suppose that at some level we all knew that attacking David was the one way we could get at Olwyn without her destroying us in retaliation. And we didn't mean to kill him, we really didn't. It just happened that way . . .'

Lucy ran her tongue uneasily over her lips.

'Don't you feel even a little bit sorry for Olwyn? After all, David was her only child, and she lost him.'

Vita frowned and spun round to face her. She was breathing heavily with rage.

'No, I don't feel sorry for her at all. And I never shall. What she did to us was criminal. It is only with my adult eyes that I can see just how criminal it was.'

'But there were other adults there,' Lucy said. 'Your parents were there. Why did they allow it to go on? Surely they're responsible in some way.'

Vita was silent. As she looked into the distance, Lucy could see a watery glint in her eyes. Then she turned, her upper lip quivering with barely contained emotion.

'Do you remember the trial of Rosemary West a few years ago? The woman who murdered those young women with her husband, and sexually tortured them? She and her husband had lots of children, and they were abused too. The ones who testified, or talked to the press afterwards, all said that at the time it seemed perfectly normal to be treated like that by their parents. They assumed that all families were like theirs, and they believed that for twenty years. They also said that they still loved their parents. Well, it was the same way for us.

'Yes, ultimately our parents were responsible. They employed Olwyn and they chose to keep her on, even after we had told them what she did. They chose to be blind and deaf about what went on because it suited them. They could get on with their lives and their children did not bother them. Which is what they wanted. They are selfish people. They always have been. They have always been wrapped up in each other and concentrated on their own careers and all their stupid causes. If it wasn't Cuba, it was the Vietnam War or battles with Camden Council, or some cause at the Camden Arts Centre. It was never us they thought about. They liked their public image as glamorous young parents of a vast family of brilliant and talented children, but they didn't really care about us as individuals. And they didn't want to put any effort into bringing us up.

'But I do love them, even if they don't really love us as parents should. And so I can almost forgive them in a way that I could never forgive Olwyn. If I saw Olwyn in the street today, I would attack her in some way. If I could poison her, I would. I'd like her to die a slow, painful death.

'And all my siblings feel the same way, particularly the younger ones. They suffered most in that monster's hands. You talk to them and see. They were all messed up by her. Not one of us has had a successful relationship: I think we're all incapable of getting close to anyone. Our parents were too remote to love us properly, and Olwyn was no substitute. All she taught us was how to survive. And to hate.

'And she succeeded: Perdita and I do not feel guilty at all about killing David. We were young, but we were all still old enough to know what we were doing when we tried to poison him – even if we didn't know how far it would go.'

*   *   *

The boy is on his hands and knees, his head close to the dog basket. The dog licks its lips and looks warily at him. The boy reaches out and pulls a thick whisker out of the dog's muzzle. The dog jerks its head away and growls gently. A warning. The boy laughs and pulls again, harder. The dog bares its teeth. The boy laughs. The dog snarls, then snaps its jaws, catching the boy's hand. The boy cries out and jumps to his feet. He runs crying to his mother who is ironing in the corner of the room. The boy holds out his hurt hand to her.

The boy's mother puts down the iron and walks across the room. The dog cringes into the far corner of the basket. The dog yelps as the boy's mother's foot kicks it hard. The boy's mother scoops up the loose skin at the back of the dog's neck and yanks the animal out of the basket. She carries the dog to the back door and throws it down the steps. The dog lands heavily. Its legs give way and its head crashes into a large garden tub filled with bright scarlet pelargoniums. The dog yelps loudly. It scrambles to its feet and limps painfully, its tail between its legs, to the bottom of the garden where it hides, trembling, under the blackcurrant bush, and licks its bruised body.

The women walked on round to Highgate ponds where the girls fed the ducks with the stale bread they had brought with them in a plastic bag. 'All my siblings are driven to do good, to protect the vulnerable in the world,' said Vita. 'You could say that's a good thing, but I think it's at the cost of any possible personal happiness.'

'What about you? You're the only one who is not in a profession, not a lawyer or doctor.'

Vita nodded. 'Yes. I am the odd one out in that way, but

I am also the only one with children. What happened to us makes it very difficult to be a parent . . .'

Her voice trailed off, and then cracked as she added softly, 'My children have suffered enough with the death of their father. But for me, every day they get older I ask myself how Olwyn could have got away with it for so long. And,' her voice cracked, 'I blame myself for not protecting the little ones, my younger siblings, more . . .'

The women said no more. Lucy had heard enough and Vita was drained. She was also now going to have to live with the revived horrors she had been forced to tell Lucy.

On the way home Lucy felt nauseous. Every time she imagined the scenes in the Valentine home, sour gorge rose in her throat. There were terrible, awful things going on in the house she had always thought was Paradise. She felt ashamed of herself for having been blinded by the glamour.

Lucy was shaken by the description of David's poisoning, and the cold clinical manner in which Vita had told her. Lucy now knew that she could never tell Vita the full impact of her and Perdita's deed. She could never tell her that the Valentine girls had not only murdered a child but they had also almost destroyed her own father. Certainly, they destroyed his career; his marriage and spirit had just about survived. She did not tell Vita because she knew that Vita would not care.

But beneath the shock of what she had just heard – both the details of Olwyn's cruelty and Vita's unrepentant hardness – Lucy felt a lightness springing up inside her. It was very strange, as if a voice inside her were singing – clear and loud – expressing an extraordinary elation.

Her talk with Vita seemed to have caused something to lift, something like a heavy dark blanket that had, for years, concealed some soft part of herself. She suddenly felt as if a wonderful space had opened up inside her, and around her, freeing her from something that had imprisoned her.

Now she could see what had happened. Andrew's request to get drugs from their father's drawer had forced her to confront something she had been running away from for nearly thirty years. Now she had turned and confronted it. She herself had done something wrong, something that had terrible consequences, and she had finally acknowledged it.

CHAPTER 20

August, 1997

The Cry of the Children

The days between Andrew's attempted suicide and his death took on a strange timeless quality. They were dreamlike, as though time were suspended. There were nine days in all. For those close to him it seemed like an eternity. Even when someone is seriously ill and obviously close to dying, he can linger on and on, waiting for the mystical moment when he finally slips from being a living person to a dead one.

Andrew's GP was heroic. He understood Andrew's terror of going back to hospital and of treatment that just kept him alive regardless of the quality of his life. He offered Andrew an alternative.

'You can declare that you want no more treatment, except that necessary to alleviate discomfort or pain. You can stay at home and be looked after by the palliative care doctor and his team.'

Andrew forced a wry grin. 'The palliative care doctor! You forget, I trained as a doctor myself. We used to call him the terminal consultant. I suppose that sounds too real.'

Thus Andrew came under the care of the local palliative care team, a group of doctors and nurses who specialised in the care of dying people. Andrew was put on a diamorphine drip which, at regular intervals, pumped its exquisite relief straight into his veins. The heroin made him sleepy and, for the most part, calm, as he lay in bed propped up against a high bank of soft pillows.

Every one of those nine days, as Lucy sat in her kitchen and drank a mug of morning coffee, she would look at the calendar on the wall. Would this be the day? Would this be the deathday that Andrew would never know and his family remember for ever?

Since Andrew could no longer be left alone, Patrick and Lucy divided up their days to look after him around the clock. Patrick obviously took the greatest share, looking after Andrew in the night as well as in the mornings before going to work in the afternoons.

Lucy took over at lunchtime and would take her work to do quietly while Andrew slept in the room upstairs.

The house was quiet for most of the day, except when the palliative care team came for their daily visit, or when friends came to sit upstairs next to the bed and whisper quietly to Andrew as his strength slipped away. Hilda and Dr Butler came every evening, driving up from south London in their car. They looked strained and subdued. They said very little on their visits, but always stayed for an hour, sitting on either sides of the bed, holding Andrew's hands.

Andrew went downhill rapidly. He gave up the fight. For the first few days he was capable of getting out of bed and coming downstairs. Once he even got dressed but it was upsetting to see how baggy his clothes were on his skeletal frame.

He had no appetite. His intestines were out of control. He ate very little and vomited up anything he did force down his throat. He became weaker and weaker.

Soon he was unable to go to the lavatory without help. He had become incontinent. The indignities grew every day. First there were the pads strategically placed to prevent him soiling the sheets. Then there was a catheter fixed to a condom pulled over his penis so he did not have to get out of bed to urinate. He had bed sores on his elbows and hips. His bottom was raw from the diarrhoea.

Lucy longed for the pneumonia to take over and kill him off. But, cruelly, it held off, refusing to come and put him out of his misery.

He talked to the doctor on the palliative care team and begged him to give him a massive dose of heroin and be done with it.

The doctor refused. 'I'm not in the business of killing my patients,' he said. And he said to Lucy later: 'I'm interested in making sure they have a good death.'

A good death! How could the death of a thirty-five-year-old, in any circumstances, be a good death? It made Lucy angry. There was nothing good about Andrew's dying. It was degrading and undignified. As she washed him down with a flannel, dressed his weeping pressure sores, changed the bed and tried not to retch if he soiled yet another set of sheets which required changing, she tried to keep her mind off the reality of it all. She tried to think of Andrew as the chubby-limbed little brother she used to wash in the bath, a little boy who needed his nappy changed, not this wizened creature who looked like a starving man of eighty, whose face was so wasted that it was impossible to read it or to decipher his expressions. Smiles could be grimaces, grimaces smiles. Her mental tricks did not work.

On the ninth day, Lucy could stand it no longer. When she arrived, she stood in the doorway of the bedroom and took a good look at her sleeping brother. She imagined coming to him afresh, trying to see him with the eyes of someone who had not seen him since he had become ill. And she was shocked. Andrew looked truly cadaverous. His body was completely emaciated so that his skin and remaining flesh hung from his long bones, his skull clearly defined with huge, sunken eyes and receding lips. When he slept, his eyelids did not close but remained half open constantly. Only the pulsating throb of his heart, faint but still visible under the thin skin stretched over his ribcage, indicated that Andrew was still alive.

For a while, Lucy tried to work at Andrew's bedside. She was copy-editing a novel, a fast-paced commercial thriller for which the publishers had high hopes. The vitality of the characters made her all the more aware of the heavy air and sickly-sweet smell of death that filled her brother's home.

Occasionally Andrew would surface into something like full consciousness. He mumbled in an incomprehensible rasping whisper. On the last day of his life, Lucy talked to him for a few minutes. He was thirsty and she lifted a beaker of water – one of the training cups that young children use when they are graduating from a bottle – to his parched lips.

'I'm so weak,' he said. His voice was raspy, like an old man's. He sank back against the pillows, his eyes half closed.

Lucy took his hand and squeezed it. 'What are you feeling, Andrew?'

He turned back to look at her. The fear in his eyes would haunt her for ever.

He struggled to lift his head and he made an obvious effort to talk so that his sister could hear. 'I'm terrified. I don't believe in an afterlife, but I'm so frightened . . .' His voice faded away.

Lucy winced and squeezed his hand again. 'Remember what Socrates said, it's just a dreamless sleep . . .'

But Andrew was frowning, his eyes shut, as if in pain. There was nothing she could say. She stared down and watched her brother as he dropped his head back on to the pillow. His breathing became steady and deep as he sank once again into sleep.

Lucy sat beside his bed for a long time. They were all so tired of this. It had been going on for too long now. She loved her brother and did not want to lose him, yet she also longed for him to be out of his misery. And there was no possibility that he could do anything other than deteriorate. His life could not get better. It could only get worse. Her sense of powerlessness made her angry.

As she sat there, she had a thought. She was not entirely powerless. She was in a position to end his suffering right then, if she wanted to. The opportunity was there. They were alone in the house. No one was expected for a couple of hours.

She glanced at the pillow on the floor and then up at her brother. Andrew's breathing was loud. His mouth lay open and a stream of saliva dribbled out of the corner to collect in a dark patch on the blue pillow.

The whir of the driver pumping more heroin into Andrew's bloodstream sounded like the roar of a train in Lucy's ears.

She knew she had to do it. As if in a trance, she lifted the pillow and clutched it to her breast for a second. Then she leaned over her brother's bed.

Andrew struggled only momentarily. He had no strength in his body left to fight. His arms flapped feebly for a few seconds. Then he managed to push himself up a few inches off the bed, his body rigid. For a horrible moment, Lucy thought that he would throw her off. She shut her eyes and pushed down harder.

Then it was over. He relaxed, peaceful at last.

Lucy's heart was pounding hard as she pushed the pillow behind Andrew's head. Leaning over, she gave Andrew a long kiss on the cheek. His eyes, still half closed, were dead and unseeing. Relaxed. At peace.

Lucy's head was clear as she rang the GP and told him that Andrew had stopped breathing. Then she rang Patrick, Simon and her parents. She went into the kitchen and put on the kettle to make some tea. She felt in complete control, breathing hard, proud of what she had done. Reaching into her handbag, she pulled out her diary. She flicked through the pages to reach the correct date. Then she wrote, 'Andrew died at four ten today.' The date was August 2nd. Andrew's deathday, the day he would never know. She measured out the tea and poured boiling water into the pot. Her eyes were dry.

It was only when Simon arrived thirty minutes later, having got a taxi from work, that she broke down and let herself cry.

She cried for the loss of her brother, both the little boy she had loved and cared for, and the adult man she had adored so much. She cried for her parents and for Patrick. She could never tell Patrick what she had done; his deep despair at not being at Andrew's bedside at the moment of death made her realise that. It had not occurred to her that he might have cared so much about such a thing. She was glad that she did not have enough room inside herself to accommodate the guilt about Patrick as well.

That evening, Andrew's family and friends gathered at the flat. Patrick was in control of himself for much of the time but every now and then he would break down and cry. Hilda and Dr Butler sat on the sofa, red-eyed and silent, while Simon held Lucy in his arms.

Lucy was relieved that there had been no suspicions about Andrew's death. The doctor filled out the death certificate. He wrote AIDS as the cause of death and gave it to Patrick so that he could register the death. If the doctor had suspected anything, he was not going to make a fuss about someone's life being ended a few hours or days before it would have ended anyway. Everyone had suffered enough. Besides, he had other patients to see. A few hours before Andrew had died, the doctor had attended the home birth of a baby girl just down the road. A nice balance that, a home death and a home birth both in one day. The balance of life, he thought as he drove home to his young family that night.

Rosie came round to the house on her way home from work. Like everyone else, she wanted to see Andrew's body. Lucy took her up to the bedroom and they stood together, staring at Andrew's face. The blood was draining away, so that his skin had begun to take on the waxy yellow look of the dead.

She touched his forehead. 'He's cold.'

'His body's still warm. It seems to go from head to toe.'

Rigor mortis was beginning to stiffen his hands.

'I suppose the virus is dead too, now,' said Rosie quietly. 'And good riddance.'

Lucy sighed. 'It's weird to think that I'm an only child now.'

The women continued to stare down at Andrew, now in silence. Rosie lifted the white sheet to look at the wasted body underneath. Andrew's penis lay curled against his thigh like a fat little worm. Rosie dropped the sheet and began to cry.

'You know I slept with Andrew once.' She sniffed loudly.

Lucy looked up in surprise. 'I didn't know that. When?'

Rosie smiled sheepishly and blew her nose. 'Yes, I seduced him when he was eighteen. I think he was hoping he would discover he was really attracted to women after all.'

She smiled ruefully. 'It failed, of course. It was hopeless all round, but we laughed about it afterwards. He still respected me in the morning!'

The two women laughed together. 'Now I understand why Andrew was so fond of you,' said Lucy. 'You were probably the only woman he ever slept with.'

'You're right,' laughed Rosie. 'I guess I should be proud of that, though maybe I put him off for ever . . .'

They stayed with Andrew's body for another fifteen minutes, saying nothing, just lost in their own thoughts and memories of Andrew when he was alive.

Lucy was tempted to tell Rosie what she had done but she decided not to. One day, perhaps, but not yet.

That night Lucy dreamed that she had given birth to twins, a boy and a girl. They were perfect. As she came out of the hospital, she held them up above her head for the crowd outside to see them. The crowd cheered loudly at her achievement and her GP presented her with a medal for her courage. It was a good dream. Lucy woke up feeling unusually refreshed and calm, and she had an uplifting sense that this dream marked the end of her childmares. Her night torments were over.

The next day Lucy rang the undertaker to arrange the funeral. She was glad to have such a responsibility. It helped to focus her thoughts during that stagnant period between the death and the formal farewell. There had to be a closing of the door, a final acknowledgement and acceptance of the end. She could suddenly understand how distressing it must be for people whose loved ones are blown to smithereens in a bomb explosion or lost in the bottom of the sea in a plane crash. It seemed to her that there was a basic need to know where a dead body was, and to have access to it, regardless of whether it finally ended up eaten by worms in a wooden coffin or burnt to grey ashes in the heat of the crematorium flames.

In many ways Andrew's death felt like a huge relief to Lucy. No longer did she have to babysit every afternoon – it had only been a couple of weeks but it felt like months – no longer did she have to feed him like a baby, help him to the lavatory, or clean his sheets. No longer did she have to carry his fear for him or have to assure him that he would be all right. She was aware of how steady she felt about his death. It was a relief because so much of the mourning had taken place as he was dying.

She did not know it yet but the missing of Andrew would not be felt for at least a year. The sharp pang of sorrow at the simple fact that he was not around to enjoy or share with her. She would think she could see him in the street, fleetingly, or hear his voice in a crowded train. She would turn in wonder and excitement before reason caught up with her and disappointment hit.

No, all that was to come. But what Lucy was aware of now was the fact that she would remember two Andrews, the healthy younger brother who was so quick and funny and handsome, and then the ill one, lying dying in his bed, his large sunken eyes looking at her with fear. Two different people, yet the same.

None of this was said to the undertaker. He was solemn

and sympathetic and arranged to come at lunchtime to take Andrew's body away.

Lucy and Simon went over in the morning to be with Patrick, and found him dressing Andrew's rigid body in his best clothes.

'He was so fond of these Paul Smith trousers,' Patrick said. 'There was a GAP shirt that went really well with them, but I can't find it. I'll have to iron another one.' And he disappeared to the laundry room. Lucy heard him rummaging around in the washing machine, then the swish-swish of the steam from the iron. Alongside the steam noise was another sound which Lucy couldn't identify at first. Then she realised that it was the sound of Patrick sniffling through his tears.

A few minutes later he came back with a perfectly ironed white cotton shirt. Lucy helped him lift Andrew's stiff body as he pulled the shirt over his wasted chest, buttoned it, and tucked the tails into his trousers. Andrew had once filled that shirt with gym-trained muscles. Now it hung loose and billowy on his torso.

The black-clad undertakers arrived promptly at twelve. They came in a black van which they had parked in the only available parking space, twenty yards down the road. They had a stretcher with them. Dressed in black, with slicked-down hair, they were dour and tight-lipped. They mumbled their respects and then asked the whereabouts of 'the deceased'.

They laid out the body and invited everyone to view Andrew before he went off. Patrick declined. Afterwards, Lucy wished she had too. It was a grotesque sight: Andrew dressed up in his oversized clothes, his eyes half shut and sunken in darkened sockets, his arms stiff across his chest, his skin grey against the brilliant white of the cotton shirt. She did not linger.

Then it was time for them to take Andrew away. The undertakers opened up the stretcher and unzipped a big black body bag. They placed the fashionably dressed corpse in it. Then they zipped it up, carried it carefully down the stairs and out of the house and down the road.

As Lucy, Simon and Patrick watched Andrew being loaded into the back of the van, they all broke down. Hugging each other clumsily and desperately, they wailed loud cries of anguish.

The morning of the funeral, Lucy went with Simon to buy food and paper plates for the gathering afterwards. The manager of the shop cheerily rang up the items – dozens of sandwiches and a stack of quiches and flans – and placed them in bags. He was a chirpy young man, no more than twenty-five years old and proud of his professional efficiency.

'Having a party, eh?'

Lucy and Simon exchanged uneasy looks.

'Er, well, sort of,' Lucy finally managed to say.

'Not going to eat them all yourselves, are you?' the young manager persisted. 'Looks like a right old beanfeast. Say, you're not getting married, are you?'

After another long, embarrassed pause, Lucy blurted out: 'Actually, it's for a funeral.'

The manager stopped dead in his tracks and looked at her with his jaw going. Words tried to come from his mouth, but he said nothing.

'Don't worry,' Lucy said. 'You weren't to know. I'll pay by Access if that's OK.'

*   *   *

The funeral was held at the crematorium in East Barnet. Lucy clutched the tape she had made from the CDs Andrew had left for her. It was a cold, overcast day with patches of drizzle.

Patrick was going to conduct the ceremony and had been holding himself together well. Rosie arrived dressed in a smart black Armani suit. Her face was puffy from crying; she had hardly stopped for the past few days.

Lucy's parents arrived in their little blue car. Dr Butler helped his wife out and escorted her into the building, holding her by the elbow as if he feared she might fall. And, indeed, Lucy thought that she had never seen her mother look so frail.

The service lasted forty minutes, which was all they had been allowed by the crematorium. Earlier in the morning Lucy had been worried that no one would come, but as the room filled up she saw that her fears had been groundless. They entered to the accompaniment of the Gypsy Kings, a mournful wail about the pain of lost love. By the time it had finished the room was packed with friends of Andrew's, several of them, Lucy noted grimly, showing signs of the same horrid disease. Nearly everyone in the room was crying.

The service was simple, with readings by friends from a selection of poems by A.E. Houseman, Walt Whitman, Mark Strand. Then the Cat Stevens song was played, with its plaintive protest against parental neglect.

Lucy glanced over at her parents to see how they reacted to this jibe from their dead son. But they either didn't listen or didn't understand. They sat staring glumly at the long coffin on the conveyor belt at the front of the room. The coffin was a spectacular sight, painted by a friend with brightly coloured scenes from the Sistine Chapel. The top was smothered with small white roses.

Lucy was beginning to feel ill. Her eyes drooped with exhaustion and she felt an overwhelming weakness coming over her. Surely she was not coming down with something, not now.

Trying to rouse herself for the final stages of the service, she rolled her head around to loosen up the stiff neck muscles. As she did so, she looked at the back of the room and was startled to see Vita and Perdita Valentine standing there together. Her mind went temporarily blank, her thoughts moving away from the service.

And then, suddenly, it was over. The blue curtains had opened and the lovingly painted coffin was being rolled into the furnace, with the ethereal music of Mozart's *Jesu Domine* soaring over the scene. As the curtain closed the music ended, and there was silence. Simon stood up to invite everyone back to Andrew's and Patrick's house, and the mourners started rising from their chairs. Everyone trooped out and stood around outside the crematorium, making small talk, lingering, some thinking about the coffin with its wasted contents burning in the fire, others thinking of the very different, healthy Andrew they had known.

Lucy stood to the side on her own. She breathed deeply, glad that the ritual was finally over and glad to get fresh air into her lungs.

She looked over at her parents who were standing together near the mass of flowers laid out carefully on the ground. They had spent a lot of time with Andrew in the end, but if only they had accepted his differences earlier, she thought. Everyone might have been a little happier.

The crowd had gathered around the sombre wreaths of flowers, scrutinising the cards to read the messages and to see who had said goodbye in this way. Lucy sighed and blew her nose and looked around for the Valentine sisters.

They had approached Dr Butler. Lucy watched them shake his hand, and then turn to Hilda and express their condolences with great respect. Then they backed away and stood a few yards away from the rest of the crowd. Lucy saw now that they were both wearing long flowing rain cloaks to protect them from the fine drizzle that had started to fall. It was chilly for August. She shivered.

The Valentine sisters were looking at her. Lucy nodded and walked over to them. She felt exhausted from the anxiety of the service. She realised how difficult the days between Andrew's death and his funeral had been. She could now see the point of a funeral, the final goodbye. It made her feel a little more settled now that it was over. Like the relief she used to feel after an important exam, she felt she could let go, if not collapse.

She felt quite light-headed.

'Well done,' said Vita with a light smile. 'It was a good service. It was personal and warm.'

Next to her Perdita looked at Lucy with her disturbingly pale eyes and nodded in agreement.

'Patrick and Simon did it all, really. And it's been hardest for Patrick, of course.'

Lucy looked at the sisters for a few moments. She had a longing to say something. The words were in her head. The women stared back at her. Lucy's eyes darted from one face to the other. She wanted to tell them what she had done. She wanted to tell them that she had killed Andrew, that she was as strong as they. She had had the courage to take away a life because it was necessary to do so. She was one of them, but there was a difference between them. What they did all those years ago had been wrong; what she did last weekend was right.

The three women stood there only for a few moments but in those moments, Lucy felt something give way. She was released from the hold these sisters had had over her for all her life. She had never realised it had been there until she cast it off.

'We must be going,' Perdita said quietly.

'You won't come back for some refreshments? You're very welcome.'

Vita shook her head. 'No, thank you. We won't stay . . .' She reached over and grasped Lucy's hand. She looked steadily at her. 'We'll see you . . .'

The sisters turned and walked away side by side. They walked in step, their long rain cloaks floating out gracefully behind them.

Lucy watched them walk down the gravel path between the gravestones towards their car. As she watched them go, she wondered if she would ever see them again. And she realised, as she wondered, that she did not care if she did or not.

She recalled vividly the deep longing to be like them, to be a Valentine child. Now she knew she no longer felt it. They were hard-hearted and cold. It was not their fault, perhaps, their childhood had made them that way. But Lucy was not like them at all, and she did not want to be, either. Not any more.

Her spirits lifted as she turned to walk back to the crowd of mourners by the flowers. Rosie came up to her. Her nose was red and she looked miserable. 'I won't come to the house,' she apologised. 'I have a lot of work to do but I also feel like being on my own for a bit.'

'I understand,' said Lucy. 'I wouldn't mind being on my own, too. Thank you for all your support – and I'll let you know what I decide about that job soon. I'm sorry I've taken so long to respond to the offer, but as you know I've been preoccupied.'

'Just so long as you tell us next week. We can't wait any longer than that because we'll have to find someone else if you say no.'

Lucy kissed Rosie on the cheek. 'Thanks a lot for your support in every way. You've been great.' She glanced at Rosie's suit. 'Nice bit of material there,' she commented.

Rosie chuckled. 'Yes, I bought it with my dress allowance. It's a perk. We're supposed to give back the designer clothes at the end of each year and they're sold in discount boutiques, or something.' She lowered her voice. 'The trick is to buy a Marks & Spencer version and swap the labels!' With that, she gave Lucy a strong hug, turned on her heels and walked off towards her car.

The gathering at the house was a mixed affair. Most of Andrew's friends were having a good time. They had been to too many friends' funerals over the past few years to be numbed by the pain any more. For Patrick, it was hard, and for the Butler family, it was grim.

Lucy longed to go home with Simon and shut herself away from the world. The buzz of conversation around her made her feel dizzy. The sip of wine had sent a wave of nausea through her.

Her father walked across the room to her. He looked tired. Lucy thought that he was looking much older than his years.

'I was surprised to see those Valentine girls,' he said. 'It was touching that they came along. I didn't know that Andrew meant anything to them.' He paused and looked thoughtful. 'Funny things, those girls. I was just thinking about the way they acted all those years ago when their housekeeper's son died.'

He stared into the distance, a puzzled expression on his face. 'I don't know why I've suddenly thought about it. I haven't thought about any of that business for a long time. Those girls were the two who were so adamant that they'd seen the boy take that medication out of my bag. I was always pretty certain that I didn't keep it in the bag at that time. Yet they were so sure of it . . .'

His voice trailed off, and he fell silent. Lucy stood beside him in silence. She owed it to him to release him from his torment. 'You were right, Daddy,' she said quietly. 'You remember correctly.'

Dr Butler glanced at her. 'What did you say?'

'I said that your memory is correct. The drugs were not in your bag.'

Her father turned to look at her, his face so tired and grey. 'You were too young. You don't know anything about what happened.'

Lucy looked deeply into her father's eyes. She was aware of some of Andrew's friends hovering behind her, waiting to offer their condolences to the old parents. She touched Gordon's forearm. 'I'll tell you about it when we meet next,' she said softly. 'This isn't the time, not now . . .'

There was no time to say more. The hovering couple engaged Gordon in conversation and Lucy moved off to talk to her mother, leaving her bewildered father in the corner.

Lucy joined her mother who was clutching a glass of orange juice, staring around the room.

'I still can't believe I'm here after the funeral of my own child,' she said quietly to her daughter. 'I can't believe that my son has predeceased me. It's just not natural.'

They stood against the wall watching the crowd of young people, Andrew's friends, talking, drinking and smoking, and laughing. They were all trying to have a good time, as they knew Andrew had wanted them to.

'They're all such nice, respectable, successful young people,' Hilda said, her voice choking. 'Every one of them has come up to your father and me to say wonderful things about Andrew. They obviously loved him a lot.'

Lucy watched the tears creep into her mother's eyes. 'It makes me sad to think of Andrew in the company of these friends,' continued Hilda. 'We've barely seen Andrew as an adult, and I know that's really been our fault.' She corrected herself. 'My fault. And now it's too late . . .' Her voice cracked again.

Lucy slipped her hand through the crook of her mother's arm. 'At least you've seen more of him over the past few months,' she said.

It occurred to her at that moment that she was so very different from her mother, and she wondered briefly if that fleeting acquaintance with the Valentines, the nonconformists, had saved her from such a fate. How could she know? But she wanted to believe that it was true.

Hilda nodded. 'Yes, and I'll cherish those moments with Andrew, and what I've learned from him in that time.' Her voice sounded wistful and sad. 'He taught me some good things, though, and I'm proud of him for that. He has made me think about things I've never questioned before, and he taught me that I can change – I hope for the better – even at the age of sixty.'

As she spoke, her husband came over to them. 'I think I'm ready to go home now, dear,' she said, turning to him. 'Let's leave these young people alone.'

Dr Butler was surprised by the gentleness in his wife's voice. She had not spoken to him like that for many, many years. Taking her by the arm, he pulled her gently to him and kissed her on the cheek. 'Let's go,' he said. 'I'm ready.' Then, turning to Lucy he touched her arm. 'We'll talk soon, yes?'

Lucy walked her parents to the front door to see them out. Simon came over to join her. They said their farewells, and as they shut the door, Simon placed an arm around Lucy and kissed the top of her head. 'I think it's going as well as it could.'

Lucy nodded. 'Andrew wouldn't be disappointed,' she said, pressing herself against him.

The day after the funeral, Lucy managed to get an appointment to see her doctor. She was certain that something was wrong. She was feeling nauseous and exhausted almost constantly. She expected the doctor to tell her that she was experiencing the normal symptoms of bereavement or anxiety, but she wanted reassurance, whatever it was.

Dr Kenny asked about her symptoms, then said she'd better have a look at her. The doctor listened to her heart and lungs and felt her neck and armpits for swollen glands. She looked down her throat and into her ears. Then she told her to lie down on the examination couch. She prodded and probed Lucy's breasts and then took a long time examining her belly, pushing it gently with her fingertips. Then she told Lucy to get dressed and sit down on the chair by the desk.

'Take a deep breath. I can tell you exactly why you're feeling the way you do . . .' She paused and smiled. 'It seems that you are pregnant. About sixteen weeks pregnant, I guess.'

Lucy felt her jaw go slack and her mouth open in amazement. For one ghastly minute she thought about her night with Giles. But that would be impossible if she was as much as sixteen weeks gone.

'Pregnant? How can I be so pregnant?' Lucy continued to stare at her in disbelief.

The doctor continued cheerfully, 'Judging from my examination I'd say you were well into the fourth month.' Dr Kenny ran her finger across a calendar. 'That means you conceived in early April.'

'But that was long before my miscarriage. It's impossible. How can that be?'

Dr Kenny nodded. 'It is possible. The likeliest explanation is that when you were diagnosed as pregnant earlier this year, you had actually conceived twins. When you miscarried, you lost one of them but the other continued to thrive.'

She looked down at Lucy's notes as she spoke, then continued: 'You had the miscarriage at home and, as I recall, you didn't come in for a follow-up examination or scan.'

'No,' Lucy said faintly. She hardly knew what to feel about this astonishing news.

'Well,' the doctor continued, 'it all looks okay to me. Chances are the baby is doing very well. It must be pretty tough to have survived the miscarriage of its twin. I'm sending you down to the hospital for a scan this afternoon and that'll confirm that everything's all right.'

Leaning forward, she touched Lucy lightly on the arm and gave her a friendly, maternal smile. 'I knew you'd get there in the end.'

Later that afternoon, Lucy lay on her back holding Simon's hand while the two of them looked at the flickering black-and-white monitor to their right. Simon was laughing and crying simultaneously at the sight of his embryonic child floating gently around in Lucy's uterus.

'It's going to be all right,' he said, hugging Lucy hard. 'Everything's going to be all right.'

Lucy laughed through her tears. Her throat was tight with emotion. 'I guess I'll have to tell Rosie that I won't be taking that job, not for the time being, anyway.'

'She'll understand,' said Simon.

'I'm not sure if Rosie will think a baby is a good reason for not taking a job, but she'll have to accept it. In fact, I was already having second thoughts about working at the same place as Rosie. Much as I love her, I think I'll love her more if I don't work with her.'

But Simon was not listening. His eyes were fixed again on the black-and-white image on the monitor. 'It's a miracle,' he whispered, 'just a miracle.'

Lucy squeezed his hand and lay back on the pillow. With a contented smile, she shut her eyes. Simon's exclamations of joy were drowned by the sound of happy children's voices echoing in her head.